To love is nothing
To be loved is something
But to love and be loved is everything

T. Tolis

Also written by Ruth Kipnis

Lane's End
A French Connection
His Name Was David Freeman

The Butterfly

Ruth Kipnis

First Edition Design Publishing
United States Canada London

The Butterfly
Copyright ©2018 Ruth Kipnis

ISBN 978-1506-907-60-4 PBK
ISBN 978-1506-907-61-1 EBK

LCCN 201866555

January 2019

Published and Distributed by
First Edition Design Publishing, Inc.
P.O. Box 17646, Sarasota, FL 34276-3217
www.firsteditiondesignpublishing.com

ALL RIGHTS RESERVED. No part of this book publication may be reproduced, stored in a retrieval system, or transmitted in any form or by any means — electronic, mechanical, photo-copy, recording, or any other — except brief quotation in reviews, without the prior permission of the author or publisher.

Chapter 1

With a gentle tap on my shoulder and the sound of a soft voice, the veil of that never-never land between deep sleep and consciousness began to part. I opened my eyes as the stewardess spoke. "Favor abrochense el cinturon de seguridad. She was smiling and pointing to my seatbelt. After almost four hours we were about to land in Guadalajara.

The trip aboard Aeromexico had been surprisingly pleasant, although nothing, not even first class seating, could make the knot in my stomach disappear. The Mexico assignment was the chance of a lifetime. Succeed and I'd climb rungs on the ladder to success. Fail and the ladder would be pulled out from under me, even if I weren't fired any hopes of making partner someday would be dashed. For better or for worse Guadalajara was to be my home and my proving ground for the next six months. Unfortunately, hard as I tried my Spanish language skills were sorely lacking, and I didn't know a single person in all of Mexico.

I collected my suitcases and passed through migration and customs with little trouble taking in the unfamiliar sights and sounds all around me. This was a whole new world. The Mexicans traveling though the overcrowded airport seemed to fall into two classes, the well dressed, attractive, almost European looking types wheeling stylish luggage and the poorer class neatly attired and well-mannered pushing their carts piled high with their belongings in boxes held together with twine or carrying old battered suitcases. Like me all heading toward the exit, but it was the group of American tourists who stood out from the crowd both in dress and attitude. They were loud, impatient, and disrespectful of the personnel who were only trying to do their jobs making me feel uncomfortable, even embarrassed.

I'd almost reached the doors leading to the outside when I spotted a short, stocky Mexican man of about forty in a black suit and cap holding a card with my name on it.

"I'm Michael Madison," I said as I approached. From the long hard stare that greeted me I knew what he was about to say. I'd seen that puzzled expression many times before.

"Sorry, Senorita," he said, speaking in heavily accented English. "I thought Michael Madison was a man," then pausing for a moment, he smiled and tipped his cap. "My name is Juan. Come this way, por favor. The car is parked in front."

Juan took possession of the cart carrying my luggage and motioned for me to follow. Outside, at the curb, a black Mercedes sedan was waiting. After placing my luggage in the trunk and helping me into the back seat, he started to drive off. In a friendly manner, Juan asked, "You speak Spanish, Senorita?"

For the past month I spent endless hours practicing Spanish using Rosetta Stone and trying to plow through Spanish for beginners without a great deal of success no matter what the advertising promised. I hesitated. Had I learned anything? "Yo hablo espanol, muy poco," my words spoken in a tentative, clumsy manner. I was embarrassed to say the least.

The pained look on Juan's face told me I had a long way to go to be even semi-fluent in Spanish.

"Don't worry, Senorita, I lived in Texas for many years so talking English is no problem. I speak good English, no?"

Traffic was heavy as we left the airport. Nearing the city of Guadalajara I began to feel a sense of excitement. I'd never been in a foreign county before. I stared out the window taking in the landmarks Juan pointed out. As we approached what Juan called the old district we passed colonial buildings interspersed with modern structures. Late model American cars were speeding along the wide tree-lined boulevards. The scenery was not what I expected, but then, I didn't know what to expect. The guide books noted Guadalajara and the outlaying neighborhoods were home to over four million people, second in size to Mexico City. Guadalajara was a far cry from the San Francisco Bay area I called home. For better or for worse, I'd be living here until I completed my assignment.

I had real concerns about accepting the position from the beginning, and they were growing by the minute as I took in the magnitude of the surroundings. The longer we drove the more I became concerned. Could I actually pull this off?

After a half hour drive, we approached a gated community in a modern, clearly expensive residential part of the city. Juan presented his identification to the guard who raised the bar so we could enter.

"This is Las Palmas, Senorita. Your townhouse is here."

The area looked new. The residences, as well as the surroundings, were well maintained. Acres of mowed lawns, colorful flower beds, tall palm trees, and sparkling fountains made a picturesque setting for the white stucco buildings with their red-tiled roofs. Juan stopped the car in front of a row of attractive townhouses on a cul-de-sac.

"This is your casa, Senorita. It's very safe here and quiet." He unlocked the front door of the two-story townhouse and held it open for me to enter, excusing himself to retrieve my luggage. I stood in the middle of the room and looked around, overwhelmed with what I saw. I hadn't expected to be staying in anything this nice. The beautifully furnished living room with its ten-foot ceilings, its wall of sliding glass doors leading to a covered patio, this was fabulous.

Juan brought my cases upstairs and handed me the keys along with his business card. "This is my cell number. I'll be your driver twenty-four hours a day. You call me, and I come and take you where you want to go." He walked toward the door. "If you don't need me, I'll be here at nine-thirty Monday morning, Senorita Madison, to drive you to your office. Have a nice weekend. Bienvenido, welcome to Guadalajara."

I plopped down on the white sofa, sinking deep into the cushions, to catch my breath. Noticing the large bowl of fresh fruit and the bottle of Tequila that graced the large glass topped coffee table I read the hand written note attached. "Welcome, from Grupo Ortega."

The large over-stuffed chairs across from the sofa were white as well. Only the large pillows on the sofa and chairs in varied shades of red, blue, and green added color to the room.

I was relieved after discovering the large television housed in an armoire in the far corner of the room thinking I'd have some way to pass the time. I turned on the set and ran through the channels, disappointed that there was only one English speaking station, CNN International with its promise of twenty-four hours of world news. I turned off the set and continued exploring the townhouse.

THE BUTTERFLY

All the furnishing looked new. I'd be surprised if it had been occupied before. This was much more than I'd expected and certainly a step up from my small, one-bedroom apartment in San Francisco.

It had been only three years since I started working for Bradley and Rowan. A prestigious old San Francisco law firm that hired me right after graduating from law school, certain the only reason I'd been given this assignment was no other lawyer in the firm wanted the job. No one wanted to be stuck in Mexico for six months or however long it took to implement the contractual details of the merger of the American company we represented with the Mexican company, Grupo Ortega.

The jitters began the moment I fastened my seat belt for the flight. Until then it has all been in the future. Now that all the bon voyage parties and well-wishers were behind me, the implications of the task before me were staring me in the face. Funny I couldn't get a scene from some old movie out of my mind. The theme song of that old suspenseful motion picture I seen years ago kept playing in my head non-stop. The scene seemed so real I could hear the music reaching a crescendo just before the car overshoots the curve and goes off the cliff. That's where I saw myself: speeding toward the curve headed for the cliff. I tried to convince myself everything would be okay, I'd navigate the turn and the car would stay on the road. Unlike the movie it would be a happy ending.

I decided the best thing I could do to settle my nerves was to unpack and make myself at home. Monday would come soon enough. By late afternoon, after I'd finished unpacking and setting things in order I was hungry, my stomach growling back at me was hard to ignore. I checked out the small, but modern kitchen. Someone had stocked the refrigerator and the cupboards with all the essentials. I scrambled a couple of eggs, made toast, a pot of coffee, and set a place at the dining room table where someone had placed a large bowl of fresh flowers and candles. Whoever it was thought of everything -- the bottle of Tequila and the six-pack of beer in the fridge all intended, I was sure, for the Mr. Michael Madison they thought was coming.

I went to bed early, hoping to get a good night's sleep, something that had evaded me the last few days. Tomorrow I would have plenty of time to go over my notes to be sure I had everything in order. Even though all the legal work had been completed already, my job was to make sure everything came together without a hitch. Deep down I felt I was in way over my head. This was the first major project I'd be handling on my own

Chapter 2

I had spent all of Sunday going over my game plan for the hundredth time, but it only seemed to increase my sense of panic. Now Monday morning found me rushing to get ready for the big day. My insecurities had reached a tipping point where I was even obsessing over what to wear. The bed was piled high with dresses I'd tossed aside. Taking into consideration the warm weather I settled on a pale-green, sleeveless shift with a short navy linen jacket. I had no idea what the dress code was in Mexican offices, but I hoped the outfit would be appropriate

The sound of a car stopping in front was followed by Juan knocking on the door, I grabbed my briefcase and laptop taking a few deep breaths as I tried to settle my nerves. I locked the door behind me and followed Juan toward the car.

He asked if I had a nice weekend. I lied telling him it was wonderful. As we drove, Juan continued to point out landmarks, and kept up a steady stream of conversation until he stopped the car in front of a multi-story modern office building in the business section of town. He came around and held the door open for me. It was ten o'clock. I couldn't believe they started work so late, but according to Juan, this was the norm. I had a lot to get used to.

"What time will you want a ride home?"

I thought for a moment, "I'm not sure what my working hours will be, Juan, but I'll call you later."

"With traffic, maybe it takes me thirty minutes to get here, Senorita. Okay?"

"I'll call you in plenty of time," I couldn't help thinking it would be really easy to get spoiled with a chauffeur at my beck and call. This sure beat walking to work or taking the bus.

I squared my shoulders and took another deep breath thinking it was now or never as I entered the building's well-appointed lobby. The sun shone through the glass dome roof, an atrium-like entrance with live trees and white marble floors. I checked the board alongside the bank of elevators and found Grupo Ortega listed on the sixth floor.

The elevator doors opened to a large, attractive reception area. The decor caught me by surprise as the walls were painted in vibrant shades of watermelon red, violet, and white with modern paintings scattered about. This looked nothing like the understated wood-paneled lobby of Bradley and Rowan's staid old law offices.

I approached the desk and said, "I am here for a ten o'clock appointment with Sr. Ortega."

The woman behind the desk asked my name.

"Michael Madison. I'm expected."

She looked at me with misgivings.

I smiled and explained, "I know you expected a male. It happens all the time."

She gave me another quizzical nod, probably thinking all Americans were crazy. "Have a seat please. Sr. Ortega's personal assistant will be with you in a minute."

Many minutes passed before a dark-haired woman approached the desk. I didn't know it then, but it would take a while before I learned "in a minute" didn't really mean "in a minute", or that "manana" didn't really mean "tomorrow." Nothing happened in a hurry in Mexico. Their concept of time was so different and hard to get used to.

The neatly turned out woman of about forty dressed in a black shirt and white blouse approached the reception desk. She also looked confused when the receptionist pointed to me as they exchanged a few words in Spanish. These were the times when I was really irked at my parents' choice of names. My father wanted a boy, but they could have saved me a lot of trouble if they'd chosen a different name and not the one they'd picked for the son they were hoping for.

The woman introduced herself in perfect English as Anna Morales, Sr. Ortega's assistant. "Come, let me show you around our facility and to your office. Senior Ortega has not arrived as yet, and I'm sure he will be looking forward to meeting you."

Anna showed me around the firm, which occupied the entire sixth floor, and was everything I expected from an international business the size of Grupo Ortega. The office assigned to me was like a dream come true, the spacious room had large windows overlooking the skyline and the Sierra Madre Mountains beyond. A far cry from the windowless cubicle I called my office at Bradley and Rowan.

I sat down at the large desk, took my laptop out of its case and placed it in front of me. Reaching into to my briefcase I removed the flowchart I'd worked on for weeks. At least an hour went by before Anna knocked on the door and announced Senor Ortega would see me now. She led the way down a long hall, past many closed office doors, to the tall carved oak wood double doors at the end. She rapped once before entering. My stomach was in a knot as I followed her into the palatial office. Senor Ortega rose from behind his massive rosewood desk.

If he was surprised to see me, I was equally surprised to see him. Umberto Carlos Luis Ortega Gonzales was not the crusty old gentleman I had pictured as the head of the prosperous company. Instead, standing before me, hand outstretched, was a forty something man, who was without a doubt the handsomest male I'd ever seen. He was tall, with a muscular build, his jet-black hair was a little on the long side, with a few stands of grey at the temples. Staring back at me were dark brown eyes and lashes any girl would die for. His flawlessly tailored, dark blue suit fit without a gap or wrinkle and his French cuffed white shirt had been starched and ironed to perfection. His maroon silk tie hung from a perfect knot. The men I knew didn't dress like that.

Senor Ortega smiled and shook my hand. "I must say I did not expect an attractive young woman to be the merger specialist. I was expecting an older man named Michael Madison."

"I'm so sorry for any misunderstanding." I tried to seem calm and sound professional. All I really wanted was to run for the door. "They should have told you I was female. My name is always confusing."

Senor Ortega took a moment to reply as he began to smile, "It's probably a good thing they didn't inform me. Our culture doesn't give much credence to women above a certain professional level, so I would more than likely objected, but now that you're here, let's get started. Anna, ask Manuel to join us."

The deep, melodic sound of his voice, and his perfect English completed a very attractive picture. I thought men like that were only seen in movies or on the cover of magazines.

Seconds later the door opened and a gentleman about sixty entered the office. I caught only a few words as the two of the conversed in Spanish at a pace I couldn't keep up with. I heard my name and *mujer,* which I knew meant woman. The rest flew by me.

Finally, Manuel shook my hand as Senor Ortega asked if I spoke Spanish.

"I'm trying to learn the language, but at the moment, I'm afraid I am still at the beginner level."

"Manuel speaks some English, but Anna will translate if need be. I had hoped your office would send someone fluent in our language, but it is what it is. Your job may prove to be more difficult without sufficient knowledge of Spanish. If you have problems you and Manuel can't resolve, I'm here.

He paused, then smiled, "I hope you will be happy here, Miss Madison. Be sure to take advantage of your stay. There is much beauty and culture to be enjoyed in Guadalajara. Our history dates back to the fifteen hundreds, and we boast excellent food, wine, and music."

Senor Ortega turned toward his desk, indicating the meeting was over. I followed Anna out the door.

Manuel, Anna said, was the head of the accounting department. The smile left has face as he closed the door closed behind us. The dismissive look he gave me left no doubt he didn't seem happy to have a female in charge, let alone an American. This could prove to be difficult.

Chapter 3

Weeks passed and the process of merging the two companies was going much slower than I'd hoped. Working hours were only part of the problem. The office didn't get underway until ten in the morning. Siesta was from one until three. The office closed at seven in the evening, the pace much slower than what I was used to in the states. No one worked overtime, much less the 60 plus hour weeks I put in.

I saw little of the city, hesitating to venture out alone. Beyond ordering a meal, asking how much something cost, or where was the nearest bathroom, my language skills were slow in expanding. While I might be able to ask questions well enough to be understood, I had trouble understanding the answers. Everyone talked too fast, and it seemed the Spanish spoken on all the tapes I listened to was Castilian, different in pronunciation and even words from Spanish spoken in Mexico.

I'd been at the office for at least a month, when one Friday evening, long after everyone else had gone home, I stayed late to finish my weekly report to the San Francisco office. I heard a knock on the door, thinking it was the cleaning lady I said, "Entre."

I heard a male voice ask, "What are you doing here so late, Miss Madison? Everyone's gone home long ago."

I was surprised to see Senior Ortega standing in the doorway. "Just finishing my weekly report."

He crossed his arms across his chest a quizzical look on his face before saying, "I hope you don't stay late often. Work is important, but time for enjoyment is equally important."

"I totally agree, but my company didn't send me here to enjoy myself." a quick look of concern crossed his face.

"What a pity. One should always make time to enjoy oneself. If you have no plans for the evening, may I suggest I catch up on your progress over dinner? I dislike eating alone."

I'm sure he recognized the hesitant look on my face as he continued, "We haven't spoken since the day you arrived. Time you brought me up to date. Come, it's time to end the work day."

It was obvious he wasn't taking no for an answer, so I quickly saved my report, reached for my purse, and followed Senor Ortega to the elevator where we rode in silence until it stopped at the basement garage.

He walked quickly to a bright red Audi convertible and opened the passenger door asking, "Do you have a favorite restaurant?"

I wasn't about to tell him I hadn't eaten dinner in a restaurant since I'd arrived. So far, my eating out had been confined to the café's within walking distance of the office at lunchtime or the food truck parked down the street.

"You choose, please." This whole thing seemed strange and I wasn't sure how to handle the situation.

He reached for his cell phone and dialed a number. I was able to understand his words even though he spoke at a rapid pace, to be reservations for two in twenty minutes. Maybe I was getting more accustomed to hearing Spanish.

Driving faster than I thought was safe and ducking in and out of traffic, he still managed to point out landmarks of the city. I guess more to fill the uncomfortable silence than anything else, I was having trouble holding a conversation. Not only didn't I know how to relate to the man next to me, I was scared stiff by his reckless driving.

We received a warm greeting as we entered the restaurant. Its modern interior was on a par with any fashionable spot in San Francisco. The owner seated us at a candle-lit table for two, the subdued lighting in the dining area was far different from the well-lit bar. The sounds of a classical guitar somewhere in the background set the mood.

The only thing I knew about Mexican food was enchiladas or tacos served with a bottle of Corona. A quick look around told me this wasn't that kind of restaurant.

I noticed a few tourists dining there, but not the jeans and T-shirt variety. The majority of the patrons were well-dressed Mexican men and exquisite looking women. The travel guides mentioned the state of Jalisco and Guadalajara, in particular, had the most beautiful women in Mexico. I glanced at my simple sleeveless blue linen dress and immediately realized my office attire wasn't appropriate. Certainly not on a par with the elegantly dressed women at the other tables, leaving me feeling self-conscious.

"I cannot keep calling you Miss Madison. It's much too formal for sharing a meal. I will call you Michael, and you call me Berto, as my friends do."

As he pronounced his name, it sounded like Bear Toe. I wasn't sure I should be calling him by his first name. This whole occasion was making me uncomfortable, feeling even more unsure when he asked what I would like to drink. I didn't know how to respond. Should I order wine or a Margarita or pass on a drink altogether? I'd never had an occasion to have dinner at an upscale restaurant with the boss before. I took the easy way out. "What would you suggest?"

"Try a Paloma. It's a favorite among the women I know and very Mexican, only foreigners drink Margaritas." He nodded toward the waiter ordering Scotch on the rocks for himself."

I sipped my drink, a delicious mixture of grapefruit juice, lime, Tequila, and soda. Still feeling ill at ease, somehow this didn't feel as if we were there for a business meeting. Nothing about work had come up as yet. The way he looked at me was difficult to understand. One moment he was disarming, almost fatherly in his manner. The next moment there was something sensual in his stare, or was I overreacting?

"So, Michael, tell me, are women lawyers common in the States?"

"Yes." I hesitated calling him by his name feeling a little strange that we would be on a first name basis. Women lawyers are becoming more common all the time. I think there are more women in law school now than men." This seemed to surprise him.

"The world is changing so fast, but in Mexico we are slow to catch up. For better or for worse, we still cling to many of the old world ideas about the roles for women. You're not married, I understand. Do you have a man in your life?"

Why was he asking those questions? More importantly I couldn't understand why I was answering them, but I couldn't seem to stop myself. Berto was charming, much more worldly than the single men I met socially. His questions were hard to ignore.

"No one special. I've been too busy getting through law school and trying to get ahead in the firm. New lawyers, like me, work more hours than you can imagine. I find I have very little time for a social life. It's difficult to get ahead. The competition is stiff and women have to be twice as good as men to climb the ladder to success."

When the waiter returned he asked if we wanted a second cocktail as he placed the menu in front of me. Berto answered yes for both us. I opened the menu horrified that it was entirely in Spanish. I hesitated a minute not wishing to appear at a loss, trying to seem at ease when every bone in my body was rebelling. Finally I asked Berto to order for me. If he realized I couldn't read the menu, he masked it well, except for a slight smile, and he ordered for both of us.

"That's what I don't understand about Americans, Michael. Work is so important you forget about living, but I thought it was only the men. You're telling me the same work ethic applies to women, now. I find that very disturbing. Women are supposed to brighten men's lives not compete with them."

I was relieved when the Caesar salad was placed before me, I was starved and maybe the interrogation would stop. At first bite the salad was better than any I'd eaten before. As expected, the entrée was slow in coming. A lesson I learned the hard way trying to grab a quick lunch. Everything was cooked to order. Microwaving was out of the question.

When the entree finally arrived the plate placed in front of me looked like work of art, the food almost too pretty to eat. Berto said the dish was called Ravioles de Pato. it consisted of won ton rounds filled with some kind of fowl. The ravioles were topped with a delicious salsa of currents, cranberries, and other red fruits. The waiter had poured a very nice glass of red wine. I had no idea pato meant duck in Spanish or I might have had second thoughts. The restaurant far outclassed any place I'd been before. I'm sure it was very expensive.

Thankfully the questions became less intrusive, but Berto never brought up the merger even once as we enjoyed the meal. I began to relax and enjoy his company. This was the first time I'd had a social evening out since I arrived. I suppose the drinks had taken the edge off. We took our time over coffee and could have occupied the table until closing. The waiter didn't appear in a hurry for us to leave. The check wasn't presented until Berto asked. This was such a different life style. In California everyone seemed to be in a hurry. Restaurants had tables to turn in order to make more money. In Mexico, dining out it seemed was something to savor something to be enjoyed, never rushed.

It was well past ten when we left the restaurant. Berto didn't ask where I lived as he drove off at breakneck speed. Minutes later he parked near one of the main plazas. He couldn't have missed the confused look on my face, because as he helped me out of the car he explained, "The city doesn't come alive until at least ten in the evening. Come, we'll stroll for a bit, enjoy the fresh air after the afternoon rain. Here in the plaza you can begin to feel the vibrancy of Guadalajara."

The area was alive with people most of them young. The café's that lined the plaza were full. The sounds of music were everywhere. After a few blocks, we settled on an ornate metal bench amongst potted trees and beds of flowers.

Turning toward me, Berto said, "Tell me more about yourself, and why you are called Michael."

For some reason I didn't hesitate maybe it was all the people milling around that made me feel more at ease. "The Michael is easy. My father wanted a son. I have an older sister, but due to my difficult birth, there would be no more children. I was destined to be the substitute son. My father taught me how to pitch a baseball, throw a spiral football pass, and fly fish. But I always had to be as good, if not better, than the boys. He demanded I excel at everything, a really tough taskmaster."

"A little unusual to be sure, but it could never happen here. Boys follow after their fathers and girls after their mothers. I could never imagine playing catch with either of my daughters."

As Berto spoke, I looked around at the sights, enjoying watching the people walking by. San Francisco had nothing like this. We had parks and green areas, but no real plazas. For the most part the summer weather didn't allow an evening stroll as the fog would be rolling in.

People seemed more carefree here, not in the least concerned about showing affection. Young couples were kissing, oblivious to their surroundings. Their openness seemed completely natural. I was so busy watching what was happening in front of me that I was surprised to hear Berto's voice.

"I find you so very different from the women in my life. I'd like to know more about you and your unconventional father. We must do this again soon, and you can tell me more about yourself."

A trio of strolling musicians' stopped in front of our bench, guitars in hand, and nodded at Berto. He turned to me and asked if I had a favorite song. When I said no, he stared at me for a long moment, then asked them to play, "El Verde de tus Ojos."

I'd quickly translated the title as, "The Green of Your Eyes." Strange. Was he making reference to the color of my eyes? After a few bars I recognized the song as an old American standard from the forties called "Green Eyes" something I heard often on the radio at my grandmother's house. It sounded so much better in Spanish, so sensual. The guitarists were better than good and the lead sang the words directly to me. This was really different. The whole performance was unforgettable. I felt like a little kid, excited by the moment. I glanced at Berto, the look he gave me was hard to decipher.

THE BUTTERFLY

When they'd finished, the lead guitarist winked at me. He must have thought there was something between us. They seemed pleased with the pesos Berto handed them and moved on.

"Shall we call it a night?" Berto stood and held out his hand to help me up, ever the gentlemen. "You do have beautiful green eyes."

Chapter 4

When the car slowed to a stop in front of my townhouse, I thanked Berto for a lovely evening. "I'll be sure and comment on how kind you've been when I turn in my report."

Turning in his seat he looked straight at me. "You are mistaken if you think this evening had anything to do with business. This was personal. I enjoyed having dinner and spending the evening with an attractive, intelligent woman. I do not relish dining alone." He paused for a moment then opened the car door. Walking around to my side he extended his hand to help me out of the car.

"Do you have an interest in art, Michael? There is a gallery event tomorrow afternoon, the works of a promising young Mexican artist. As my family is out of town, would you care to join me? I could give you a tour of the city as well."

I hesitated. I had no plans for tomorrow, just another dull Saturday alone going over the week's accomplishments. I couldn't help but wonder if it was a good idea. After all he was a married man, the wedding ring on his finger had been obvious. But what was the harm. He was my boss. Why not?

"That sounds quite exciting. Yes. I'd enjoy that."

"It's settled then. I'll be here at one in the afternoon."

As I reached my door I said goodnight and thanked him again for the evening.

The next morning, I slept in and took my time getting ready, looking forward to the day's events. Since my arrival, my time had been spent either at work or by myself in the townhouse. The weekends were long and I felt lonesome. I missed my friends and my family. I was very much alone in a strange city.

I put aside the concerns I had telling myself Berto was good company, a business associate, a family man. No reason to have turned down his generous invitation, besides being friends would help if some problem had to be resolved regarding the merger. I slipped into a green silk sheath. It showed off the color as my eyes and was dressy enough for a gallery showing and comfortable enough for the warm weather. I put an umbrella in my bag. Afternoon downpours, I was learning, were to be expected this time of the year.

I watched from the window as Berto arrived at exactly one o'clock, dressed casually in tan linen slacks, a white starched shirt and tan belted linen jacket. He was quite dapper in a very European sort of way.

Draping the matching jacket over my arm I reached for my purse and opened the door. It was hard not to stare. Berto was incredibly handsome

"Buenos tardes, Michael. Ready, I see. Something I must say I'm not used to. Mexican women are notorious for never being ready on time. We can take a quick tour of the city if you like, and then on to the gallery. The showing doesn't start until two. Anything special you would like to see?"

"No, I'm happy to have such a knowledgeable guide."

Starting the engine, he asked "I meant to inquire earlier, are your accommodations to your liking?"

"Oh, yes, they're perfect. Far better than I expected."

He seemed pleased. "You have Anna to thank. She took care of everything. I could not get along without her."

I turned toward Berto curious to know more about Anna. "Has Anna been with you a long time?"

"A very long time. Ever since I took over the business. She started working for my father shortly before his death."

I could tell by the catch in Berto's voice that the mention of his father's death was painful, something he didn't want to talk about, so I simply said, "I'm sorry.

When we neared the center of the downtown area, Berto began to point out the numerous neoclassical buildings, many dating back to the seventeenth century. We passed plazas with fountains along the tree lined streets and numerous impressive Gothic structures. I tried to take in everything Berto was pointing out, realizing just how fascinating Guadalajara was.

By now we were in the older section of the city. Our first stop was Liberation Square. Then on to the Rotunda de los Jalisco, dedicated to famous artists, musicians and politicians. We drove past the Guadalajara Cathedral built in the sixteenth and seventeenth centuries. Berto was giving me a fascinating history lesson, but my brain was on overload. There was so much to absorb. Our final stop was Hospicio Cabanas, a Unesco heritage site dating back to the eighteenth century. We toured the building, a former hospital and orphanage. Now the walls were lined with a collection of art made even more interesting as Berto was as knowledgeable about art as he was about Mexican history.

His enthusiasm helped explained the artwork that graced the walls of the office. He took great pride in pointing out the famous frescos by Jose Clemente Orozco. I had to admit I'd never heard of him as I tried to explain art history hadn't played a part in my education.

All this was new and exciting. I told Berto how different this was. "Compared to San Francisco, which has only a few buildings that survived the 1906 earthquake, this was a lot to take in. The history and beauty are overwhelming. I can't thank you enough for the tour, for taking the time to show me so much of your beautiful city."

Berto looked at me with a warm smile, an expression that showed in his eyes. "I enjoyed showing you a small bit of the city. You remind me of a child in awe of all you see. I'm delighted you're enjoying yourself. What a pity if you returned home with little or no appreciation for our culture or heritage, but it's getting late. Time to be off to the gallery."

Gallery Renaldo, was located in an old earthen toned colonial house. Berto opened the door to the sound of music and the voices of people. The room was filled with an interesting assortment of what I assumed were lovers of art. Well-dressed men and women speaking Spanish and an assortment of what I'd call aged, ponytailed hippies. A grey haired man in an over-sized white silk shirt open to the waist and gaucho styled black trousers, his hair pulled back into a ponytail, looking like a character in some play rushed to greet us extending his hand to Berto. "Como estas, Berto. Bienvenida. Hace mucho tiempo, que no?"

"It has been a while. Speak English please, my friend, Miss Madison is new to our language. Michael, this is Renaldo. The owner of this fine gallery."

Renaldo kissed me on both cheeks, European style and asked "From where do you visit?"

"I'm an American. I've been working here for the last several months."

"I'm surprised. I think maybe you are French. You are too slim and too sophisticated to be an American. Are you interested in art?"

What an odd thing for him to say. Was that how educated Mexicans see American women? Slightly flustered I said, "Yes, but not as a collector."

Renaldo beckoned a young woman carrying a tray filled with flutes of champagne over to us and handed both of us a glass.

THE BUTTERFLY

"Come, Berto, bring your drink. I have the new collection to show you, and I want you to meet the artist. I think you will like what he has produced."

As we were steered through the crowd, several people greeted Berto warmly as we passed by, until finally we reached a large group encircling a slim, dark-skinned young man seemingly ill at ease.

"Jorge," Renaldo said, reeling off a long introduction in Spanish. Berto shook hands with the young man speaking at length with him. The words I caught were relating to art, but the artist's attention seemed to be drawn to me.

Berto smiled in my direction. "Michael, Jorge thinks you are very beautiful, and he would like to paint you, but I wouldn't be surprised if he might have other things besides painting in mind."

I felt my cheeks redden. "Please tell him, thank you, but I really haven't the time." I'd heard Mexican men were anything but shy in their attitude toward women.

Berto smiled and repeated what I said. Jorge gave a shrug as if to say, "If you change your mind."

Renaldo suggested we view Jorge's work as he moved on to greet other guests. I followed along as Berto studied each of the framed paintings hung on the white stucco walls of what must have been the parlor of the old house. Most of the work was modern and colorful, but was nothing I could understand. I thought if you gave my sister's two kids a canvas and a lot of paint they could do as well. I couldn't tell from his expression whether Berto liked the paintings or not.

We moved on to the adjoining room where the artist's style changed. The paintings were still modern in that the nudes were not portraits, but distorted bodies whose faces were masked with splashes of color. I was embarrassed as I realized what Jorge was suggesting when he said he wanted to paint me.

Berto caught me starring at one of the paintings. "It's not too late. You can still be one of Jorge's models."

"Thanks, but I'm really not interested."

Berto took me by the hand as we walked back to the main part of the gallery. "I've seen enough of Jorge's artwork. Another glass of champagne, perhaps?"

More people were arriving, many stopped to say hello. Some referred to Berto by his nickname, others as Senor Ortega. I seemed to be of great interest and was introduced as an American business associate. Many smiled at me in a knowing way, the women in particular, which I found uncomfortable, especially when they went on to inquire about his wife and family. .

We were about to leave when Renaldo approached Berto asking what he thought of Jorge's work. "Give him a few more years and we'll see."

Renaldo seemed disappointed, probably expecting to make a sale. He patted Berto on the back and thanked him for coming.

As we walked to the car the streets were still wet, trickles of water still ran in the gutters. The afternoon rain had come and gone taking the humidity with it. Berto asked if I was hungry.

"I'm starved!"

"Good. It's still too early for dinner. The only ones who eat at six are American tourists, but I may have just the solution."

Berto parked at the entrance to another of the many plazas. We walked past a large fountain, a steady stream of water spraying from the mouth of a horse and stopped in front of El Caballo, Vino and Tapas extraordinaire. With his hand on the small of my back he led me through a bright red door. Inside the place was alive with throngs of young people and not a tourist in sight.

This wasn't really a restaurant, but one long wine bar that wrapped around the entire room. The only food served was Tapas, which Berto explained were the small almost bite-sized savory dishes favored in Spain. He ordered and the bartender placed glasses of red wine and a small platter of various varieties of cheese and paper thin slices of bread in front of us.

Raising his glass, Berto said, "To a delightful day, Michael. I hope you enjoyed yourself. I seem to never grow tired of your company."

"It's been exciting. I've never been to a private art showing before and the tour of the town really peaked my interest. There is so much to take in. I couldn't have had a better guide. I don't know how to thank you."

He seemed pleased. "Watching you enjoy yourself and your enthusiasm was thanks enough. I think I spend too much time around older and jaded people."

The bartender began to place small dishes of food in front of us, while the mellow-sound of a saxophone played somewhere in the background. The bar was filled mostly with singles. Everyone around us was friendly and many spoke English. The young women, about my age, were attractive in their short skirts or dresses, heels and makeup. Berto explained the university was nearby. This was definitely not the typical bar scene near a California university on a Saturday afternoon.

By nine o'clock I was back home having had a full day. Once again I thanked Berto.

"Nothing to thank me for, Michael. I had a most enjoyable day as well."

There was something sad about the way he spoke. I felt touched by his expression. Somehow he reminded me of a troubled little boy longing for happier days. There was no way could I inquire when his family was due to return. Berto had kept his personal life to himself, always directing the conversations toward me, but I couldn't help but wonder what his home life was like.

I changed into sweatpants and a t-shirt and called my parents. I hadn't spoken to them in a couple of weeks. We chatted for a long time. My dad was full of questions genuinely interested in everything I was doing. They made me promised to call more often.

I hung up the phone, thinking it was too early for bed and turned on the television finding a Mexican news station. Television was proving to be a great way to improve my Spanish. I'd even begun to enjoy the telenovelas, the Spanish version of our soap operas.

Hard as I tried I couldn't concentrate on the television, my mind was on the last two days spent with Berto. They'd been a refreshing change. While the women in the office were respectful, always pleasant, there was an invisible wall between us. I was never invited to join them for lunch, never privy to their gossip or any details of their personal lives. I was the American, an outsider, and from a different social class. The caste system was alive and well in Mexico. You didn't have friends outside your social or financial class. The men were married, and again I didn't fit into their social construct.

Almost two weeks passed before I saw Berto again. He stopped by my office just before the end of the day and invited me to have dinner with him. I didn't give it a second thought I enjoyed his company and looked forward to an evening out.

We went to a different but equally pricy restaurant and again had a pleasant meal. The conversation was light this time touching on the merger. When I could eat no more and had my fill of wine, Berto thought the evening was too young to end and suggested he show me Mariachi Plaza. The plaza was home to the mariachis. Several of the sombrero-wearing, colorfully dressed groups of musicians were playing their traditional music for the crowd. This time, the crowd was mostly tourists and like any tourist, I was enthralled by what I saw and heard.

There was that sense of sadness to his voice as Berto, speaking just above a whisper said, "I haven't been here since I was a child. It takes me back to happier days to see you enjoying the musicians as I did ages ago."

Once again I found myself wondering about the man at my side. Our relationship would be so much better if I could scratch the surface and get a peek at what lay behind the sense of melancholy.

It soon became a pattern, two or three times a week Berto would ask me to have dinner with him. I wasn't sure how to handle the situation, knowing we were spending way too much time together, but he was always the perfect gentleman. On occasion, he'd reach for my hand or put his arm around me as we walked, he never went further. Nevertheless, I was beginning to worry about our evenings out. If it hadn't been for Berto, I'd have no social life at all, but my concerned was the more time we spent together, the more I knew our relationship was anything but a normal business connection. A nagging voice in the back of my head said this was dangerous. This would never be allowed under any circumstances in our law firm and I had no idea where we were headed.

Chapter 5

Little by little, I understood the strong powerful businessman had another side to his personality. Berto seemed lonesome, sad, as if something was missing from his life that family or friends couldn't provide.

One evening, as we sat in a quiet corner of Berto's favorite restaurant, I asked the obvious question. Looking over the glass of wine I held in my hand I mustered the courage and said, "Why me, Berto?"

"I'm sorry. I don't understand your question, my dear."

"I wonder why you spend so much time with me? You must have other friends, and you do have a family. We're miles apart in so many ways."

My question must have taken him by surprise as he starred right through me, a far off look in his eye. His body was there, but his thoughts were elsewhere. It took some time before he spoke.

"If you must know, Michael, you remind me of a young woman I knew eons ago when I was a student at Yale, a time in my life when I was the happiest."

That came as a surprise. He'd never spoken of Yale before and I said as much.

"I spent four happy years at Yale. After I received an undergraduate degree I stayed on hoping to achieve a master's in international economics. My father's sudden death required I return home at once."

My curiosity peaked I asked, "Were you serious about the young woman?"

"I suppose I was in love with her. I thought so, anyway. I know she cared for me, but my world was suddenly upended. Being the eldest son, and according to law and custom, I inherited the majority of the estate and the sole responsibility for the family business. Suddenly I had no time for the beautiful young American woman. She had no place in my new world."

I finished what was left in my wine glass and nodded yes as Berto tipped the bottle in my direction and refilled my glass.

"And I remind you of her?"

"Oh, not in looks or anything I can put my finger on, Michael. Maybe it's only that you are a young, beautiful American woman, so different in attitude from Mexican women. Free to go where you want and do as you please. Women my age and of my social class were most often educated by the nuns in expensive Catholic schools, in some ways deprived of the joys and excitement of life. They were taught church and family are all that is important. The blithe spirit American women exhibit, their sense of independence, is not found among the women I know."

Berto reached for the half empty bottle of wine and re-filled his glass.

"I love to hear your laugh, to see the way your eyes light up when you see something new. I enjoy watching your freedom to have serious conversations about whatever crosses your mind, and to hold your own with men."

Just then, the waiter arrived and began to serve our entrées. The conversation abruptly changed and at that moment I knew our relationship had as well, though I wasn't sure exactly what was happening between us. I only knew our time together no longer seemed like just two business friends meeting each other two or three evenings a week.

At times the way Berto looked at me set off warning signs in my head as well as a flush of heat running down my spine. I had no idea how to put an end to it. If I was being honest, I wasn't sure I really wanted to. I rationalized the situation would resolve itself when my assignment was completed and I returned home. For now, I liked being with him, regretting he was married.

Toward the end of September, Berto mentioned that this time of the year the staff readied the beach house in Puerto Vallarta for the season. Guadalajara's winters could be cold while Jalisco's beautiful beaches stayed warm. He said his family would be leaving on Friday for the extended Mexican Independence Day vacation and invited me to spend the week at the beach as well.

The more I thought about it, the better the idea seemed. I needed to meet his family. It would make our spending time together more acceptable. I could tell some in the office were becoming aware of our all too friendly relationship. Anna, in particular, let me know in subtle ways she didn't approve. Being friendly with the family might make the time spent together seem more normal.

THE BUTTERFLY

I was packed and ready when Berto arrived at ten on Friday morning, excited about seeing more of the state of Jalisco and enjoying some much needed time away from the office. By now I'd gained a great deal of confidence in my ability as the project was going well, but I was working hard and under a great deal of stress to finish within the time allocated.

I opened the door and laughed to myself, rather than admire the handsome man who stood at my doorstep decked out in a starched navy blue shirt and creased starched white cotton shorts, the man who looked like an ad for GQ, all I could think of was "who did his laundry?"

As Berto took my suitcase, placing it in the trunk, I noticed the convertible top was down.

"If you wish I'll put the top up," as he started to do just that.

"No, please leave it down. The fresh air feels wonderful."

"You're not worried about your hairdo?" His expression showed that wasn't the answer he expected.

I laughed as I assured him, "Not at all. Let the breeze blow through it. I can always brush it out later. How long will it take to reach the coast?"

"Good question, my dear. The first part of the trip will go very fast as it's all on beautiful toll roads. The second part of the trip winds down the mountain on a two-lane road. It's more than a five thousand foot drop to reach the coast, passing through many pueblicitas. You might call them small villages. If the traffic moves along, it will take about five and a half hours. If we get stuck behind a slow moving bus or heavy traffic, it could take much longer, but there's so much to see the drive is worth it. Much better than flying."

The multi-lanes of the toll road were as modern as anything in the States, though they were without much in the way of traffic. Berto explained the reason why there were so few cars on the road was because the locals used the old roads rather than pay the tolls. The scenery was spectacular, mile after mile of Agave Cactus, with its distinctive blue color glistening in the sunshine.

"Agave is the plant from which they make tequila. The Mexican government, Michael, restricts producing tequila anywhere but Guadalajara. It's a real boost to our economy. Would you believe three hundred million plants are harvested near the town of Tequila alone every year? More are grown in the highlands. When we get to the beach, I will introduce you to tequila magnifico. The kind of tequila you sip like the finest brandy, not down with salt and lime."

Most of the time we drove in silence, stopping only at the toll stations every few miles. The radio was playing popular love songs I recognized only they were sung in Spanish. When we came to the end of the freeway, everything changed. Instead of miles of cactus we passed through small villages. The road was clogged, as Berto feared, with slow moving buses belching diesel fumes and old decrepit cars, with black smoke pouring from their tail pipes.

Every time Berto gunned the engine and passed a line of slow moving traffic, I held my breath. I knew the double yellow line in the middle of the road meant no passing. The road curved, leaving no clear view of what was ahead. Paying no attention Berto would pull out and floor the engine, ducking in and out between oncoming vehicles. This was no longer a pleasant drive to the beach as we zigzagged between cars, just one heart-stopping incident after another. I was terrified. Was Berto crazy? Each time he pulled out to pass, I saw my life pass before my eyes. What would my parents think when they learned I'd died in a car crash, let alone in the company of a married man.

Sensing my anxiety Berto explained, "Don't worry. I've driven this road a million times. I know every turn and every bump. If I don't pass, we'll be traveling at thirty miles an hour for days all the while inhaling deadly fumes."

I didn't feel any better knowing he knew every turn. If I were religious, I'd have prayed. I was sure we were going to be killed in a deadly accident or I'd be seriously injured. Instead of praying I clutched the top of the car door until my knuckles were white and hoped for the best.

Hours later, though it seemed like years, the traffic lightened as the road improved. We passed the towns of San Francisco, which Berto said they called San Pancho and Sayulita. He explained they were funky beach towns overrun with surfers, and promised to stop on the drive back to Guadalajara.

We were now about an hour from Puerto Vallarta, the fashionable tourist town I'd read about on the coast. Berto promised we'd stop there for a late lunch. Now that my nerves had settled all I could think about food. I was starved.

As we approached Puerto Vallarta, everything changed once again. We drove past the modern airport, luxury hotels facing on the beach, and the entrance to the famous marina full of boats from all over the world. Rows of shops and cafes lined the left side of the boulevard. An inviting walkway wound along the waterfront, called the Malecon. We'd entered the heart of the city turning left onto a narrow cobblestone street stopping in front of a café located in an eclectic looking art museum. I sighed a breath of relief we'd made it in one piece. After the long drive it felt good to stretch my legs.

Berto led the way. "This is my very favorite place for lunch. You'll like the artwork better than in Renaldo's gallery, and the food is great. You must try the fish. I guarantee it will be fresh from the bay this morning. Before John Huston and the movie industry made Vallarta famous it was a sleepy fishing village."

THE BUTTERFLY

I sat at a small table and watched Berto return carrying a tray, He sat down beside me and placed a small plate before me.

"What's this?"

"It's called Ceviche. Try it it's a delicacy."

I hesitated, "I don't think I'll like it."

"How will you know if you don't give it a try? Take a bite, then if you aren't pleased you won't have to finish what's on the plate."

I had to laugh he sounded just like my mother urging me to try calf's liver or some other food I rebelled against as a child. Feeling squeamish my reaction changed with the first taste of the thin slices of raw fish with fresh squeezed lime juice. In Mexico, limes are called limons. Lemons weren't to be found anywhere. As I tasted each bite, I began to savor the delicate flavor. I hated sushi, but this was different. If nothing else my time in Mexico was opening up a whole new world of experiences.

Berto had ordered fish tacos and Carta Blanca beer for two. The cold beer, warm chips, and fresh salsa tasted wonderful. Five hours in a convertible with the fresh air swirling all around me wetted my appetite as well as my thirst.

The plate placed in front of me was not at all what I expected, it consisted of shredded lettuce, chopped tomatoes, slices of tender pan fired fish filets, with warm corn tortillas folded in half on the side. Not the fried taco shell filled with hamburger Taco Bell called tacos at home.

Berto kept staring at me, smiling, as I devoured the food. "Are you enjoying yourself, Michael?"

"More than you can imagine," I drank the last of my beer, taking in my surroundings, enjoying the music coming from somewhere. I realized I was beginning to like the Mexican attitude, that life should be lived at a slower pace, so different from rat race in the states. Here life seemed to be all about food, drink, friendship, and family. There was time to enjoy life. Even I'd begun to slow down and enjoy my time in Mexico, hardly missing home at all.

We walked through the art gallery after lunch. A few paintings hung on the walls, as well as framed posters of famous artwork, jewelry, ceramics, and pottery all produced by Vallarta artists. We left the car parked on the street, and walked to the Malecon strolling along the wide curved walkway facing the water. White sand as far as my eyes could see.

"Is this the Pacific Ocean, Berto?"

"No, the ocean is twenty six-miles from here. This is the Bahia de Banderas or the Bay of Flags or Banners, protected from the ocean weather and home to the whales who come in the spring to have their calves."

We walked for some distance without the need to talk. I loved the feel of Vallarta. The smell of the water, the miles of sand beach, the old buildings. People seemed different here. Maybe the weather and the more casual beach clothing had something to do with it. Or maybe it was the police dressed in white Bermuda shorts and pith helmets.

"Notice the police have pistols at their side," Berto said. "It is unlikely they could shoot anybody. They are issued guns, but have to buy the bullets themselves. If there is trouble they call the Federales the federal police."

The American tourists, much to my embarrassment, stood in sharp contrast to the well-groomed locals. Too many looked like they'd just gotten out of bed. Unshaven men in T-shirts with ridiculous sayings stretched across their overweight torsos, the women didn't look much better.

Berto glanced at his watch. "Time we were on our way. It's still a bit of a drive to the beach house. We can come to Vallarta again while you're here and spend as much time exploring as you like."

The divided road became two lanes as we came to what was called Old Vallarta. Shops and cafes were off to the right side of the road that wound its way down to the beach, on the left large houses were built on the hillside with fabulous views of the bay. We drove for about forty minutes, past Mismaloya Beach where "The Night of the Iguana" was filmed, until we reached a long stretch of beach with three large houses spaced a great distance apart. Berto turned off the road and parked in front of a white stucco wall surrounding an enormous white stucco house. "Welcome to El Borde del Aqua. My favorite place in all of Mexico, maybe in the entire world."

"Translate it for me?"

"It means Water's Edge in English."

I didn't know what to expect. I wondered what the week with Berto's family had in store for me. I'd find out soon enough.

Chapter 6

Putting the top up on the car and retrieving the two cases from the trunk, Berto motioned for me to follow. He opened the massive ancient wooden doors, and we entered a large courtyard with tall palm trees and beds of hibiscus, dracaena, and bougainvillea all in full bloom. A tile set every few inches along the wide Saltillo pathway had a metal design of a fish embedded in the middle as they led the way to another set of old wooden doors. Berto unlocked them and motioned me to enter.

I couldn't believe my eyes. What was before me was not what I'd expected of a beach house. The interior was spectacular. I looked in awe from the high peaked ceiling of the immense living room to its Saltillo tile floors. A glistening wall of glass doors that opened onto an enormous Saltillo tiled patio. Berto pushed back the glass doors folding them against the side walls until the whole room became part the patio and the rear garden. I could hear the water as the tide was coming in, and the smell of the bay, feeling a slight breeze. How unbelievable. I'd never seen anything quite so beautiful.

The house was dead quiet. Where was the family?

"Berto where is everybody?"

He looked at me for what seemed ages before he spoke. "There's no one here but you and me."

"I don't understand," I couldn't quite grasp what he was telling me. "You said you family was leaving for the beach house on Friday, but now you're saying they're not here. Tell me the truth."

"I was being truthful when I said the family was leaving Friday for vacation. My wife has taken the girls to visit with her parents in Mexico City. She never comes here. She hates the beach house."

I couldn't think straight. He'd lied to me. At that moment there was only one thing I knew for sure, I knew I didn't belong here alone with Berto. Feeling a sense of panic I tried to appear calm. "Please take me back to town. I'll get a hotel room and fly back to Guadalajara tomorrow." Hard as I tried to seem in control of the situation the alarm in my voice gave me away.

"Please, I beg you to stay. Michael, by this time you know me and have come to trust me. You are safe here with me. I give you my word of honor. I know you will love the beach house just as I do. I hate being alone." Even his eyes pleaded with me to stay.

"I can't stay. You know that as well as I do."

I didn't know what else to say. Too many warning signals were going off in my brain. Feeling a need to be alone I stepped out onto the patio, trying to get my head around the circumstances and walked past the blue tiled swimming pool, down a few steps leading to a tall ornate metal gate. Opening the gate I found myself on the white sand beach. I kicked off my shoes and started to walk along the water's edge having no idea where I was going only that I needed to get away. What was I going to do now? I had no way of returning to Vallarta on my own. Staying here, alone with Berto, didn't seem like a smart thing to do. I knew he wasn't going to take advantage of me, but I still knew I shouldn't stay here. I'd walked a long way lost in thought, trying to understand why Berto had lied to me until the beach suddenly ended against a tall cliff that jutted a great distance out into the bay, waves crashing against it. I'd reached an impasse, not unlike the one awaiting me. Having no place to go, I turned and started to walk back to the house.

Berto was sitting at an ornate wrought iron table under the large palapa across from the pool, two glasses filled with gin and tonic, a bowl of chips, and fresh salsa in front of him.

He stood and pulled out a chair. "Come sit down, Michael. I apologize. I should have told you the truth, but I knew if I did you wouldn't come. Stay the night and we'll talk about what you want to do tomorrow."

I had no choice but to join him, maybe a stiff drink was just what I needed.

"I know you will love this house and the beach. It's my little bit of paradise, but it's not the same by myself. It cries out to be shared."

"What about your family, your children? Can't you share it with them?"

"I used to bring my son with me. He loved to spend time here, but he's in England at prep school. The girls won't come without their mother so the house sits empty, begging to be enjoyed. Enjoy it with me, please. We'll talk about it in the morning and I'll abide with whatever you decide. I put your suitcase in one of the guest rooms."

I sipped my drink and began to relax. Berto never crossed the boundaries before. I'd have to believe he wouldn't cross them now.

"The house is spectacular. I can't believe you can walk out a gate and have the whole beach all to yourself. I'd love this place, too, if it were mine." I began to relax as the drink began to take effect.

"I swim in the bay every morning before breakfast, sort of a ritual. You can join me if you like. The water's warm, the bottom sandy, you can walk out for some distance before it gets deep. I know you will enjoy my way to start the new day."

We'd finished a second drink before I was given a grand tour of the house, all six bedrooms and seven bathrooms. That didn't even include the servant's quarters. So this is how really rich people live. I'd never seen anything like this before, not even in magazines.

Berto asked if I was hungry, announcing he was the chef tonight. As usual I was starved. I watched as he barbequed steaks on the grill, a part of the massive outdoor kitchen. It was still quite warm so we dined outside under the palapa. The serene atmosphere of the house facing two miles of white sand beach made it seem as if the whole world had disappeared. The only sound was the water lapping against the shore. Finishing the last of the red wine, we brought the dishes into the main kitchen leaving them in the sink for the maid to deal with on Monday. Berto said that's just the way things are done as he suggested we have an after dinner drink by the pool.

The warm breeze had given way to the night air, and it began to cool off a bit. I'd gone to the guest room to get a sweater, when I heard Berto calling, "If you want to see the sun set, you had better hurry."

He was stretched out on a double chaise alongside the pool, motioning me to join him. I hesitated for a moment, then settled in beside him just as the sun was beginning its descent. I'd never witnessed anything quite like it before. The sun, a brilliant orange in color, glowed as it dipped toward the horizon. Its reflection on the still waters of the bay was an incredible sight, then all of a sudden the sun disappeared, seeming to sink into the ocean, and the sky began to darken.

The chaise we shared brought me in close proximity to Berto, closer than I'd ever been before. I could feel the heat of his body, the aroma of his cologne. I was afraid to speak or move. I began to feel warm all over, ashamed of what I was thinking.

"This has been one of the nicest days I've spent in a long time. Thank you for sharing it with me, Michael."

"Berto, I still don't understand. You have a family, friends, you don't need me." I was desperate to understand the man next to me.

"Ah, yes. You are right. I do have a rather large family."

I waited for him to go on. The silence was uncomfortable, but I didn't know what else to say.

Finally Berto turned on his side facing me and asked if I like stories?

I nodded yes, not sure what he meant.

"Good." He paused. "Let me tell you a story about a young college student who was just beginning to know himself and what he wanted from life when he is suddenly called home due to the death of his father. He is expected to assume responsibilities he isn't ready or prepared for. While the young man has older married sisters the wealth and responsibilities fall to the eldest son."

Maybe at long last I was about to learn more about the man. I hung on every word as he continued.

"The first thing the young man must do is marry and produce a son so the family wealth, position, and business remains safe. In Mexico the country's wealth and power rests in the hands of about ninety families. They marry within the families as a sort of protection.

"A young woman of suitable means and family was selected by the young man's mother, being sure the bride to be brought with her a large dowry."

Berto's story was finally coming to the surface. I needed the patience to listen and not interrupt if I was to get a glimpse at last of what was hidden beneath the aura of competence and sophistication. I hadn't noticed the two large snifters on the small table next to the chaise until Berto handed me the one only a quarter full.

"This is Roca Patron, one of the finest tequilas made. Sip small amounts ever so slowly to enjoy the taste, the full body. I promise you will sleep well tonight."

I picked up the glass and swirled its dark amber liquid before I took my first taste asking, "The rest of the young man's story please, Berto." With the amount of liquor I'd already consumed that day, I was sure I'd have no trouble sleeping.

Berto was sipping his tequila watching for my reaction, but I wasn't interested in Tequila. "You can't stop now I'm sure there is more to the story."

"The story. Ah yes, the story. At twenty-three years of age, the young man was married to a nineteen-year-old young woman he barely knew, having met her only once. The grand wedding took place in Mexico City with every prominent figure in society and politics attending. By twenty-four, his first child was born. A daughter. Thirteen months later a second daughter. Eighteen months after that a son, named after his father, as is the custom. If more children followed their sex didn't matter. For now there was a son to carry on the family's name and business."

The tone of his voice was tearing me apart. There was no joy in what he was relating.

"The young man had little time for family or friends he was consumed with work. The fortunes of his large extended family depended on the continued success of the business. He never really got to know his wife, though She did what was expected of her. She oversaw a well-run household, saw to the children's needs, was the perfect hostess when they entertained, and was ill with bouts of depression the rest of the time. And so ends the tale and existence of our young man, now no longer young, he is a family man with a family in name only."

I took another sip of tequila, letting it rest in my mouth before I swallowed as a real sense of sadness came over me. Here was a man of considerable wealth, who was well educated, charming, handsome, and worldly. He was heading a successful international business and seemed to have what every man strived for, and yet in this unguarded moment, his unhappiness was all I saw.

What he said next wasn't directed at me, but was his unconscious speaking out in a hushed tone just above a whisper. "She should have been a nun, much happier married to Jesus rather than to me. She'd be well on her way to sainthood by now."

I didn't know what to do. I'd never been in this kind of situation before. Should I speak or just let the conversation end? I couldn't help myself as I voiced what to me seemed the obvious solution.

"No one should be that unhappy in a marriage. Why don't you just get divorced?"

Berto reached over and took my hand in his, smiling. "My dear, charming Michael, what I love most about you is your naivety. I never should have spoken as I did. I am wrong to play on your pity, but to answer your question, I'm Catholic, as is my wife. Divorce is impossible. She would never agree. Even if I attempted to sway the church I have no basis for a divorce. Unhappiness is not a consideration. Our vows were made to God and cannot be broken."

Taking the last sip of my drink, the warm taste of the tequila lingering on my tongue, left me with nothing more to say.

Berto brushed away a lock of my hair that had fallen out of place, reached over and kissed me on the forehead. "Go to bed, Michael. I'll sit here a bit longer and finish my drink. If you're awake, we can swim together in the morning. I promise a happier day tomorrow."

I said goodnight and hurried to the guest room and closed the door, leaning against it. For some strange reason I'd never felt closer to Berto. I wanted to reach out to him. Take him in my arms. Only my better judgment kept me from doing so.

I undressed and readied for bed, bringing my toiletries into the bathroom, which like the rest of the house, was unbelievable. Everything was in a grayish-toned marble, the floors, the walls, the counters. The back wall of the oversized shower was glass looking out onto a private walled garden. I stood before the double sinks with their impressive hardware and starred at my image in the mirrored wall above. What was I doing here? Michael, I said to the image in the mirror, keep your emotions and any feelings you have for this man in check. Remember he's a married man.

I smiled back at my image, "If you're smart, you'll leave first thing in the morning."

Stepping up onto the king-sized bed that sat almost a foot off the floor, its ornate black-iron headboard and footboard designed in a unique ivy leaf design, I sank deep into the feather bed. The large guest room with its tasteful decorations was far more glamorous, almost regal, than anything I'd ever experienced. So this is how really rich people live. I turned off the light.

Chapter 7

I slept like a rock and only awakened when Berto tapped on the door. "I'm going for a swim. I'll wait if you want to join me."

Rubbing the sleep from my eyes, I called out, "I'll be with you in a sec. A swim sounds wonderful."

I threw on my bathing suit, wrapped a pareo around my waist and opened the door. Berto was waiting in the living room. He reached out his hand and kissed me on the cheek. "Good morning, Little One. Did you sleep well?"

"I've never slept better, but after all the tequila I'm looking forward to a swim to clear my head."

"Come along." He glanced at my bare feet and grinned.

As I walked beside him, I couldn't help but notice how well built he was, fascinated by the tufts of dark hair forming an inverted v on his chest.

I ran through the open gate toward the water hoping to catch up with Berto who'd dashed ahead. Dropping my pareo on the sand, I took a few quick steps leaving Berto standing at the water's edge and dove into the bay. I expected the water to be cold, but was surprised to find it warm. The tide was coming in with only small waves breaking toward the shore. This was heaven. I swam for some distance before Berto caught up to me.

Laughing as he swam alongside me. "No bathing cap, or shoes. You dive in head first and swim off like a fish. Come, let's swim to the end of the beach and dry off on the walk back."

By the time we reached the cliff and could swim no further I was winded. It had been a while since I'd had time to swim and keeping up with Berto had sapped all my energy. Wading through the shallow water to the shore I ran my fingers threw my hair and shook off the water. The sand felt warm beneath my feet.

I walked along side Berto, surprised by how delightful the weather was so early in the morning. "That was fabulous. It's hard to believe you can have all this beauty to yourself."

"If you choose to stay we can do this every morning."

Closing the gate behind him as we re-entered the property, Berto pointed to an outdoor shower. "Come, Little One, let me rinse the salt water and sand off."

He playfully sprayed warm water from the top of my head to the tips of my toes. "Your bathing suit doesn't leave much to the imagination. Not an ounce of fat on your body. You're beautiful in every sense of the word."

"Stop. You're embarrassing me." I could feel my cheeks redden.

"Nothing to be embarrassed about. A man should always compliment a woman on her beauty. He handed me a plush towel asking, "Are you hungry?"

"I'm always hungry."

"Yes, I am well aware. We can breakfast here or drive to the hotel in Mismialoya. Which do you prefer?"

"Let's stay here."

"Then you have plenty of time to change while I fix an Umberto special."

I towel-dried my hair, and changed into shorts and a sleeveless green linen top while trying to decide what to do next. Had I overreacted? So far there was no reason to be concerned. It would be nice to spend a few days here at the beach. We'd been friends up to this point, no reason why Berto and I couldn't remain just friends.

Berto was busy in the kitchen still in his swim trunks busy with pots and frying pans on the stove. He'd opened the glass doors so a slight breeze filled the living room. He called to me. "If you set the table under the palapa, our breakfast is just about ready. It's too nice to eat indoors. Everything you will need is in the cupboards outside."

I had just finished putting the silverware in place when Berto walked out carrying a large tray, smiling as he placed it on the counter. "Breakfast ala Berto, specialty of the house."

With a flourish he set a pitcher of Mimosas down in the middle of the table, placed a glass and a large plate piled high with some sort of creation at each place.

Pouring drinks he noticed my quizzical look. "You've never had Huevos Rancheros before? Well then, you are in for a treat."

THE BUTTERFLY

I started to slice through the breakfast before me, a warm tortilla on the bottom covered with a layer of black beans, two fried eggs covered with a warm sausage and tomato salsa, topped off with slices of avocado, shredded cheese, cilantro and sour cream. As promised, it tasted delicious.

"What do you think? It's a traditional Mexican dish served on special occasions like brunch after church on Sunday."

"It's incredible." Taking another large bite, I asked if he was missing church on my behalf.

"Not to worry, Little One, I haven't been near a church in years. You're not keeping me from anything. Enjoy your meal. Here, let me refill your glass."

When every bit of food was gone from my plate and I had my fill of Mimosas, we took the dishes back to the kitchen. I fully expected to help with the clean-up, but Berto wouldn't listen. We left them alongside last night's dishes. Maria would have her work cut out for here tomorrow. Berto assured me this is how it is done in Mexico. The patron would never be expected to do menial tasks.

All I wanted at the moment was to stretch out and take a nap. My stomach was full, and once again I'd had more than my share of alcohol. I laid down in one of the chaises by the pool, loving the feel of the warm sun. I must have dozed off, when I awoke I had no idea how long I'd slept. I glanced to my left and saw Berto sitting on a chaise beside me with a sketch pad in hand, a magnificent blue butterfly resting on his shoulder.

"I'm so sorry, that was rude. I didn't mean to fall asleep."

"Nothing to be sorry about. You're here to enjoy yourself and I'm happy to just sit here and look at you."

When I started to get up Berto said, "Please. Don't move. Stay as you are for a few more minutes." He looked at me, then down at the sketch pad as he held a pencil between his lips. He stared at the drawing, so serious about what he was doing, oblivious to time. After what seemed an eternity, I started to change position, but Berto begged for just one more minute, saying, "I'm almost through."

At last he closed the pad, rose, and started toward the house.

"Don't go," I pleaded. "I'd like to see what you've drawn."

He tucked the pad under his arm. "It's nothing really. Just something I wanted to have for myself." He continued walking toward the house as I jumped up and ran after him.

"Please, that's not fair." I reached out my hand and he handed me the pad. Opening the cover I was overwhelmed by what I saw. I turned several pages of excellent sketches before I stared at my portrait. His talent was undeniable.

"Berto, this is amazing, but it's much too beautiful to be me."

"You're wrong, Little One. It is how I see you. Not many women have your natural beauty. They need the enhancement of makeup to make them appear attractive. Much of your beauty comes from within. To me, the picture is who you are. I see a youthful, unspoiled woman, not jaded by the passage of time. I hope you never change."

Tears began to roll down my cheeks. The way he looked at me, the words spoken were unlike anything that had ever happened to me before. I held my breath and threw my arms around him, happy to have him hold me close. Now more than ever, I was confused. What was happening? Clearly we were moving to a different place. Could I really ignore all the warning bells going off in my head?

Chapter 8

We spent the rest of the day by the pool. It felt good to be doing nothing. I'd dive in for a swim or to cool off. The pool felt like a warm bathtub. Floating on my back I was surprised by how peaceful the surroundings were. Every once in a while I'd see a boat sailing far off shore or a wind surfer in the distance, but there was nothing to disturb the beauty and solitude of the beach house. A truly enchanted place. The sun had set and the hour was late. Berto suggested we have dinner out. He spoke of a restaurant on the beach in Old Puerto Vallarta.

After a pleasant drive to old town, we parked on a side street and walked a block down to the beach. The hostess showed us to our table, which much to my amazement was on the sand close to the water's edge, close enough to the water to see and hear the waves lapping the shore. We sat under an umbrella made of palm fronds, a flickering candle the only light except for the full moon. The tourists were long gone. We had the place almost to ourselves.

I'd never been to such a romantic spot. I couldn't believe this was real rather than a set from some romantic movie. We sipped champagne and dined at a leisurely pace, no reason to hurry. Strolling musicians added to the ambiance if that was even possible. What could be more splendid than dining under the stars on a warm evening in what felt like paradise? Nothing at home could ever compete with this.

Hours later, driving back to the beach house with the top down, a warm breeze blowing through my hair, romantic guitar music played from a CD, I couldn't help thinking this was an evening I'd never forget. Never in my whole life had I experienced anything like this. I felt a warm glow, the aftermath of champagne, and I couldn't remember how much wine.

It was quiet as we entered the darkened house. Not a sound to be heard until Berto opened the glass doors,

"This has been a glorious day, Berto. I'm glad I chose to stay."

"And I am glad as well. The past two days, without a thought to the office or responsibilities, only time to enjoy your company. It has been as you said, glorious. Join me for an after dinner drink and a swim before we call it a night."

"That sounds absolutely wonderful. I'm not ready for bed."

"Go change, Little One, and I'll wait for you by the pool."

I closed the door to my room and started to change out of my clothes. A swim before bed would feel good. Maybe it would cool the feelings running though my body, dangerous images I didn't want to think about. I hung my dress on a hanger in the closet and stepped into my bathing suit, wrapping the pareo around my waist, Tahitian-style. The only light besides the stars and the moon was the small pool light, illuminating the dolphin set in tiles at the pool's shallow end. I could make out Berto's profile from where he sat on a chaise in the semi-dark. God he was handsome.

I sat beside him as he handed me a snifter half-filled with Roca Patron. I really didn't need any more to drink, but I took a sip anyway and for some unknown reason the title Berto had written at the bottom of his drawing of me popped into my thoughts.

"You wrote "La Mariposa" on the drawing. I meant to ask you earlier what that means."

Berto looked at me and smiled. "It means, My Butterfly."

"Butterfly? I don't understand."

"I'm quite sure you don't. To me you are as beautiful as a butterfly and just as delicate. The butterfly's only defense when it perceives danger is to fly away." He paused for a second and then continued, a touch of sadness in his tone. "Which I am sure you will do one day."

"How strange. Is that really how you see me? I would hardly call myself delicate." I took a gulp instead of a sip of tequila and regretted it. My throat was burning as the sensation reached my toes. "I have a career. I support myself. I expect to be successful."

Berto stood and started to walk toward the pool, "All that is true. You've done as good a job, even better than any man could in helping the merger to succeed. But my butterfly, I don't believe you've yet experienced great love or great sorrow. Will you be brave enough to handle either without fleeing?"

With that he dove into the pool and motioned me to follow. I dove in behind him. At least there wouldn't be any more psychoanalyzing. After slowly swimming several laps, I turned over and floated on my back, with my eyes closed enjoying the warmth of the water only to be surprised when Berto swam up behind me and placed his arm around my waist drawing me to the shallow end. Startled when Berto took me in his arms and kissed me with greater passion than I'd ever been kissed before. I knew then and there I'd wanted him to kiss me for a very long time. He gently gathered me in his arms and carried me out of the pool setting my feet on the ground and wrapping me in a towel. His nearness, his touch, the way he looked at me sent shivers down my spine.

Before I could say a word, he kissed me again, picked me up in his arms and carried me to his bedroom, whispering in my ear, "Don't say a word. You will spoil the mood, my little one, if you speak."

The bed was unmade, the covers pulled back over the foot of the ornate iron bed, and the mosquito netting tied back.

Berto pulled down the straps of my wet bathing suit. I stepped out of it and left it lying where it fell on the marble floor. His eyes never left my body.

"You are so very beautiful. Your breasts still small and firm, your stomach flat, absolute perfection. I've never seen anything lovelier.

He laid me on the bed, leaving his wet trucks alongside my suit and lay down beside me. "It's time for you to become a woman."

I couldn't catch my breath. I wanted him to kiss me again.

I knew what was about to happen. Whatever it meant didn't matter. For the moment all I wanted was for him to make love to me, and I wanted it more than I'd ever wanted anything in my life.

I wasn't a virgin, but I'd never experienced anything like this. Berto was like an artist. His every touch was like a brush stoke on a grand painting. My body was the canvas that came to life with every touch delivered with love until, at last, the beautiful picture was complete.

A feeling I'd never felt before encompassed my being as I lay in his arms. He ran his fingers through my wet hair, kissing me with such tenderness.

"You've made me very happy. I feel like a young man again, in love for the first time, but I've never been as vulnerable as I am at this very moment." He brushed a lock of hair from my forehead as he whispered, "Thank you for making love to me, my love. Treat me kindly as I've given my heart to you.

I fell asleep in his arms thinking only of how content I was. For the moment, nothing else mattered.

I awoke with a start. Berto was fast asleep lying on his back beside me. Morning and its moment of truth set in. I climbed out of bed, put on my bathing suit, still damp from the night before, and tip-toed out of the bedroom.

Unlocking the gate I walked out onto the sandy beach and started to jog, my thoughts a jumble of mixed emotions. I'd never had an experience like last night. I doubted I would ever again. If there was an art to lovemaking, Berto was a master, but he was married. I couldn't allow myself to fall in love with him. He could never promise marriage.

I began to pick up the pace knowing the faster I ran the harder it would be to think. The adrenalin began to kick in and I ran until I was out of breath. Panting, my heart pounding as I tried to catch my breath. Wiping the beads of perspiration from my forehead I began to walk slowly toward the end of the beach. The thoughts I'd tried to avoid came tumbling back. I knew this would never have a happy ending, but damn it, I'd never felt like this with anyone else. The sky had never looked bluer, the sand whiter, the sun brighter. Every part of my body was on sensory overload. All I wanted to turn around and rush back into Berto's arms.

By the time I reached the cliff at the end of the beach I still had no idea what I should do as I dove into the water and began to swim back toward the house.

Wading ashore I saw Berto standing on the sand near the gate. He ran toward me gathering me in his arms.

"Thank God. I've been worried sick something had happened to you, or you'd left. Are you all right?"

"Not really. I don't know what comes next."

He kissed me, and held me in is arms. "Until we return on Sunday we don't have to think of anything or anyone except ourselves. What comes next? I don't know, Little One, but we will work it out. For now it's you and me alone on our own special island with only our joy at being together. The outside world can't touch us here."

He took my hand as we walked back to the house. Stopping at the outdoor shower, he waited while I rinsed off the sand and salt. "Time to get dressed, Maria will be here soon."

I heard a female voice mumbling in Spanish as I walked into the living room. Maria was busy in the kitchen. The large square dining table on one side of the room was set. Red Bougainvillea petals were floating in a large bowl in the middle of the table. A pitcher of fresh squeezed orange juice, a platter of pineapple slices and mangos cut in quarters, and a dish of sweet rolls awaited Berto. He was nowhere to be seen.

I felt uncomfortable as I waited for him, trying to avoid Maria's questioning glare. After what seemed like ages of listening to the sound of my growling stomach, Berto appeared in a white linen shirt and navy shorts, freshly shaven.

THE BUTTERFLY

He was by far better looking than Diego Luna or Antonio Banderas or any other Hispanic movie star I could remember. Just the sight of him made my cheeks reddened as the memories of last night returned.

"Sorry I kept you waiting." He led the way to the table.

Maria appeared pouring coffee. Berto thanked her but neglected to introduce me, which I thought was odd. We ate in silence. It wasn't until Maria had cleared the table that Berto asked if there was anything I wanted to do today. I knew I had to get out of the house. I found Maria a disturbing presence. Maybe Berto could ignore her, I couldn't. "I'd love to visit Puerto Vallarta again."

We left shortly after breakfast. Before reaching Old Town Vallarta, Berto drove up the winding hillside to Conchas Chinas, which meant Chinese shells, a mostly American residential area of large million dollar homes overlooking the Bay of Banderas, one more beautiful than the next.

Berto was more than happy to let me explore the shops and attractions, one being the former home of actress Elizabeth Taylor which she purchased when Richard Burton was filming the *Night of the Iguana*, the film that changed Puerto Vallarta from a small, sleepy fishing village into a world class vacation site. The house wasn't anything special. What made it interesting was Burton's house across the street with a bridge he'd had constructed over the street to connect the two houses. Rumor had it they fought like cats and dogs, spent a great deal of time living apart, then made up and lived together again. No wonder they'd both been married and divorced so many times.

We had a light lunch at a café overlooking the Rio Cuale. Despite the tourists this felt like Mexico. Berto was encouraging me to practice speaking Spanish with him. Insisting that words of love sounded so much more beautiful in his language. He wasn't wrong they did have a different more romantic sound.

We arrived home shortly before four, just as Maria and her husband Guillermo, the gardener and handyman, were leaving for the day. I was relieved they wouldn't be staying. Their suspicious looks were unnerving. With them gone the house was ours

.

We settled by the pool. Berto poured two tall glasses of gin and tonic and we spent the rest of the afternoon talking. Berto wanted to know all about me. He was curious about where I went to school, about my boyfriends, wanting to explore every nook and cranny of my life. We had a second drink and waited for the sun to set before reheating the dinner Maria had prepared.

Hand-in-hand we strolled on the beach after dinner. I'd never been more relaxed or content. I had a sense of wellbeing I'd never felt before, happy to just spend time with Berto. My usual need to be accomplishing something had long gone by the wayside.

We spent the night together in Berto's bed with the doors wide open so he could hear the sound of the water, keeping the netting in place against the bugs. We made love as if we couldn't get enough of each other. I lay in his arms in the afterglow as he ran his fingers through my hair, kissing me on the forehead as he whispered, "If I could keep you here with me always, I would be the happiest man alive."

"I'm here and I'm not going anywhere,' I whispered, as I began to make love to him something I'd never imagined I'd ever have the courage to do.

The days flew by way too fast. The original plan was to leave on Saturday, but we put it off needing every moment of every day we could manage to be together. Berto even gave Maria and her husband Saturday off telling me he wanted us to spend the whole day in bed. We did just that.

Chapter 9

A sense of sorrow crept over me as I packed to leave, like the curtain coming down on the last act of a tragedy. Nothing would ever be the same. I knew I loved Berto with all my heart and soul, but I had no illusion that my heart would not be broken. I believed he loved me as well, but how could we make this work? I'd never pictured myself as the other woman, the mistress, yet how else could I be described.

The long drive back to Guadalajara was hell for both of us. We'd made love that morning as if it were the last time. I clung to him so tight I couldn't breathe, wishing I could understand every word he spoke in Spanish as he gently wiped away my tears.

The world was closing in on us as every mile clicked off on the odometer. The music no longer seemed romantic. There were no words spoken between us, anguish filled the silence. I felt as if I was on my way to a funeral. My own.

Berto kissed me slowly and tenderly as he left me at the door of my townhouse.

"Tomorrow will be busy for me, and probably for you as well. We will have dinner together on Wednesday and maybe I'll have a plan by then."

I heard the sound of sadness in his voice and that stopped the questions I was about to ask. How would we get through this would have to wait for another day. I clenched my firsts digging my nails into my palms trying to hold back the tears.

"I love you, Little One. You are the joy of my life. I'll find a way. I promise." He turned and walked away.

I shut the door behind me, slid to the floor, and cried my heart out. I'd never felt so alone.

Jose dropped me off at the office the following morning. Glancing in the rearview mirror he asked if I'd had a nice vacation. Good God, did he know? Did everybody know?

The office was bustling when I arrived. My desk, as expected, was full of folders with yellow Post-it notes attached, questions from Manual. I needed to put everything out of my mind and concentrate on my job. There was only two months left of my six-month assignment and still a lot to be accomplished. No matter what, I couldn't jeopardize the job I'd been sent here to do. The busier I was the less time I had to think about Berto.

I didn't see or hear from him all day, nor did I hear from him on Tuesday. The time I spent alone at night seemed bleak as the sleepless hours dragged on. I missed falling asleep in Berto's arms and waking up next to him.

He called me on Wednesday sounding business like suggesting I take a cab after work and meet him at our favorite restaurant. The tone of his voice sent off alarm bells. Was he regretting what had taken place between us? Had I been used? I had a hard time concentrating on work after his call. I hardly accomplished anything.

As I entered the restaurant I saw him sitting at the bar. I wanted to rush into his arms, but I couldn't. This was his home turf. He was always running into someone he knew, either a friend, a relative, or business associate, making me feel ill at ease. Even more so now as I imagined myself as Hester, a huge letter A hanging around my neck.

Berto stood and reached for my hand, he leaned close and kissed me on the cheek. "I thought you'd never get here, Little One. I've been miserable ever since we parted on Sunday. I miss you. It's as if the thing that gives meaning to my life has been ripped away."

Just the way he looked at me made me feel better. Everything between us remained the same.

"I've missed being with you, as well. Feeling quite alone I must admit. Have you been waiting long?"

"No, I arrived just a few moments ago. Berto picked up his drink and motioned to a small table in the lounge. The conversation never touched on the beach house. After cocktails and dinner Berto drove me home, walked me to the my door and asked if he could come in. Of course I said yes. As soon as the door closed behind him I was in his arms.

THE BUTTERFLY

"God I've missed you, my Little One. This can't go on like this. I've got to find a way for us to be together." His kiss was passionate. I returned it in kind and led his upstairs to my bedroom.

After making love I'd fallen asleep in his arms only to awaken when I felt him climbing out of bed. I opened my eyes to see him scrambling to get dressed.

"Where are you going?"

"I can't stay. I must return home. I'll call you. We'll make plans."

When the door closed behind him I was alone, feeling cheap. My married lover had just left my bed and gone home to his wife. Crazy thoughts were running through my head. Did they share a bed? Did he make love to her as well? Did they share cocktails and dinner on the evenings we weren't together? God, how could I have been so stupid? None of this should have happened. I should have stopped it, but I didn't.

I thought the weekend would never end. I felt even more alone and confused not knowing where this was leading or how it would end? Could I deceive myself into thinking it would never be over. I knew deep down it had to end badly.

I was sitting at my desk on Monday morning signing off on another portion of the agreement that had been successfully completed when Anna knocked on the door.

"Senior Ortega wishes you to bring the files on employment to his office now." The coldness in her voice left me to wonder why the pleasant relationship that had grown between us had suddenly taken on such a sudden hard edge.

Opening the file cabinet, I reached for the documents and wondered what the problem was. I thought all those conditions had been met long ago.

I tapped on the door.

"Adelante."

Taking a deep breath I pushed open the door and walked in. Berto stood and moved quickly from behind his desk to the door and locked it. He took the file from my hand dropping it on the floor. Before I could catch my breath I was in his arms.

Holding me close he spoke of having a miserable weekend. "My days mean nothing without you. My bed is a lonely place. But I have wonderful news for you. Come sit down."

I leaned back in the chair, as Berto perched on the corner of is his desk. "I'm leaving for Italy on business on Saturday afternoon and I've purchased a ticket for you to join me. We will have a whole week in Rome together." The look on his face was one of pure joy.

"Berto, I can't. How will I explain leaving? I've already taken a week's vacation that was questionable."

"Don't worry. I'll think of some excuse. No matter, we leave at three in the afternoon. I was so excited I couldn't wait to tell you." He picked up the files, and handed them to me, "I'll call later with the details. Just one last kiss before I let you go."

I sat beside Berto in the first class section on Delta Airlines as he spoke with excitement of all the wonderful sights I would see and all the romantic places we'd visit together. His whole demeanor had changed and he was as happy as he'd been at the beach house. He couldn't stop smiling as he held my hand. I didn't ask how he arranged for me to accompany him. I didn't want to know

Just as he promised, I walked down the Spanish steps, visited the Vatican, the Coliseum, the Roman Forum, and dozens of plazas and more fountains than I could remember. Some sights I saw with a private guide while Berto was in meetings. As soon as we'd checked into the hotel Berto had insisted I go shopping mentioning Prado, Versace, or Gucci as shops I might want to visit. He wanted me to have something special to wear on our evenings out.

We dined in style, sometimes alone, sometimes with clients. Among Berto's many talents was his mastery of the Italian language, which he spoke like a native. This surprised the American wife of one of his business associates. She must have assumed I was Berto's wife. When I didn't enter into the discussions she probably thought I didn't speak English. I was glad not to take part in the conversation, there were to many pitfalls. I almost gave it away trying hard not to laugh when she mentioned how much she admired the Mexican people, describing in great detail the wonders of her Mexican gardener.

As Saturday was our last night in Rome, Berto suggested a charming café with outdoor seating in the plaza across from the Trevi Fountain, the only place left on my list of places to visit. "We can dine and you can view the fountain to your hearts content."

After dinner we walked across the plaza. I was surprised to see how large the fountain was or that there were tiers leading down to the water. I remembered a scene from an old movie I'd watched on television called, *Three Coins in the Fountain,* and wanted to drop a coin into the water. The coin was a promise of my return to Rome. I hoped the promise would come true.

Berto joined me as I sat on the stone steps. The autumn weather was warm during the day, but cool as the nights grew longer. Noticing I seemed cold, Berto took off his suit jacket and placed it around my shoulders

"I promise I'll bring you back to Italy again. You will love Florence and Venice. When I retire, I'll buy you a villa in Tuscany, and we'll spend our days

THE BUTTERFLY

looking out over vineyards and olive groves, and I'll paint your picture a thousand times."

It all sounded so perfect, our own villa in the countryside as soon as he retired, maybe twenty years from now? Until then, I wondered, what would my life be like?

"Berto, I'm not sure I can wait that long. I'd like to marry someday and have a family."

"Please, Little One, don't speak like that. I'll give you a child if you wish and when my wife passes on you know I'll marry you."

Our week in Rome was ending and reality was beginning to set in. I reached for Berto's hand. "Oh, my love, can't you see how impossible this is? You have a family, your wife is young, I'm sure she will live a long time. What am I to do in the meantime?" The realization of what I'd gotten myself into was there staring me in the face. I was scared. What he was proposing wasn't my idea of a solution.

Berto held tight to my hand as we began to walk down a quiet street of old residences converted into apartments. A few couples passed us by without so much as a glance. Neither of us said a word until Berto broke the silence.

"Let me try to explain something about our culture, which you might find difficult to understand. Something so different from what you are used to, but not unlike most of the European cultures. Our attitudes are different from you Americans. Among my friends and in our social class, having an affair or a lover can be considered acceptable. Many of us marry for power, not for love. Being with a woman who is not our wife, but who you love is understood. Yes, one needs to be discrete, but no one really cares."

"Please, Berto, you're not going to tell me your wife wouldn't care. What about your children?"

"She would care least of all. My children understand they must accept whatever their father does as long as I hold the purse strings. Please, I beg you, don't end our beautiful time together in Rome with your concerns. I'm working on a plan to solve all our problems. Don't be the frightened Butterfly. Don't fly away. I would be lost without you."

Chapter 10

December was fast approaching, and my six months in Mexico would soon be coming to an end. The thought of leaving Berto was tearing me apart, but staying was out of the question. My law firm expected me to return.

His plan involved extending my time in Mexico. I discovered he'd been in contact with my office and arranged for me to stay for an extended period of time, offering to pay my salary. Giving him more time to work out a solution.

We kept our distance at the office, never speaking or meeting. Twice a week we met for dinner followed by time making love in my bed. I worried about what I would do if my stay in Mexico was extended. It wouldn't solve anything. There were only a few minor details to be worked out leaving my end of the project completed. Everything was getting more complicated by the day. Whatever final plans Berto had in mind, he hadn't revealed.

At his insistence, and over my objections, I accepted the invitation I'd received to attend a large charity ball. Berto said it was an opportunity to meet some of his family. He'd spoken of me so often they were curious. Anxious to meet me. The very idea of meeting his family seemed fraught with risk. I'd tried to beg off saying I had nothing to wear to such an affair. Telling Berto meeting his family, under the present circumstances, was more than I thought I could handle. Of course I lost the argument.

I felt like Cinderella as I awaited Juan's arrival to drive me to the ball. Having given in to please Berto my expectations of what he'd described as a gala event were tempered by the nagging thought that this evening could prove a disaster.

Berto assured me it would be a change not only to meet his family, but to mingle with the elite of Guadalajara.

One last glance in the mirror to be sure nothing was out of place gave me pause. I had a hard time believing the image in the mirror was me. I'd never looked so glamorous, but then I'd never owned anything as beautiful as the expensive gown Berto had surprised me with. The floor length, form-fitting dress of green silk, with a matching shawl and shoes was beyond anything I'd ever dreamed of owning. The note said for El Verde de tus ojos. Green eyes.

Juan knocked on the door. Berto had apologized for not being able to escort me, but He promised to be on the lookout for my arrival. When I opened the door Juan handed me a small gift box. "Senior Ortega said you were to open it before we go."

I invited Juan inside and untied the wide silver ribbon that encircled the box. Resting on a bed of white satin was a spectacular necklace consisting of three strands of beautiful pearls bound together every few inches by a small gold bar with a diamond in the center of each bar. I'd never seen anything more exquisite. It must have cost a fortune. Lifting the card out of the envelope I read the words Berto had written.

> *The ancient Greeks believed pearls*
> *were the tears of the gods. I believe*
> *they weep as a sign of my love for you*
> *Always yours,*
>   *Berto*

I excused myself and left the room, not wanting Juan to see my tears. When I returned, I picked up the necklace and handed it to Juan to fasten around my neck.

"Ready, Senorita Michael. You don't want to be late." As Juan helped me into the car he said, "I'll be waiting for you outside the hotel at midnight for your drive home." Midnight I thought, just like the fairy tale.

True to his word, Berto walked toward me as I entered the ballroom of the hotel, handsome as ever in his tuxedo. With a smile on his face and an outstretched hand he whispered, "Little One, you look even more beautiful than even I expected. I see you received my gift."

"Berto, you shouldn't have. It's much too costly. I'm not sure I should keep it."

"Do you like it, my dear?"

"Like it? I've never seen anything lovelier in my life."

"Good, then you must keep it. It was given with love. My love, like the necklace, is yours to keep forever."

"Please Berto, not now. I'm afraid I'll start to cry again and I'd have no way to explain why."

He took my arm and led me to a large table in the ballroom. A group of beautifully gowned women and men in tuxedos looked up with interest as we approached. My heart began to beat faster. I was beyond nervous. I wanted to turn and run.

"May I introduce Michael Madison, the young American I have spoken of. Michael, the woman on your left in the scarlet dress is my sister, Roberta. Next to her, her husband Alberto. Then my Brother Tomas and his wife Clara. Next is my mother, the Grande Dame of the family. Next to her, my sister Elena and her husband Felipe, and my dear wife Carlota."

He pulled out the chair next to his. Berto's sister Roberta spoke first. "Berto speaks highly of you, my dear, and how instrumental you've been in implementing the merger. Were glad to meet you at last. Though he never mentioned how attractive you are, or how young. Do you speak Spanish my dear?"

"I'm improving, but I still worry about making a mistake."

"Then we will speak in English. I'll translate for my mother as she is the only one who speaks and understands only Spanish."

I lifted the glass in front of me and sipped the champagne. A little alcohol might settle my nerves. I felt terribly uncomfortable to say the least. Berto's wife kept staring at me. Was she simply interested in me, or did she know about my relationship with her husband.

Roberta was explaining that the ball was given annually to raise money for the large number of orphans in the area. How many young girls carried on with men without the benefit of marriage, became pregnant and then abandoned their children. Was she giving me a morals lesson or was I imagining it.

I struggled to follow the speeches in Spanish given from a small stage at the back of the room during the meal. When everyone had been served dessert, an orchestra arrived. People began to fill the dance floor. Berto stood and asked his wife if she cared to dance. She declined saying she should keep his mother company. He turned to me and asked if I cared to dance. I smiled, "Yes, thank you." I'd do anything to get away from the table, anything to stop the family from glaring at me. I felt as if I'd been stripped naked and they were picking me apart piece by piece.

THE BUTTERFLY

Berto put his arm around me taking my hand in his. We'd never danced before, but of course he danced beautifully. It was strange being in his arms with so many people, including his family, watching.

"Are you all right, Little One? Not too uncomfortable I hope?"

"I have this horrible feeling they all know about us."

"Don't be silly. How could they? We've been discreet." We did a few more turns around the dance floor when I suggested it might be better if we return to the table.

"I'm not letting you out of my arms until the music stops." He pulled me even closer until there wasn't any space between us, so close I could feel his heart beating, as he whispered, "Can you sense how my body aches for you?"

When the dance ended, Berto excused himself saying he needed to visit with guests at a nearby table. Assuring everyone he'd be right back, while looking directly at me. As soon as he'd walked away his wife leaned over and asked if I was enjoying my time in Mexico, a rather sarcastic tone to her voice. I assured her I was. I couldn't quite figure her out. Was she normally this cold and unfriendly, or was it all about me.

I found Carlota very attractive. Thick jet-black hair that might have been touched up a bit was pulled back off her face and fastened in an elaborate bun at the nape of her neck. She had flawless pale skin, huge dark eyes and long lashes. Her make-up had been perfectly applied. Her figure was mature, what one might expect having given birth to three children in a short period of time.

The more Carlotta stared at me the more uncomfortable I felt sitting next to the wife of the man I was sleeping with. She had to know. There'd been married long enough that she must know his moods and habits. Feeling self-conscious, as Berto's mother and his wife were the only ones left at the table, I excused myself and walked toward the rest room. I needed a few minutes to pull myself together. After washing my hands, I fussed with my hair and reapplied my lipstick. I was about to leave when I saw Berto's sister Roberta, her back to me, speaking in Spanish with another woman. I understood the woman's question as she asked, "Who is she." Berto's sister answered. "La Casa Chica. Americana."

The disgusted tone of her voice told me her answer wasn't meant as a compliment. I waited a moment before I started to walk past them, making my presence known. The women stopped talking. The smile Berto's sister gave me seemed less than genuine as she asked if I was enjoying myself. Before I could even answer she commented on the beautiful necklace I was wearing. I'm sure she knew where it came from. Obviously I was in no position to afford anything as costly. I could feel my cheeks redden, as I smiled and walked away. More than anything I wanted to leave, to go home. I glanced at my watch, eleven o'clock. How would I make it through another hour?

When I returned to the table, Berto asked where I'd gone.

"To the ladies room."

"Are you all right? You seem upset."

"No I'm fine. Just a little overwhelmed."

"If you don't mind, my mother would like to meet with you."

I followed Berto to the other side of the table.

"Mamacita. Esta is Senortia Madison, Miguel."

Berto translated her words. "She says you are very beautiful, very young. What do you know of love?"

Berto said something to her in Spanish and she replied with a sternness in her steely stare, coldness to her voice as she stared in my direction.

"She says she's glad to meet you."

I knew Berto was lying to me. Whatever she'd said he wasn't willing to share.

After telling Berto's mother, in the few phrases I knew in Spanish, how pleased I was to have met her, all I could think of was escaping. God, I needed some fresh air. I grabbed my shawl from the back of my chair and hurried toward the lobby. The last thing I wanted was to return to the table. Maybe my best option would be to wait in the lobby until midnight when Juan would arrive. It had been a mistake to let Berto talk me into coming.

I heard Berto call my name as he came running after me. "What happened? Why did you run off?"

"Tell me the truth, Berto. What did your mother just say?"

"Nothing, Little One. She's an old lady. It wasn't important. Is that what has you upset."

I pushed open the door to step out into the night air. Why wouldn't he tell me what she said? I could only imagine the worst. Berto followed me.

"What does 'Casa Chica' mean?" I mean really mean. Obviously your sister wasn't calling me a little house."

I could tell from his reaction he was upset. "My sister used that phrase?"

"Yes. She was speaking to another woman who seemed like a friend." I wrapped the shawl around my shoulders not sure if the chill I felt was night air or a warning.

"Forget it. It doesn't mean anything."

"Please, Berto, I need to know. If you won't tell me I'll find out another way."

"I said it's nothing, believe me. Let it go. It's not important. Come back inside."

"No. It has some other meaning. From the tone of your sister's voice I could tell it wasn't meant as a compliment."

Berto seemed nervous as he said, "It's just a slang expression. Nothing important."

"Meaning what?"

"If you must know, meaning mistress." His tone was hushed as he looked away.

I stared at him clearly not understanding. "How does 'Casa Chica' translate to mistress?"

"It's a colloquial expression going back to the days of the haciendas. The man of the house lived with his family in the Casa Grande, the big house, and his mistress lived at the far end of the property in the little house, the Casa Chica."

"Good God. Don't you understand what this means, Berto? Your whole family knows."

"Knows what? That I love you."

"Knows that I'm your mistress." The ugly meaning of the word that now defined me made me feel ill. "Please, Berto, go back to your family. I need to be by myself. I can't think straight. I can't talk anymore."

He started to reach for me, but I pushed him away. "Please go. Please, please just leave me alone."

Berto realized the conversation was over. "If you insist, Michael, but never forget for a moment that I love you more than life itself. I will find a way." With a look of despair he turned and walked away as bits of salted love dripped down my face.

Chapter 11

My cell phone rang every hour on the hour. Knowing it had to be Berto I turned it off and let it go to voice mail. I couldn't bring myself to talk to him, still reeling over last night's discovery that Berto's sister knew about our relationship and wondering what his mother really said? Did she know as well? What did Carlota know? How many others knew?

I wasn't due to return to the States until mid-December although by now there were only a few loose ends that could be wrapped up in a day or two. How would I manage to get through the remaining weeks?

Juan drove me to the office on Monday as usual. The moment I got off the elevator I could sense something out of the ordinary. The place was abuzz with people gathered in small groups, heads together, worried looks on their faces. I wondered what was going on. I saw Anna at the far end of the room and walked toward her hoping for an answer.

"Anna, what's happening?"

"I would have thought you already knew."

I wasn't prepared for the bitter tone of her voice. What was I supposed to know? "Please Anna, I have no idea what I'm supposed to know. Please, what's going on?"

"Senior Ortega's wife is in the hospital. They don't know if she will live."

"For God's sake Anna, what are you talking about?"

"Senora Ortega fell down a flight of stairs at their home last evening. She may die."

THE BUTTERFLY

I felt the color drain from my face. I reached for a chair, unsteady on my feet, mixed emotions running though my brain. Die. Anna had said she might die. I tried to reject the thought staring me in the face. I kept seeing the look of desperation on Berto's face as I pushed him away. No, it's not possible. He couldn't. He wouldn't. He'd never do anything like that, but the notion crept back into my thoughts again and again. This couldn't be his solution, his "I'll find a way."

"My God, that's awful, Anna. If he calls, please tell him my prayers are with the two of them." The look on Anna's face told me she wasn't convinced I meant it. Then, like a bolt of lightning I understood. Of course she knew about us. She was Berto's assistant. She was the one who made the plane reservations, the one who booked the hotel suite in Rome. I couldn't look her in the eye. I hurried to my office and shut the door. I didn't know what to do. I couldn't call Berto or his family. I began to cry. Was this my fault? My God, what had I done? Unfortunately, I'd have to wait, like everyone else, for the outcome.

I tried to work, but couldn't concentrate. I kept picturing a terrifying image of Carlota tumbling down a long staircase with Berto watching from the landing, a smile on his face.

On Tuesday and Wednesday, we were told her condition was still touch and go. By Friday, Anna announced to everyone in the office that Senora Ortega had suffered a concussion and a spinal cord injury. She was paralyzed from the waist down, but the doctors said she would survive. Anna looked straight at me as she spoke the words, "She would survive."

I didn't hesitate. I knew there was only one thing for me to do. Closing the door to my office I picked up the phone and called San Francisco. When Harry Baker, the head of my division, came on the line, I explained that my work here was done, and I was ready to return to the States. I'd like to leave on Monday to be home in time for the Christmas holidays.

"I must say this comes as a surprise, Michael. I had a long conversation with Senor Ortega just last week, and he suggested you stay on for a few more months to handle a couple of remaining items. He gave a glowing account of your performance. The only thing left to work out regarding your staying on was financial."

I had no choice but to feign ignorance. "I had no idea Senor Ortega had spoken to you. He never mentioned the possibility of my staying past December. If you'd ran it by me, my recommendation would have been that Senor Ortega would be better off hiring a local attorney. Obviously, I have no understanding of Mexican law. Any relevant questions that might come up I could handle by phone. My job here is done and I'm really anxious to return home."

"Fine, if you think that's best, I'll take you at your word. To be honest, I look forward to having you back in the office. You've done yourself a world of good by the way you've handled this project. I see great things ahead for you, Michael."

I hung up and called the airport making reservations for Monday afternoon, charging the non-refundable fare to the company's credit card before I could change my mind. The few things left to resolve were so minor in nature and I could check them off the list today.

By Sunday, I was packed and ready to leave. Berto continued to call several times during the afternoon and evening. I didn't answer and deleted all his voicemails without listening to them. I knew I couldn't face him. Knew I couldn't take his calls. Saying goodbye was something I wasn't brave enough to do in person, but I owed him an explanation. Having put it off all afternoon I finally willed myself to do what needed to be done. I sat down at the dining room table, opened my laptop, and began to draft a letter. After numerous attempts to say what needed to be said, to express my feelings, I realized I'd spent too much time writing legal briefs. Now when I wanted to write a love letter, I didn't know how. I pressed delete, closed the laptop, and walked out onto the patio trying to gather my thoughts. I could hear voices and laughter coming from one of the houses across the large expanse of manicured lawn, the sound of a stereo in the distance. All I felt was sorrow at leaving this behind. I knew returning home was the right thing to do, but it still hurt. What was it Berto had said about experiencing great love and great sadness? Was I fleeing like the butterfly in his story?

Returning to the dining room with stationary in hand I started to put pen to paper, hoping my teardrops wouldn't stain the page. I poured the last of a bottle of wine Berto had brought several nights before and the words began to flow as I let my heart instead of my head dictate what I wrote.

I put the pen aside, drank the last of the wine, and read what I had written.

My Dearest Berto,

I am taking the coward's way out to say goodbye. You once told me I'd never be a woman until I'd experienced both love and sorrow. I now know that to be true as I love you with all my heart There are no words to describe the deep sorrow I feel, but this has to end.

Rightly or wrongly your wife's injury was a cause for alarm.

THE BUTTERFLY

I know you would have fulfilled your promise and bought a charming little house for us and we'd have spent every Tuesday and Friday evening together until you had to leave my bed in the middle of the night to return home. I'd accompany you when you traveled, and we'd spend precious time together at the beach house whenever you could sneak away.

I've envisioned our relationship after the passing of twenty years or so. My youth gone, as would be my child bearing years, still waiting for you to retire to the house in Tuscany where you promised we would spend our golden years. By then, I'd be consumed with worry that another younger butterfly would cross your path and rest upon your shoulder. Would Tuesdays and Fridays belong to someone else who had become a captive of your irresistible charm?

If I tried to say goodbye in person I know what would happen. You'd hold out your arms and whisper,

"I promise I'll never let you go, Little One." I'd press my body close to yours as you held me tight, forever caught in your net.

But just as you predicted, I'm frightened and my only defense is to fly away.

With love,
La Mariposa, The Butterfly

By the time I'd finished reading the letter, the teardrops were a steady stream and they wouldn't stop. There'd never be anyone like Berto in my life again. It had been a magical dream, a beautiful fairy tale, but unlike most fairy tales, this one didn't have a happy ending.

I placed the letter in an envelope, sealed the flap, then placed both the letter and the necklace resting in its satin box into a large bubble wrap mailer I'd carefully addressed to Berto at the office. I planned to ask Juan to deliver it for me. Drying my tears I spent my last night in Mexico curled up in bed alone.

Chapter 12

Monday morning I heard Juan's car stop in front of the townhouse. My suitcases were waiting at the door. I'd packed everything except the dress from Italy and the ball gown, which I left in the closet. One more remembrance better left behind. Juan seemed surprised as he placed the cases in the trunk. "Are you leaving Senorita Michael?"

"Yes, Juan." I smiled and tried to sound upbeat. "My job here is done. It's time for me to go home. I'll be going to the airport rather than the office this morning."

"I am sorry you are leaving."

"Me too. I'll miss seeing you."

I settled in the back seat gripping my oversized purse in one hand, the mailing envelope in the other. "This has been a wonderful time for me. My ideas about Mexico have changed. I've learned to love so much about your country. Maybe I'll return someday."

The car slid to a stop in front of Aeromexico. Juan placed my cases on the curb as I reached into my purse and drew out a hundred dollar bill handing it to him.

"I need to ask you for a very big favor." I handed him the mailing envelope. "Please give this to Senor Ortega. Not to Anna or anyone else. You have to promise me you'll place it in his hands no matter how long you have to wait. It's very important."

Juan tried to hand back the money, but I insisted. "Do you promise me this will be given to Senor Ortega and to no one else?"

THE BUTTERFLY

"I promise. I will place it in his hands. De mi mano a Senor Ortega's mano solamente. Gracias para todo, Senorita Michael. Vaya con Dios."

As I wheeled my cases to the check-in counter, a sinking feeling grew in the pit of my stomach. Nothing in my life would ever be the same.

The plane landed on time at the San Francisco airport. It seemed so strange to hear the conversations all around me in English. I hailed a cab. Even the weather was different. Cool with a low hanging fog. Its bleak feeling matched my mood.

I opened the door to my apartment, leaving the cases in the hall. Looking around at what should have been familiar seemed unfamiliar. I was tired and emotionally spent. After changing into sweatpants and a T-shirt, I curled up on my bed letting the recent events wash over me and cried myself to sleep.

I awoke early still on Jalisco time. It took a minute to get my bearings as I wandered into the kitchen. My apartment at 101 Lombard was a small one bedroom, efficient and conveniently located within walking distance of the financial district and my office.

I opened the refrigerator to find a vacuum-sealed package of Peet's coffee. The freezer held a loaf of sliced rye bread, an unopened jar of strawberry jam in the cupboard. Good enough for breakfast.

After showering, and changing into jeans and a warm sweater I called the office to tell them I was back and was taking a few days off to get settled.

I needed to do some grocery shopping and unpack. It seemed strange to be home. Somehow I didn't feel like the same person who left six months ago. So much had changed. I had changed.

I put off calling my parents. I wasn't ready to spend time with them and I didn't want to talk about Mexico just yet. I really didn't feel like seeing or talking to anyone.

By the end of the day, with my chores done, I nuked a frozen dinner, had a glass of wine and turned on the television. It took a moment to realize the voices were in English. In some small way I missed hearing the rapid pace of news in Spanish. I had no idea what was happening in the States feeling disconnected from everything and everyone.

Though I promised myself I'd never think of Berto again, that was easier said than done. I could only imagine how he would take my letter. Fortunately, he had no way of contacting me. He didn't have my home address and only had my cell number. I could transfer his calls to the office and direct to my voice mail, which I could delete with out hearing them. I set his e-mails to auto delete. I needed to put him out of my life.

Still feeling tired, I went to bed early only to be awakened in the morning feeling an alarming sense of nausea. I almost didn't make it to the bathroom. Had I picked up a bug on the airplane? I vomited until there was nothing left in my stomach and continued to experience dry heaves. I crawled back into bed exhausted.

By ten, I felt much better and decided I needed a change of scenery and thought I'd go for a drive. The building maintenance man reconnected my car's battery and I took a long drive to the beach. I parked alongside the Cliff House and watched the waves crash against the rocks, listening to the sounds of the foghorns. I had to put the pieces of my life back together before next Monday. Once I started back at work there would be no time for self-pity. Mexico and all that encompassed was behind me. My life and my job were here in San Francisco.

I drove home and changed into running pants and shoes. The Embarcadero was only a block away. A good run would clear my head. I ran past Fisherman's Wharf with its familiar aroma of fresh caught seafood, and continued running until I reached Ghirardelli Square and the pleasing smell of chocolate. A good place to turn around. I felt much better by the time I reached home. I showered, nuked another frozen dinner, and promised to call my parents in a few days. I sat down in front of the television and at ten I went to bed.

The same damn thing happened early the next morning. I vomited until I was exhausted. I thought I'd die. Whatever this bug was I needed to see someone. I needed a prescription or something before this got worse. I didn't have a regular physician so after getting dressed I did the next best thing and drove to an urgent care center in the Marina.

After filling out pages of information, I waited in the crowded reception area for over an hour to be seen. At last I was ushered into an examining room. A young Asian woman entered introducing herself as a nurse practitioner and proceeded to take my temperature, my blood pressure and pulse, finding everything normal. In answer to one of her many questions, I mentioned my return from Mexico a few days earlier and the thought I might have picked up a bug or something on the plane. She asked me to describe my symptoms. Listening with care, she asked if I had sexual relations in the last ninety days.

When I answered yes she reached into a cupboard retrieving a small plastic container writing my name on the outside.

"The restroom is down the hall on the right. You may leave the urine sample in the box next to the scale and return here to the examination room."

THE BUTTERFLY

She left the room leaving me holding the container. I had no choice but to follow her instructions, then waited and waited and waited for her return. At least thirty minutes passed before the door opened.

"I've checked your urine sample, Miss Madison. You don't have a bug. You're pregnant. I suggest you make an appointment with an ob-gyn."

I felt lightheaded. I thought I'd pass out. Pregnant. No I couldn't be. The nurse must have been concerned as I barely heard her voice as if in an echo chamber say, "Here, let me help you. Just lie down on the table." I felt her put a pillow under my feet "You'll feel better in a minute. Just rest. I'll be back."

I could feel my head begin to clear as the word pregnant still rang in my ears.

Chapter 13

I sat behind the wheel of my car in the parking lot, the motor off, still in a daze. I had no idea how long I sat there not knowing what to do or where to go.

I finally drove off surprised to find myself near Old Fort Point. I parked the car and walked to the end of the path, starring out over the bay at Alcatraz. The afternoon was chilly, a high fog over the bay, but I didn't notice. I felt numb. Even the eerie sound of foghorns in the distance failed to penetrate my feelings. Dear God, what do I do now? I looked down at the waves breaking against the cliff as if I'd find the answer there.

I don't know how long I stood there lost, mesmerized by the crashing of the waves and the sound of the seagulls, until I felt a gentle tap on my shoulder that caused me to look up. A female police officer was standing at my side.

"Are you feeling all right?" she seemed concerned.

"I beg your pardon?"

"We received a 911 call. A passerby was worried about you."

"I'm sorry. I don't understand. Are you telling me I can't stand here without someone complaining to the police? I'm fine, I just needed some time alone."

"Hey, somebody was concerned enough about you to make a call, afraid you might be considering jumping into the water. Let me walk you back to your car."

Even though I objected vigorously the officer tucked her hand under my armpit making sure I got into my vehicle. "Can I call someone for you? If you'd like to talk, I'm happy to listen."

I was beginning to get annoyed. "There's nothing to talk about. I had some things I wanted to think about that's all. Believe me, I wasn't considering suicide." I slid into the driver's seat and rolled down the window. "Now if I may, I'd like to leave."

"Could I have your name and address for my report."

"No, you may not." I started the engine and drove off.

I parked in my assigned space in the garage and took the elevator to my floor, holding tight to the prescription the pharmacy had filled for what the doctor described as morning sickness.

I walked down the hall and unlocked the door to my apartment still trying to come to terms with the brutal fact that I was pregnant. Flopping down on the sofa, I felt my whole life unraveling. What would I tell my parents? "Yes, folks, Mexico was wonderful and I brought home a gift for all of us." That would go over really well.

God, what was I going to tell my boss? "Because I did such an outstanding job in Mexico, guess what I received as a bonus?"

Unable to move, I sat on sofa until dark. Turning on the lights I walked to the kitchen and, standing at the sink, I smeared gobs of peanut butter and jelly on raisin bread. When that wasn't satisfying enough I opened the refrigerator and took out a pint of Ben and Jerry's dark chocolate ice cream, grabbed a spoon, and returned to the living room. I turned off the lights, sat down on the sofa and ate the whole container of ice cream through my tears.

Hours later, I stood naked in front of the bedroom mirror looking at my stomach. It felt the same to the touch. The same was true of my breasts. How long would that last? Grabbing an old T-shirt out of a drawer, I crawled into bed and pulled the covers over my head, but sleep wouldn't come.

I tossed and turned as my world came tumbling down like a house of cards. I'd expected to have kids someday, just as I expected to be married. Being a single mom was something I never imagined could happen to me, but somehow I'd gotten myself into this mess.

Thoughts kept running through my head like tumbleweeds carried on the wind, spinning in all directions. I had only two options neither one I was ready to accept. I wasn't ready to be a single mom, but could I face the idea of an abortion? I'd always been a pro-choice supporter, but now that the option was there could I even begin to consider abortion? Dear God, what do I do now?

Nothing had changed by morning, except the pills worked. My stomach felt woozy, but I didn't throw up. After two cups of black coffee and a piece of toast, I scrolled through the listings I'd pulled up on my laptop for an ob-gyn. Finding a female doctor with offices within walking distance I called for an appointment. The call was answered with a recorded message, "The office is closed for the weekend. Please call back on Monday morning." My life was so messed up I hadn't realized it was Saturday. I listened to some additional information about emergencies before I hung up.

Next, I called my parents. I needed to let them know I was back in town, but there was no need to tell them anything else yet. I agreed to drive down to Burlingame for dinner the next evening. My mother was so happy to hear I'd returned. How happy would she be when she learned I was pregnant was another question.

I moped around the condo for the rest of the day, not bothering to get dressed, still no closer to a solution.

Sunday went well under the circumstances. My parents were eager to hear all about Guadalajara, wanting to know what I'd seen and where I'd gone. Whenever I could I managed to turn the conversation back to them. I asked my father how things were at the university. How many classes was he teaching? When was his sabbatical? Did he have any plans? My mother was still teaching English at a private school in town, so I asked about her students. Anything to change the subject regarding Mexico.

I escaped early saying I had to drive back to the town and get ready to return to the office in the morning, promising to visit soon.

I choose to walk the seven or so blocks to the office on Sansome Street. Though it was nippy, the fresh air felt good and the walk gave me a chance to settle into my old routine. As I entered the office, I was greeted with smiling faces, everyone anxious to know how I liked Mexico. I kept my answers short and asked if I still had the same office. When I was told yes, I walked down the hall to my tiny space, no bigger than a broom closet. It was nothing like the spacious office with its extraordinary view I'd enjoyed in Mexico. I found a folder on my desk with a note from Harry Baker, my boss, asking me to research a case.

The first thing I did was call the doctor's office and was given an appointment for three o'clock on Friday. Harry's research project took up most of my workday leaving me little time to think about the looming doctor visit.

I looked through the state bar association's publication for job openings. It was obvious I couldn't stay employed here. It would be too embarrassing for everybody, mostly me, when they found out I was pregnant. While I knew they couldn't fire me they sure as hell could make me feel uncomfortable. My life under those circumstances would be miserable.

I called a headhunter, having come to the conclusion I needed to leave the area. That was the only way I could hide the facts from my parents, and my

THE BUTTERFLY

friends, buying me time to figure out how to handle the situation. My license allowed me to practice law anywhere in the state. My only stipulation was the employer had to provide health insurance. I knew my situation was going to make it hard to find a job. It would be one thing to get pregnant after I was hired. It would be difficult enough to find an employer willing to hire a pregnant woman if she was married, but who was going to hire a pregnant woman without a husband.

I arrived at the ob-gyn's office promptly at three. The reception room was filled with women in various stages of pregnancy. I looked at one woman with a bulging stomach and was horrified to think that would be me in a few months. I filled out pages of forms and nervously waited my turn.

Finally a nurse accompanied me to an examination room and she began the whole routine of taking my vital signs. Once all my information was entered into a computer the nurse handed me a hospital gown and told me to undress.

As she headed out the door she smiled and said, "Everything off. The doctor will be with you, soon."

After few minutes, there was a knock on the door and a slim, attractive dark-haired woman of about forty entered, reaching out her hand she said. "Hi, Michael, I'm Doctor Hastings. How are you feeling?"

"Fine, thank you."

"Good. Hop up on the table and let's have a look."

She asked me to scoot down a bit as she placed my feet in the stirrups, raising my gown. I closed my eyes and let her complete her examination.

"You can sit up, now. I would guess you're about six to seven weeks pregnant. I noticed from your paperwork that you're unmarried? Is the father part of the picture?"

I felt my face redden. I hesitated, should I answer. Why was that information necessary? Against my better judgment I answered her. "No. He doesn't know, nor will he. He doesn't reside in the States."

In the same detached tone Dr. Hastings continued. "Do you plan to keep this baby or are you considering adoption?"

"I haven't given anything a thought. I'm still trying to process the fact that I'm pregnant. I had no idea until last week. Clearly, adoption hadn't crossed my mind."

"I only mention the option as we handle cases differently if adoption is the choice. There are legal hurdles that can be challenging. Anyway, you have a while to decide."

She smiled as she began to enter the updated data into the computer. "You appear to be a healthy young woman. I see no reason to expect anything but a normal pregnancy. I want to see you once a month for the time being. No smoking, no alcohol, and of course no drugs of any kind. I can recommend a counselor if you think that would be helpful. Do you have any questions for me?"

I shook my head no. My thoughts were so confused at the moment I couldn't think of a thing.

"I'm glad to have met you, Michael. You can go ahead and get dressed now. I'll see you in a month. Stop at the desk on the way out to make an appointment." With that she was gone.

I started to put on my clothes. Adoption? One more option to consider.

I stopped by the office on my way home to see if there were any messages. There were two. One was from the headhunter, the other from Berto, which I deleted. I closed the door to my office and called the headhunter. He said the only thing he had at the moment was an opening for an attorney in a small non-profit in Monterey called the Mexican Alliance run by a Maria Alvarez. He gave me her telephone number saying the salary was small, but it met all of my criteria.

I hung up and called Maria Alvarez. She came on the line, a slight hint of an accent. "Good Afternoon, My name is Michael Madison. I understand you have a position open for an attorney. I received your name from Jobs USA."

"Yes, we do have an opening." Maybe luck was with me. "Have you passed the California bar?"

"I have. I've been working for a law firm in San Francisco for almost three years and just returned from six months working with a company in Mexico."

"Interesting. Do you speak Spanish?"

"Some, but I'm willing to expand my capabilities in the language."

"You do realize how small the salary is? We operate on grants and we're limited in what we can pay."

"Yes, I was told what you were offering."

There was a long pause on the other end. I wasn't sure we hadn't been cut off, and then she spoke again "Would you be willing to come to Monterey for an interview?"

"I could come this weekend. I'm interested in leaving the Bay Area as soon as possible."

Again a pause and I sensed she was hesitant. "All right. I could meet with you in our office on Sunday afternoon." She gave me the address and we agreed on

THE BUTTERFLY

the time. I said I was looking forward to our meeting and hung up. Would this be my opportunity to escape?

Chapter 14

It took almost three hours to drive to Monterey. The offices of the Mexican Alliance were located in a storefront on a side street off East Alisal, far from the tourist attractions of the area.

The bell over the front door announced my arrival. The interior of the office was as unimpressive as the exterior. A quick glance around allowed me to see pretty much everything, Three tired looking metal desks, old file cabinets, bookshelves that were nothing more than unpainted 2x4s resting on concrete blocks, with what appeared to be a small office located in the back of the room. A far cry from the first rate firm I worked for.

A woman, who appeared to be in her fifties, reached out her hand to greet me. Her dark hair streaked with grey, her figure mature, her demeanor standoffish.

"You must be Miss Madison. I'm Maria Alvarez. Come into my office where we can chat."

I sat on a wooden chair opposite her as she sat behind her desk. She looked at me long and hard making me feel uncomfortable. "I've been thinking about you all morning, Miss Madison. The headhunter tells me you graduated magna cum laude from U.C. Berkeley's, Bolt Hall. I know it to be a most prestigious law school. Something doesn't add up. You're employed by a large law firm in San Francisco, and you want to come to Monterey to work for peanuts. Are you about to be fired, or are you facing disciplinary proceeding with the bar association? What's the story here?" She folded her hands on her desk and sat back watching and waiting for my response.

THE BUTTERFLY

I thought for a long time before I answered. The only thing I could do was to tell her the truth.

"You have every right to be suspicious, Mrs. Alvarez, I do have an ulterior motive."

Maria's look seemed to say 'I knew it.'

"I'm two months pregnant. I haven't told my family knowing it will be an embarrassment to them and to me. Staying on at my law firm would prove to be embarrassing as well. I'm looking for a safe haven."

"Well that explains a lot and I must say I appreciate your honesty. What about the child's father? Are you running away from him as well? The office doesn't need any more drama than we already have. Is he likely to present a problem?"

"He has no idea and I have no intention of telling him. As he lives in Mexico, it's unlikely I'll run across him."

Maria paused as if trying to weigh the pros and cons of the situation before she spoke. "You realize the salary is $24,000 annually, probably a quarter of what you earn now. There are no paid vacations, no forty-hour weeks, and no bonuses at the end of the year. Our last lawyer had retired some years ago and was just looking for something to occupy his time after his wife died.

"With just four of us to run the office, a paralegal, a receptionist, a lawyer, and myself, the workload can be overwhelming, but we do have health insurance. Can you live with that?"

"I have some savings, my car is paid for, and my needs at the moment aren't great. I can promise you I'll work as hard as if you were meeting my present salary. As I said, my only needs are a place to live, and a job that's far enough away from home giving me some distance from family and friends."

"Well, if it were me under your circumstances, I'd want my family around me, but if you can start immediately, I'll take a chance on you. We're really shorthanded."

"You won't be sorry. I have nothing pending at the office so it's not as if I'm leaving them in the lurch. I'll give my two weeks' notice and be ready to start work after the first of the year."

She reached in her desk drawer and pulled out several pages of legal-sized paper all stapled together. "Fill these out and bring them back with you when you show up for work. I hope this pans out for both of us. Oh yes, I forgot to mention. We don't offer paid sick leave or paid maternity leave either." Maria stood, the meeting being over and walked me to the door.

I thanked her and left. I decided to drive around Monterey. I hadn't been in the area in years, not since my sorority spent a weekend in Carmel. I was familiar with Pebble Beach, and all the wonderful touristy waterfront areas like Cannery Row, but I had no idea where the working people lived. With my new salary, I wouldn't be living high on the hog.

I decided to take the long way back to the city along Highway One, the two-lane scenic route that curved along the Pacific Ocean. I had a lot to think about. I needed an excuse for leaving that my folks might buy and an understandable reason to give the law firm. Two weeks meant I could spend the Christmas holidays with my parents and I'd still be able to collect my year-end bonus.

What had to be accomplished in a little more than two short weeks was beginning to sink in. I had to find a place to live, pack and move my belongings, and then begin a whole new way of living making $126,000 less.

My life had always been easy, with someone always there to smooth my path. I'd never had financial worries. My parents paid my way through college and law school. I'd been lucky enough to find a great paying job right after graduation. While my lifestyle hadn't been extravagant, I'd never really wanted for anything. The new circumstances would be hard enough even if I wasn't pregnant. I'd almost forgotten that for a moment. I knew nothing about babies and had no idea about what costs might be involved.

The magnitude of my situation was just beginning to take hold. For the first time, I'd be without my family or friends to lean on, completely on my own to face the biggest crisis in my life not sure I was up to it.

When I was almost home, I called the Fog City Diner across from my apartment on my cell phone. I was hungry and desperate for something special. Maybe one of my favorite foods would help calm my mood as wine was now out of the question, ordering calamari with their avocado salsa to go.

I parked the car in the garage and walked across the street to the diner. Handing the hostess my credit card, I signed the slip after adding the tip, and began to realize I'd better start cutting corners and soon. Pricy eateries had to go.

The alarm went off awaking me from a wonderful dream. Berto and I were running along the sand toward the beach house after an early morning swim. We were both laughing at how fast we were going to strip naked and make love before breakfast. Everything seemed so real before the sonic sound of the damn clock brought me back to reality. Would Berto always remain a part of my unconscious thoughts? Would it be impossible to forget him?

Arriving at the office, my resignation letter in hand, I knocked on Harry's office door. He looked up from his desk as I entered. "Thanks for the research, Michael. Good work as usual"

"What's this?" he asked as I handed him the letter.

"I'm leaving the firm. I've accepted a position with a non-profit."

"You're kidding of course?"

"No. I've been thinking about doing something like this for a long time. I'm single, without any responsibilities, so the timing couldn't be better." I hoped I sounded convincing.

Harry glanced at the letter. "I'm disappointed to say the least. I hope you know what you're doing, Michael. Your name came up at the partner's meeting last week. They were pleased at how well you represented our firm during your stay in Mexico. In fact I planned to ask you to be second chair when the case you just researched went to trial."

I couldn't look him in the eye afraid I'd give away how I really felt. This was everything I'd dreamed about, everything I'd worked so hard to achieve.

"You've a great future ahead of you with the firm, Michael. If you quit now, it's all out the window. We have a no return policy. Once you leave, you're out for good."

He carefully folded the letter and placed it in his inbox. "You know you can't get rich doing public service. Think it over for a few days. You may want to change your mind." He sounded almost fatherly. "I'll hold your letter for a day or two in case you want to change your mind."

"I've already accepted the position, Harry. It might prove to be a mistake, but only time will tell."

"Well, I can't stop you. I only wish you'd spoken to me first. I might have talked you out of leaving, even given you a much deserved raise. I wish you the best of luck." He looked down at a stack of folders on his desk, indicating an end to the conversation.

I closed Harry's office door behind me and walked back to my desk, glad the meeting I dreaded was over. The realization of what I was tossing away was gnawing at my insides, but I had to keep moving forward. There was no turning back now.

The next item on my list was finding a place to live, having searched on Google for rental agencies in Monterey I started calling only to find nothing I could afford. One by one, the agencies brushed me off saying they didn't handle low income housing. At least the call to the management of my building went better. They had a long waiting list for apartments and could care less about the short notice. My substantial deposit would be returned if I left everything in order. I needed every dollar if I was to make this move work.

Next, I contacted a small moving company setting up a moving date with a delivery address unknown. Telling my parents could wait until Christmas dinner.

I drove to Monterey again on Saturday desperate to find a place to rent. I planned to stop by the office to see if Maria could help and arrived in the nick of time as the office closed at noon. There were still a few people waiting to be seen.

The pretty young Hispanic girl at the reception desk asked if she could help me.

"Hi, I'm Michael Madison. I'll be starting to work here in January. I was hoping to see Maria. Is she available?"

"Sorry, she's not here. She's giving a speech at some luncheon. Can I help?"

"Maybe. I'm trying to find a place to rent and I'm not having much luck. I thought she might have some ideas."

"Stick around. Elena, our paralegal, might know of something. By the way, my name is Clara. I heard you were coming to work for us, but I thought you were a guy."

As the two people seated at the corner desk got up to leave, Clara pointed to the last man seated in one of the folding chairs lining the wall then in rapid Spanish, told him siguiente por favor. I understood that to mean next.

I stayed out of the way waiting for the office to close.

Finally, Clara introduced me to Elena, who said she might have a solution. Her sister was moving out of her townhouse in Seaside Village. There might be a chance I could rent her unit. The complex manager was a relative.

Elena knew the one bedroom unit was affordable as it was in a government low income controlled housing project. I did the figures in my head. The rent according to Elena would be thirty percent of my salary. If it was calculated on gross income it would be six hundred a month, less if it was based on salary after deductions. At any rate, it was something I could manage.

"If the unit was available that would be great. If it isn't too much trouble maybe we can drive out and see the place."

"No trouble at all. We really need you in the office. I'm in way over my head and way overworked. Hold on, I'll call my sister."

I followed Elena as she drove the four miles toward Seaside and the complex of about one hundred townhouses. More trucks than cars were parked in the driveways. The streets were full of mostly brown-skinned kids, a far cry from my condo in the fashionable 101 Lombard building or the townhouse in Mexico.

Elena walked to the front door and rang the bell. A very pregnant young woman opened the door. The two exchanged hugs as Elena introduced me. We were invited into the small townhouse consisting of a living room, a small kitchen, one bedroom, and a tiny bathroom. I looked around trying to visualize where I'd put my furniture. After a quick glance, I knew I had way too much stuff.

The place was immaculate. Rosa, Elena's sister told me she and her husband were moving as she was expecting their second child and the place was much to small. "The neighborhood is safe and the neighbors mostly friendly." She told me they planned to move out before January first when their rent was due. She spoke with her cousin and the townhouse was mine if I was interested.

The place wasn't perfect, but it would be one more thing I didn't have to worry about. If it didn't work out, I could always look for something else later.

With that settled we drove over to the manager's office. I signed a six-month renewable lease and gave the manager a check for twelve hundred dollars, first and last month's rent.

I said goodbye and thanked both of them. Elena said she looked forward to seeing me in January and let her know if there's anything she could do.

As I opened my car door, I heard Elena say, "I hope you speak Spanish, Michael."

"I shouted back, "Mas o Menos.*"*

Chapter 15

I'd been too busy to think about anything other than moving. My living room was lined with boxes containing my belongings, having no idea where I'd put all my things in the tiny townhouse. My dining room table and chairs were already at a consignment shop along with a couple of side tables, and the large chest that sat under my flat screen. I hated to part with them, but I had no choice. My life had become a never ending series of hard choices all spiraling downward.

Christmas morning I slept in. After showering and dressing, I grabbed my family's Christmas presents and took the elevator to the garage. This year my sister, her husband, and their two girls would be spending the holidays with my parents. I hoped having the kids around would leave less time for questions about my move.

Parking in front of my parent's house I could see the exterior was decorated with Christmas lights, an inflatable snowman stood on the front lawn, and a wreath of holly was at the front door. I heard Christmas carols playing throughout the house as I entered. The usual tall Christmas tree stood in the living room with dozens of presents underneath, all my mother's doing. Christmas was wasted on my father.

I wondered what next Christmas would be like. There'd be a baby I couldn't explain. Would I still be welcome?

I took a deep breath and called, "Hello. Anyone home?"

"I'm in the kitchen, dear."

THE BUTTERFLY

My mother was busy placing marshmallows atop a baking dish of candied yams. I gave her a hug and asked, "Where is everybody?"

"Your father piled them all in the car and he's taken them on a drive to see the neighborhood decorations. I needed some quiet time to finish up in the kitchen."

I gave Mom a hug. "Anything I can do."

"No, dear. Everything is just about ready, though you could open the cans of cranberry sauce and put them on a plate." She stopped what she was doing as she looked at me.

"How is everything, Michael? You look a little tired."

My heart skipped a beat. Although I didn't show could she possibly tell I was pregnant. "Everything's fine. I've just been working hard."

Thankfully, I heard footsteps and the infectious sounds of over-stimulated children heading toward the kitchen. They were both talking at once. "Grandma, you should have come along. The decorations were wonderful. We even saw a real sleigh with Santa sitting in it on somebody's front lawn. It was really so cool."

My sister Jean greeted me with a hug. We weren't close as sisters being as different as night is to day. I got a big hello from her husband, Frank, and hugs from both my nieces.

We were all ordered out of the kitchen and into the living room for eggnog, spiked for the adults, and the opening of the gifts. The majority of the presents were for the girls. When the gift opening was completed it was time for Christmas dinner. I'd managed to pour the eggnog down the kitchen drain without anyone noticing before we sat down. I was waiting for the right moment to break the news, but so far it eluded me.

Mother was busy serving the pumpkin pie with a scoop of vanilla ice cream on the side as my father proclaimed, "This was the best Christmas ever." He said the same thing with the same lack of enthusiasm every year. Holidays upset his structured routine.

Finally, there was a lull in the conversation and it was just the opportunity I'd been looking for. "I have some news. A bit of a surprise."

My sister with her usual enthusiasm blurted out, "You're engaged?"

"No, Jean, not that kind of a surprise. I'd have to have a boyfriend first." I tried to sound excited. "I'm moving to Monterey in January. I'm going to be working with a non-profit helping low income Spanish speaking residents."

I'd dropped a bombshell. No one said a word. After a minute, I said, "Come on you guys, you must have something to say."

My mother seemed overcome. She'd learned years ago to wait for my father to set the tone. How many times had I watched her look to him before voicing an opinion.

"Well, this does come as a surprise." Dad's facial expression had me guessing. Was he really going to approve? "I suppose this has something to do with your recent stay in Mexico."

"In a way, but aren't you going to wish me success?"

"Of course, dear," my mother said. "You know we wish you the best in whatever you choose to do. It's just as Dad said. A bit of a surprise, and"

Before Mom could finish he interrupted, "Well, it's more than a surprise, Mother. It's the most ridiculous, damn fool thing I've ever heard. You're leaving a prestigious law firm, throwing away the chance for a brilliant career for what? A bunch of people who most likely aren't even here legally."

Unfortunately this was what I expected. "My reasons are hard to explain, Dad, but legal or not they have rights. I was hoping you'd wish me luck."

"You'll need a lot more than luck, Michael."

I tuned out the rest of his diatribe, at least the announcement was over. If my dad was unhappy with my decision, I could only imagine how he'd handle my next surprise announcement.

The moving men arrived at eight o'clock the morning of January second. I'd made arrangements for maintenance to inspect the apartment later in the day so my deposit could be refunded. The check would pay for quite a few months' rent.

By the time the movers had everything out of the apartment I drove on ahead to see what might be needed at my new digs. As I drove down the highway I knew there was no turning back now. I'd sink or swim. The outcome was up to me.

By early afternoon I arrived at my new home and parked on the street. The units didn't have garages. Climbing the few steps I unlocked the front door and felt a sense of despair as I came to grips with just how small the rooms were and how depressing the place was. With only a few windows, the room was a dark bleak reminder of what I had gotten myself into and how far I'd fallen. No more ladders of success to climb. I'd spent one week allowing my heart to rule my head. One week was all it took to turn my life into a shambles. Had it been worth it?

I sat down on the floor as the tears rushed down my cheeks in a wave of self-pity.

THE BUTTERFLY

When I finally pulled myself together I began to look around. Rosa had left the place spotless. Every inch scrubbed clean with a familiar aroma in the air. I tried to recall where I'd encountered it before. Yes, it was Fabulousa, the same purple-colored cleaning liquid they used in Mexico. I tried to push back the memories, not wanting to be reminded of a moment in my life that was over.

I tried to visualize where my furniture should go in the living room and moved on to the bedroom. My queen-sized bed and double dresser would overwhelm the small space. I could feel my eyes filling with tears again. The knock on the door told me the movers were here.

By the time they left, I had little room to move around with all the boxes that were piled high against one wall in the living room. Somehow, I had to get organized before I started my new job on Monday.

Chapter 16

Monday morning, Maria gave me a quick indoctrination. Most of my responsibilities would consist of giving legal advice, trying to resolve problems by telephone, or writing letters on a client's behalf. Only a few cases involved filing a lawsuit, and most disputes could be handled in small claims court. Elena had a stack of files she saved for me to review as a handful of people began to trickle in.

It was Clara job to take basic information and explain the fees. Although our funding came from grants and charity, the Alliance charged a small fee for our services. Maria felt any advice given free had little value. The majority of the clients wanted to pay their way. They weren't looking for handouts, only help.

Clara also decided who the clients should see. Previously she ran them all by Elena, but now she'd be leaving the difficult cases for me to handle.

I spent most of the day reviewing the files that had accumulated after the last attorney left. Deciding which to handle first, returning a lot of the files to Elena. She could help clients fill out the paperwork for small claims court and go with them if the case went that far, or if they needed a translator. The day flew by leaving me no time to think about anything but work and exhausted by the time I returned home.

The days and weeks passed by without notice, each day the same as the last. I kept busy, which I was thankful for. The office ran well, and we all got along. Clara and Elena went out of their way to be helpful and Maria was fast becoming a good friend. She was in fact my only friend. I'd intended to find a local ob-gyn, but so far I hadn't had the time. The busier I stayed, the less time I had to think about the child I was carrying. The solution was simple. If I ignored the situation, I didn't have to deal with the reality.

Maria kept after me until I gave in and finally found a doctor and after being informed everything was progressing normally I was put on monthly visits, which were hit and miss at best. My time was fully occupied with my job. Taking time for doctor's appointments was a low priority. I began to stay late most days, lessening the time I spent at home. I hated the place.

One prenatal exam called for an ultrasound, once again assuring me everything looked normal. I chose not to know the sex of the baby or to view the ultrasound, just as I tried to tune out the sound of sloshing water as the nurse moved the small probe across my abdomen. The whole idea of watching what was growing inside me was freaking me out.

Throwing myself into my work, I began to take casework home at night. I'd gained only a small amount of weight, and the only sign of pregnancy was a little thickening of my waistline and the need for a larger bra.

I spoke with my mother now and then, always too busy to drive home for a visit, assuring her I was happy in my new job, and loving what I was doing. She was glad I was happy, but the few times my dad came on the line he wanting to know when I'd come to my senses and find a job that reflected my talents. I let his lectures go by without a response. Arguing with him never got me anywhere.

By now I was far into my seventh month and I had no way to hide the fact that I was pregnant. God bless Clara and Elena they never asked a single question. One evening after the office had been closed for over an hour, I was still going over papers when Maria stopped by my desk.

"My husband is going to a business meeting this evening. Why don't you and I grab a bite to eat? I apologize, Michael, for not making more time to spend with you, but I've been working on a large grant. If it comes through, we'll be secure for some time to come. How about it? Will you join me for dinner?"

"I'd like that." I placed the files in a neat stack on my desk and grabbed my purse.

Maria drove the short distance to Carmel chatting about a small café she enjoyed. Being mid-week, she was sure it wouldn't be crowded with tourists. Parking in Carmel was always difficult as the hotels and many of the houses were without garages forcing everyone to park on the street. Making it next to impossible to find a spot on the weekends with the influx of tourists. Even on a quiet night we were unable park close to the café. Maria asked if I was game to walk. She offered to drop me off first.

I laughed. My first real laugh in months, a walk would do me good. The small cafe was a quiet contrast to the glitzy tourist spots on Cannery Row. When we were seated the hostess handed us menus and asked if she could bring us anything from the bar. I smiled, knowing Maria would understand my not joining her in a cocktail.

The waitress returned rattling off the specials of the day as she placed Maria's cocktail on the table. Maria picked up her drink, swirling around a plastic toothpick with two green olives attached and smiled at me. "How is everything going? Is your apartment working out? You're not feeling too lonesome I hope."

"Everything is fine." I lied. "I don't have time to feel lonesome."

"I'm glad to hear that, Michael. You've proven to be a wonderful addition to our small group. I must say, I'm delighted at how well you all get along despite the difference in your education and upbringing. I hope you plan to stay with us for a long time, which brings me to a subject we need to discuss."

That caught me by surprise. "There's nothing to discuss. Why would you think I have plans other than staying?"

"I was hoping to discuss the baby, of course."

I honestly had no idea what difference a baby would make and said as much.

"Why should that make a difference?"

Maria looked at me in disbelief. "Michael, either you're terribly naïve, or you're refusing to come to grips with the situation. Have you given any thought at all to what happens after your baby is born?"

"What do you mean?"

"I mean, what do you plan to do with the infant while you're at work?"

"Well, a nanny or daycare I guess. I'm ashamed to admit I hadn't given it a thought "

"A nanny or daycare on your salary, really? Do you have any idea of the costs involved? Unless of course, you have unlimited funds."

That caught me off guard. "To tell the truth, I guess I've been too busy to think about anything other than work."

"Well, if my count is correct, you have less than six weeks before the baby's arrival. That doesn't give you much time to make arrangements. Have you done anything about purchasing a crib or clothing for the child?"

"No, not yet. As I said I haven't had time."

The expression on Maria's face was easy enough to read. "When are you going to come to grips with reality Michael? As your friend, as well as your boss, I suggest you start making time. I don't know anything about the situation regarding your pregnancy, nor am I interested in prying into your personal affairs, but denying the inevitable is not the answer."

I began to feel uncomfortable, glad the waitress came to take our orders. Maria was right. I'd put off confronting the inevitable. Hard as I tried, ignoring the fact wasn't going to make it go away. I felt my eyes fill with tears, as my throat began to constrict. The thought of food was more than I could handle. The wall I'd built between denial and reality began to crumble leaving me exposed to the fate that awaited me. My stomach was in knots and as if on cue I could feel the baby began to move around a gentle kick to remind me. I ordered a small mixed green salad not sure I could handle even that.

I nibbled at the food. Less than six weeks" kept ringing in my ears. I wasn't ready. Truth be told, left on my own, I'd never be ready.

"There's a small storage room next to my office, Michael. We could clear it out and it could become a quiet place for the baby to sleep while you're working. It's not a permanent solution, but it will give you a little time to get your act together."

Maria had finished her meal and the last of her glass of Merlot before she spoke again. "Is your mother or some friend going to be with you when your time comes?"

"No. My mother has no idea I'm pregnant." I had to answer honestly although I could tell this shocked her.

"Again, Michael, none of my business, but when do you intend to tell her?"

The conversation was becoming more uncomfortable by the minute. "Sometime after the baby's born. Then she and my dad will have to accept the fact. They aren't the most understanding when it comes to things like this."

"Look, Michael." Maria had folded her napkin placing it alongside her dinner plate and pushed back her chair. "I have two sons, and I remember how scared I was the first time I delivered, even though my husband was there at my side. It's not something you want to go through alone. If you'll let me, I'd like to be there for you."

That caught me off guard. When I felt I could speak without breaking down, I said. "Believe me, I'm not naïve. It's just this isn't how I'd planned my life."

"Michael, believe me. I can't begin to imagine how difficult this has been. I doubt I could have handled the situation as well as you have all by yourself."

I pushed aside the half-eaten salad realizing the time had come to face the truth, I was a few weeks away from delivering a baby. The thought terrified me as I tried to hold back the tears. "I'd like it if you were there with me. Deep down I'm scared to death. I really need a friend."

"Good. We'll see this through together, I promise. Saturday, if you'd like, we can go shopping for the things you'll need. For me, it will be like having another grandchild." She smiled. "It will all work out, Michael." The way she said it I knew Maria would be there for me every step of the way. For the first time in seven months I didn't feel alone.

My due date was drawing closer and the kicks getting stronger. I was convinced the baby was a boy and bound to be a soccer player. Clara and Elena threw a baby shower and Clara's husband helped assemble the new crib Maria helped me pick out. There was hardly enough room in the bedroom to accommodate even a small piece of furniture much less a crib. After pushing my bed up against the wall there was still practically no space to walk between the bed and the crib.

Everyone pitched in to clean out the storage room on the following Saturday after work. We scrubbed down the walls and floor, turning it into a temporary nursery. Maria found a large wooden crate and using one of my shower gift cards, I purchased a small mattress to create a bed of sorts. I'd finally faced the fact there would soon be another person in my life, someone I'd be responsible for taking care of for years to come. I hoped I was up to the job.

Chapter 17

Even though we'd been busier than usual on Friday, I had to drop everything and drive to Salinas to settle a long standing dispute. I spent the best part of the morning threatening a landscape contractor with a lawsuit over his underpayments of wages to his Mexican laborers, finding it difficult to convince him I was serious. The rough looking, gruff speaking owner of the company seemed unable to understand that just because his workers were here illegally, didn't mean they had no rights.

My ace in the hole was my threat to turn him into ICE for hiring undocumented workers. If he paid them what was rightfully theirs and continued to do so, I told him, I wouldn't make the call.

I handed him a list of the employees and the amounts due them in back pay. Once we agreed on the details, I walked back to my car. Feeling woozy, I sat behind the wheel with the air conditioning running on high, mad at myself for running out of bottled water.

I'd been standing in the hot June sun far longer than I'd planned. My back hurt and my feet and ankles were swollen to twice their normal size. It would take a good thirty-minutes to drive back to the office, and I was exhausted as well as thirsty.

Driving down the dusty dirt road that had taken me to the landscaper's growing fields, I'd just reached the freeway when I I felt a small twinge. I thought it must be my back acting up. It stopped as quickly as it started.

I lucked out finding a parking space in front of the office, eager to tell everyone an agreement had been reached and seven Mexican laborers would be receiving a tidy sum. As I opened the car door, I felt another twinge. Could this be the start of labor? No, it couldn't be. I wasn't ready. I needed more time.

I knocked on Maria's door. She looked up from her desk as I entered. "Jesus, Michael, you look like hell. Are you feeling okay?"

"I think I'm going into labor. How can I tell?"

"You can't miss the contractions. They feel like a tightening cramp. They start off mild but increase in intensity and frequency. Tell me what's happening."

"I think I've had contractions about thirty minutes apart. What should I do?" Even I could hear the panic in my voice.

"First thing, call your doctor's office. They'll probably want you to check in at the hospital when the contractions are fifteen minutes apart."

I did as Maria suggested, my hand shaking as I dialed the phone. The nurse said fifteen minutes apart just as Maria predicted, but to come to the hospital at once if my water broke. I remained seated at my desk unable to move as visions of every movie I'd ever seen, with women screaming, sweat pouring off their faces as they went through labor, while some idiot kept telling them to push. Was this about to be me, starring in my own movie?

Maria grabbed her purse and told the girls to hold down the fort. She was taking me home to pack an overnight case and await the baby's arrival. With more excitement than I could muster,

Elaine and Clara each gave me a big hug and wished me a safe delivery. Maria followed me home. I felt both helplessness and dread. There was no stopping now and no way to turn off the inevitable.

Maria parked behind me and followed me into my unit. She'd never been there before and looked around curiously.

"Cute place, Michael. A bit small, but you have really nice things. I'm sure it's a big change from your last place."

"It's serving its purpose."

"If you haven't packed already, I'll sit down and wait. You won't need much. They're going to send you home the morning after delivery. Do you have everything you need for the baby? How about food? Do you have plenty of groceries in the house? I'd be happy to shop for you if you give me a list."

I gave her a hug. "You've been wonderful, a real friend. If you hadn't spoken that night at dinner I'd have never knuckled down and gotten organized. Thanks, but I think I have everything I need."

After packing a few thing in a small case, Maria and I sat together in the living room timing my contractions, which were getting closer to the twenty-minute mark.

THE BUTTERFLY

"I'm a good listener if you want to tell me about the baby's father. It's none of my business, but are you intending to tell him after the baby's born?"

"No, I have no intention of ever telling him. He must never know."

I saw a look of concern on Maria's face. "Are you afraid of what he might do?"

"Oh, no, Maria, you've got it all wrong. I know exactly what he'd do. He sweep me up in his arms and take me back to Mexico and treat me and his child like royalty."

"Then, for God's sake what's the problem? Why all the secrecy?"

"He's the most wonderful man I've ever met. Cultured, smart, handsome, from an important and wealthy family. His behavior toward me was always an act of love, but he's married. I can't be his mistress, waiting for his wife to die, or for the time when family pressures are so great that parting is the only answer. No. It's better this way."

I realized I hadn't thought about Berto in months, but I thought about him now as a sharper contraction took hold.

Maria took my hand in hers. "I hope you know what you're doing, Michael. Being a single mother isn't easy. Especially when the father, from what you tell me, would gladly meet his responsibilities, although I don't have a great deal of respect for men who cheat on their wives." "

As the contractions hit the fifteen-minute mark, Maria took my overnight case, unlocked the door to her car, and helped me in. The drive to the hospital didn't take long. The contractions were beginning to be more than a little uncomfortable. Little did I know what was to follow.

I walked to the reception desk and after signing a pile of papers, an attendant pushing a wheelchair arrived. With Maria following, I was whisked off to labor and delivery.

The small room was pleasant enough if a little sterile. Maria helped me undress and stayed with me as I sat on the bed wearing the hideous blue-patterned cotton hospital gown, waiting for something to happen.

It seemed to take forever before a nurse arrived and checked everything from my heartbeat, blood pressure, and temperature, she seemed uninterested in how I felt, prodding my belly, while informing me it wasn't time to alert the doctor yet. She said it would be quite a while before I was ready to deliver, but everything seemed normal.

The nurse proceeded to help me into the bed putting up the guardrails and dimming the lights. Now, I was really getting scared. I'd never been in a hospital before, much less been seriously ill a day in my life. All of this was new and totally out of my control and the damn contractions were growing more intense. How much longer could I ignore them? The nurse's comment that it would be quite a while, wasn't helping.

Hours passed. The nurse would come in every fifteen minutes or so, and check what was happening. I finally told Maria to go home. I was no longer good company and the last thing I wanted was to carry on a conversation. I just wanted it to be over. Maria seemed reluctant to leave me alone, but I insisted. I wanted to be by myself.

Alone in the darkened room, time passed at an even slower pace. The contractions were closer and more painful. I grabbed the guardrails so hard my knuckles turned white and bit down hard enough for my lip bled. God, was this never going to end? I wanted Berto one minute and never wanted to see him again the next. My feelings were so conflicted at this point, all I wanted was for this to all be over.

At last, having been proclaimed fully dilated, the obstetrician checked everything and broke my water. By now the contractions were stronger, and things were moving along. Just not fast enough for me.

I was pushing as hard as I could, but not hard enough to satisfy the doctor who I was beginning to hate. She spoke to me in a soft voice, and I screamed back at her and gave one big push then bingo, a wet little creature was placed on my stomach, it's umbilical cord still attached. I heard the doctor say it's a boy. Tears flowed down my cheeks. If I'd been scared before I was terrified now, the sense of panic that sweep over me was like a giant wave crashing against a sea wall then carrying me out into deep water, where I was drowning in the fear of the responsibility I had for the child resting on my chest. Knowing that this little boy was God's way of keeping me tied to Berto forever.

Chapter 18

Having little recollection of what happened next only of being exhausted and thinking Berto would be so happy to know he had a son, I dropped off to sleep. I remember being aware of a nurse entering the room and then falling back asleep.

I was awakened by a knock on the door and a tray being placed on the table alongside me. I picked at the unappetizing breakfast of cold scrambled eggs and dry toast, drinking the vapid coffee and waiting for what would happen next. Time passed slowly.

After a visit from a doctor on morning rounds, I was informed I'd be discharged at ten o'clock. Still feeling a bit tired, but otherwise okay, I dressed, combed my hair, and put on lipstick, then sat on the bed waiting for something to happen. Every time I heard footsteps in the hall, I thought they were bringing my baby. I'd not seen him since delivery, but I assumed this was normal. No one had told me what to expect.

About nine o'clock, after a soft rap on the door, a tall, athletic looking doctor in blue scrubs entered the room. I couldn't help but notice his full head of red hair. I stood up as he entered.

"Good morning, Mrs. Madison. How are you feeling?"

"Fine, but I've already been discharged. I'm just waiting for someone to bring my baby."

"I'm Doctor O'Malley. I'm not an obstetrician. I'm a pediatrician. I've just come from examining your son." He looked around the room noticing I was alone. "Is your husband going to be here, soon?"

"I'm not married." Why was he asking about a husband?

"I see. Are you expecting your significant other or some family member? I'd like to discuss your baby's condition, and it would be better if some other person was here."

"There's no one. Just me, but you're scaring me to death. What condition are you talking about?"

He motioned to the only chair in the room, and I sat down, my heart beating a mile a minute.

"Both your obstetrician and the attending nurse noticed your son's coloring was abnormally blue. It was recommended he be sent to the neo natal ward for further observation until I could examine him." He paused allowing me to catch my breath before he went on.

"Let me explain this in the simplest of terms. I ran a few quick tests and concluded his oxygen level is low. I'd like to run some additional tests, but in all likelihood from what I've observed, your son will require surgery in the next few days to correct what I suspect is a hole in his heart. I've had him moved to the neo natal intensive care unit."

If the doctor was still talking, I couldn't hear a word. Heart. Surgery. Those were the only words my brain heard. Everything else was a blur. My thoughts were a jumble of words. Moments passed before I could reply, wondering how could this happen?

"I don't know what to say. Should I call a specialist?"

"Pediatric Cardiology is my specialty. That's why they called me. This is not a completely uncommon abnormality and a capable pediatric surgeon can close the hole. Until I do a further examination, the size of the hole is yet to be determined, but I need your permission to put the child in my care. The long term prognosis is excellent as is the survival rate from surgery. These babies lead normal lives, but without the closure, normal development due to lack of the proper level of oxygen, is guarded at best."

It felt like someone had driven a stake through my heart. What was I supposed to do now? "What happens next, Doctor? I'm sorry I don't remember your name."

"O'Malley. Doctor O'Malley. I'd like to run a few more tests, and then, depending on what I find, get in touch with a pediatric surgeon at Lucille Packard hospital at Stanford. He's the best at this type of surgery. All with your permission of course."

"Doctor O'Malley, I don't have a great deal of savings, and I'm not sure how much, if anything, my insurance would cover." By now, tears were running down my cheeks. "I don't know how I can pay for this."

"Don't worry. A successful outcome is the only thing that's important now. If you feel up to it, we can walk down the hall to see your son. He's a fine looking boy." Something about his confident manner made me trust him.

I walked along in silence, a million things running through my mind. After entering the neo natal unit, I was given a gown and a mask before being allowed to enter the intensive care section. Doctor O'Malley led me to the crib nearest the nurse's station, and I glanced down at the tiny figure in the bed, a plastic tube attached to his nostrils delivering oxygen. He looked much too small to have heart surgery.

Doctor O'Malley put his hand on my shoulder, and in the most reassuring tone, told me everything would be fine. "Your baby will stay here until a decision is made as to the next step. We'll do an electrocardiogram this morning, the results will give me a better idea of the size of the opening."

Try as I could, most of the words were going right past me. That anything could be wrong with my baby was something I'd never even considered

"He'll be well taken care of here. In my opinion, the nurses in this unit are the most dedicated staff in the whole hospital. Try not to worry."

Easier said than done, I thought. "I'll wait to hear from you, Doctor O'Malley."

"I'll call as soon as I have more information to share, and again, try not to worry,"

I walked back to my room alone, called Maria, and asked if she could pick me up. I was shaken to my core and ran into her arms as soon as she arrived.

I explained the circumstances between sobs, on the drive home. Maria was my rock of Gibraltar, assuring me everything would be fine. She'd check the policy, but not to worry. The baby would have the surgery he needed. God would provide.

The drive home was a blur. Maria put a casserole in the refrigerator along with an assortment of salad fixings and fruit. Motioning toward the bedroom she urged me to lie down.

"You'll need all your strength. I'll tell the girls what's happening. As she opened the door to leave, she called over her shoulder, "Call me as soon as you hear anything."

I stretched out on the bed exhausted, my eyes drawn to the empty crib. Guilt, like a school of piranhas, was eating away at my being. I'd never given much thought to God, but if there was one, was this my punishment?

I must have fallen asleep, awakened by the sound of my cell phone. I couldn't believe I'd slept so soundly.

"Miss Madison, it's Doctor O'Malley. I sent the cardiogram results to my mentor at Stanford and spoke with him just a short while ago. He's agreed to do the surgery the day after tomorrow. The good news is the hole is small in size."

"That's wonderful news, but I haven't had time to figure out how much coverage I have."

"That's the last thing you need to be concerned about at the moment. I've made arrangements to transfer him by ambulance. He's fine and strong in every other aspect. If you meet me at the hospital emergency exit at eleven, we can be on our way."

"You're going with us?" For whatever reason I felt reassured.

"Of course. The baby's my patient. Besides, the surgeon, Doctor Hoffman is a good friend. I don't have the opportunity to visit with him very often. See you then and don't worry. We'll see this through. The odds are with him."

Chapter 19

How I got through the rest of the night I'll never know. I couldn't stop blaming myself. I hadn't been good at keeping my doctor's appointments. Maybe I'd worked too hard, didn't get enough rest, didn't eat properly. If only I'd been more responsible.

I arose early. having spent the night thinking about the surgery. I showered and dressed in clothes I hadn't worn in months. I swallowed a cup of coffee and drove to the hospital.

After parking the car I walked across the parking lot to the emergency exit. And spotted the ambulance backed up to the exit door, I tried to remain calm. About ten minutes passed before Doctor O'Malley arrived alongside a nurse wheeling a crib. They lifted it into the back of the ambulance.

Doctor O'Malley smiled as he saw me standing there. "Good morning. Ready for a ride?"

I nodded yes. He pointed to the open door and I climbed into the ambulance and sat on a bench along the side watching the crib being secured to the opposite side. The baby seemed to be sleeping. The nurse exited as Doctor O'Malley sat down next to me. The back doors were closed and the ambulance pulled away from the hospital.

"With any luck, we should be at Stanford in and hour and a half. Have you named your son? I can't keep calling him Baby."

"Yes. His name is Bertram Tyler Madison. I plan on calling him Tyler."

"Great name. I can't keep calling you Miss Madison either. We're going to be interacting a lot until Tyler is out of the woods."

"Right. My name's Michael, and no remarks please."

"Michael Madison." That name sounds familiar. Something about you seems familiar as well. Are you from around here?"

"No, I'm from the Bay Area."

"Where?"

"Burlingame, why?"

"You didn't go to Burlingame High by any chance?"

"Yes. I graduated ten years ago."

A smile lit up his face. "Are you one of Professor Madison's daughter's? Do you have a sister named Jean?"

"Jean's my older sister."

"Wow, that's crazy. What do you imagine the odds are that I'd know your sister? My brother Terrance dated her their junior and senior years in high school. Now I remember you. You were three years behind me. Gosh, what a small world."

I started to laugh. "I remember Terrance. He had red hair just like yours. Jean was crazy about him. Then I don't know, guess they went off in different directions, to different colleges. I only remember being sick and tired of hearing about him. He was all she ever talked about. He practically lived at our house. My sister rated him number one in kissing."

A broad grin broke out on Dr. O'Malley's face. "Somehow that doesn't sound like my brother Terrance."

We rode along for some distance before he asked the next question.

"So what did you do after high school, and what brings you to Monterey?"

"After graduating from San Francisco State I received my law degree from Bolt."

"Whoops, a U.C. Berkeley grad," he groaned. "That could be the end of our friendship before it even begins. I graduated from Stanford."

The rivalry between the two schools wasn't lost on either of us, as we both laughed.

"And you're in practice here. Why not in the Bay Area?"

"It's a long story, but I started working in Monterey for a non-profit called The Mexican Alliance seven months ago. And you?"

"Nothing too exciting, Stanford undergrad and Stanford med school. When I finished my residency and passed the boards, the hospital in Monterey was looking for a Pediatric Cardiologist. I applied and was accepted. I became a partner in an established pediatric practice a little over two years ago. That's my history to date."

He leaned over to check the monitor. "All's well. He's doing fine. Seeing as we have so much in common, why don't you call me Pat? All my friends do."

We were making good time. Traffic was light. Pat had one eye on Tyler all the time he was talking to me. We entered the Stanford campus and drove straight to the Lucille Packard Children's Hospital. After the ambulance came to a stop, Pat hopped out and said, "Wait here. I'll let them know we've arrived and have Tyler transferred to their neo-natal ward."

It felt strange being alone for the first time with my baby. I'd never so much as touched him since the delivery. I noticed the slight covering of dark hair just like his father's. I wondered what color his eyes would be.

Minutes passed, wishing Pat would hurry back. I felt nervous being left alone with the baby. What would I do if he started to cry? I stopped myself. He wasn't the baby, he was my baby. Hard as I tried, adjusting to the fact that Tyler was mine was proving difficult.

At last, Pat, a nurse, and an attendant arrived. After removing the crib they wheeled it toward the ambulance entrance as Pat started to accompany them. He walked past me saying, "I'll come and find you in the waiting room after I'm sure he's settled."

A long hour passed before Pat returned. "Everything's going well. The surgery is scheduled for five this afternoon. Nothing for us to do now but wait. He's in good hands."

Pat sat down beside me. We were the only ones in the waiting room.

"How about we grab a bite to eat? It's bound to be a long day. We can either eat in the hospital's cafeteria where I can tell you from experience, the foods just food, or we can walk over to the Stanford Shopping Center. You can have your pick of a bunch of great places to eat."

Food was the last thing on my mind. "I'm not sure I can eat. I'm really not very hungry."

"I'm starved. Come on." He smiled, grabbing my hand to pull me up. "If nothing else you can watch me eat. Besides a walk in the fresh air will do you good."

We settled at an outside table at Max's Opera Café, a large umbrella protecting us from the sun. Most of the lunch crowd had come and gone by the time we arrived.

"How about something to drink? It'll settle your nerves, and I'll bet you haven't had a drink in months."

"You're right. A drink does sound good."

Lunch went well, almost like two old friends we exchanged stories. I learned all about his brother Terrance and Pat seemed genuinely interested in hearing about my sister. It felt so good to talk to someone I could more easily relate to.

We'd been in no hurry to leave, but by now it was almost three o'clock. Pat finally stood and suggested we should head back to the hospital. He wanted to check on Tyler and make sure everything was still set for five.

Pat introduced me to the head nurse. After donning disposable gowns and masks, the nurse took us to Tyler's crib. "He's a little bit cranky. Hungry for his bottle, but unfortunately he can't have anything before his surgery. You can hold him for a while if you like."

I turned toward Pat and whispered, "I've never held a baby before in my whole life. I don't know what to do."

Pat reached down with complete ease and picked Tyler up handing him to me. I can't explain the feeling that came over me. I held him tight to my breast for a moment before I cradled him in my arms. I felt his little heart beating. I reached out to touch his small hand and his fingers gripped mine. I realized I was crying. The little bundle in my arms was truly mine.

Pat excused himself, saying he wanted to check with Doctor Hoffman, the surgeon. A short time later, the nurse returned and took the baby from my arms. She needed to prep him for surgery.

I stood in the hall outside the unit and waited for Pat's return. Hospitals were new to me and they evoked a sense of tension, like waiting for the other shoe to drop. Not knowing if the day would end on a happy note or one of high drama?

We returned to the waiting room, but no longer had it to ourselves. A grayhaired woman, surrounded by what seemed like family, occupied one side of the room keeping their voices low. An older man sat alone by the window, his hands folded in his lap as he starred at a blank wall. Pat pointed to a couch, and we sat down.

"Doctor Hoffman seems confidant, Michael. He's the best in his field. This is going to take at least three hours. Don't let that worry you, it's the norm."

Something about the positive tone of Pat's voice helped. For the first time, looking past the thick thatch of red hair, I saw the man, the delightful scattering of freckles across the bridge of his nose and the bluest of blue eyes. With the name Patrick O'Malley, he had to be Irish. Tall and angular, he had the body of an athlete. Pat wasn't what I would call handsome, but he was damn good looking. Something about his warm smile and easy manner made him even more attractive.

THE BUTTERFLY

The only sound in the room was the ticking of the large clock on the wall until Pat broke the silence asking where I worked before coming to Monterey. I mentioned the law firm in San Francisco.

"It's none of my business, but what caused you to leave San Francisco for Monterey?"

"You're right it's none of your business." I regretted the sharp tone of my voice as soon as the words left my lips. "I'm sorry, I didn't mean to sound rude."

"You were right. I was off base."

"I guess I'm just on edge. All I can think of is opening up Tyler's little chest to mend his heart." I took a deep breath trying to get myself under control. "I can't believe you've taken so much time away from your practice to be here. Do you do this for all your patients?"

"No, not really, but I understand how traumatic this can be especially without anyone to lean on. I wanted to see this through, and besides I don't take many days off. This was a great opportunity to visit with Doctor Hoffman again. One of the perks of being in a partnership is that I can ask the receptionist to transfer my patients to Ron, my partner."

We ran out of conversation as the hours dragged on. The family seemed to receive good news from the doctor who spoke with them, as there was much hugging and smiles before they left. The lone man was still waiting. He hadn't moved from the window.

Almost four hours later, a short, unimpressive looking man wearing green scrubs, a mask hanging around his neck, entered the waiting room. Pat stood and went toward him. The two embraced and walked to where I was standing.

"Doctor Hoffman," Pat said with a smile, "I'd like to introduce my fiancée, Michael Madison."

Pat put his arm around me, tightly squeezing my hand. A warning to stay silent. "I can tell by the look on your face its good news."

"The hole was as expected, rather small. I stitched it closed and with any luck he won't need any additional repair as he grows older. If there are no complications, you can take him back to your hospital by noon tomorrow. I know you'll watch him carefully, Pat. I would suggest two more weeks of neo natal care before you send him home."

Doctor Hoffman shook my hand. "I'm glad to meet you, Michael. Pat here was one of my favorites. You have a fine looking son, but I am surprised at you, Pat. I thought you'd put marriage first before you fathered a child."

"That was our plan, but accidents happen. Michael wanted to wait for her parents to return to the States so her father could walk her down the aisle.

They're missionaries in China. They were due here three months ago, but they've been delayed. They should be here soon."

My cheeks were bright red by now, part embarrassment and part pure anger. How dare Pat concoct such a story, such a bunch of damn lies. I hardly knew the man. It was all I could do to keep quiet.

"Well, the best of luck to you both. Now that you two have a fine son, get married."

Pat thanked him. I tried, but I was so mad the words wouldn't come. After the doctor left the room, I turned toward Pat, my anger unchecked. "What the hell was that all about? You just told a bald faced lie to that man and embarrassed the hell out of me."

Pat looked at me with smiling eyes, a mischievous grin on his face. "The story had a purpose, Michael, and it worked. I spoke with Dr. Hoffman earlier about us and he waived his fee. You're receiving a courtesy discount for the hospital services as well."

I didn't know what to say. I should be grateful. "But you just strung together a huge pack of lies. Doesn't that bother you?"

"Well, not lies exactly, sort of, shall we say, embellishments?" Feigning an Irish brogue Pat continued. "When I was a mere lad, my dear mother used to call all young boys lads, she'd say, 'Patrick Christopher O'Malley, you remind me of your dear departed grandfather, who just like you, could string together a remarkable tale. It will surely get you into trouble one day for there is a fine line between tellin' tall tales and lying'. With a broad grin on his face, Pat said. "I choose to think of my words as a tall tale."

What could I say? He had my best interest at heart and he did have a certain innocent charm.

"We have ourselves a bit of a problem, Michael. No car and no place to stay. Do your folks still live in Burlingame?"

"Yes, why?"

"I'll call my dad and have him pick us up. You can stay at with your folks and I can stay at mine. We can meet at the hospital tomorrow for the ambulance ride home."

How was I going to deal with this? I couldn't suddenly show up at ten in the evening without an explanation. I wasn't ready to face my parents with the truth, but how was I going to explain this to Pat without sharing more than I wanted to.

Pat picked up on my concerns. "Is there a problem, Michael?"

"Let's just say I haven't told my parents about being pregnant and leave it at that."

THE BUTTERFLY

"Problem solved. Wait here while I call home. I'm sure my mother will be glad to have a houseguest."

"No please don't do that. I can stay here, I'll be fine. I can't impose on your mother."

"Of course you can. Knowing my mother she'll be more than happy to have you."

Doctor Daniel O'Malley, Pat's father, stopped the car in front of a large two-story white stucco house in the foothills of Burlingame abutting the large estates of Hillsborough. He let us out in front and drove the car into the garage. Pat opened the front door. "Mother Molly, I'm home."

A handsome woman in her seventies came out of the kitchen. With bright red hair and flawless complexion, what my mother used to refer to as peaches and cream, Pat's mother smiled, as her eyes lit up at the sight of her son. Her mature figure was reflected not only her age, but the birth of six children. Her blue eyes sparkled as she greeted me.

"Welcome to our home," she said. I realized where Pat's ease with speaking in an Irish brogue came from. She sounded as if she arrived from Ireland yesterday.

Pat embraced his mother saying, "If you remember Terrance's old girlfriend, Jean Madison, this is her younger sister Michael. Michael, my mom, Molly O'Malley."

"Your father said something about you both needin' a place to stay the night. Patrick, you told your father something to do with a surgery patient."

"More or less, but we do need a place to stay."

"Come along children," she said as she headed toward the kitchen. "I'm brewing a cup o' tea."

"Really, Mrs. O'Malley I just need a place to sit and rest. The sofa will do just fine."

She dismissed my concerns with a smile. "Nonsense. We've a big house full of empty bedrooms. Come along, Patrick and tell me what you've been up to."

The four of us sat at a large, round oak table in one corner of the kitchen drinking tea and eating homemade sugar cookies. Pat's mother was delightful, bubbling over with news of her other children and grandchildren. His father, looked at me with suspicion, uncertain of the limited details Pat had given him.

I stretched out on the bed without undressing, dead tired. There'd been too many things to cope with in one day. I fell asleep and didn't awaken until well after eight the following morning. A bathroom connected my room to another bedroom. I did my best to freshen up and went downstairs. Voices and the aroma of coffee led me to the kitchen. Pat's father had already left for morning rounds at the hospital. Pat and his mother were chatting away. "I hope you slept well, my dear."

"Thank you, Mrs. O'Malley. I slept like a log."

"Mother Molly is going to drive us to the hospital when were ready. I haven't made arrangements for the ambulance as yet. I'm waiting for the okay from Dr. Hoffman."

"Patrick tells me you were accompanying a surgery patient."

"It's a long story, Mom. Not for today."

I ate a hearty breakfast of oatmeal and homemade scones as Pat and his mother did their best to make me feel comfortable. As promised, Pat's mother dropped us off at the hospital.

I sat alone in the waiting room, unable to relax as I waited for Pat to return. He'd gone to check on the baby's status. Pat was all smiles as he approached. "Master Tyler is one tough little character. Everything looks great. He's off the oxygen and his color is improved already. Arrangements for an ambulance have been made, and we'll be on our way in about an hour."

We had little to say to one another on the ride home. The pent up anxiety of the last few days was beginning to take their toll. I thanked Pat for everything he'd done, saying how I couldn't have managed without him.

"Nothing to thank me for. I do get attached to my little patients and the bigger ones, too. I'm just glad it turned out so well. You'll be hearing from me with updates, and if things continue as expected, you can take master Tyler home in two weeks."

I thanked him again and walked to my car, somehow still not really feeling like a mother.

Chapter 20

In the two weeks that followed, nothing had changed in my life. Yes, I'd had a child, but he was somebody else's responsibility. I stopped by the hospital on Sunday and still felt a stranger to the child in the crib.

Pat called every evening with an update, assuring me things were going well and the release date was still on schedule.

Two weeks to the day, I found myself all alone at home with Tyler. He was so little I feared touching him, scared I'd do something wrong, and terrified out of my wits with no one to turn to.

I tried to follow the detailed instructions the hospital had given me. The six o'clock bottle went as well as could be expected as I fumbled my way through the process. The ten o'clock bottle went a little better. When I crawled into bed I found sleep impossible. I kept checking on Tyler, aware of every small sound or movement. I finally dozed off, only to be awakened at two o'clock by a crying baby. I fed and changed him, and tried to go back to sleep, but the crib was so close to my bed I heard every peep Tyler made.

Up again at six to the sound of his fussing, I repeated the routine all over again, wondering how long the four-hour schedule would last. Weren't babies supposed to sleep all night?

An hour later, Tyler had finished his bottle and I faced the next step, bathing him. I read the instructions again, scared to death at the prospect. I was about to make a pot of coffee, hoping it would settle my nerves, when the doorbell rang. Who'd be at my door at that time of the morning? I opened the door a crack to see Pat standing there. "What are you doing here?"

"I'm making a house call. May I come in or are you going to leave me standing out here?"

"I'm sorry. Come in. Is something wrong? Are you worried about Tyler?"

"As a matter of fact, it's you I'm worried about. The little tiger is doing great. He's already proved to be a tough character. But you, Michael, how are you doing? You look tired. By the way, I like your outfit." Pat handed me a cardboard container. "I brought breakfast."

I'd glanced down realizing I was barefoot, wearing the grey sweats and Bolt Alumni T-shirt I'd slept in. Aware I must look like something the cat dragged in, my hair uncombed and no makeup. "My God, I must look like hell."

"I'll make coffee while you change. Don't be long. The muffins are fresh out of the oven."

Throwing on jeans and a turtleneck, I brushed my teeth, combed my hair, and put on a quick swipe of lip gloss and mascara, then hurried back to the kitchen.

Pat had removed all the baby stuff I'd piled on the table and placed two plates and mugs in their place. "Sit down. You look exhausted."

I starred at the blueberry muffin on my plate, the steaming coffee in my cup, and wanted to cry. "This looks wonderful. Thank you so much, but you really didn't have to do this."

"Did you sleep at all last night?"

"To be truthful, not really. I was afraid if I slept to soundly I wouldn't hear Tyler cry."

"Believe me, you'll hear him. He has a powerful set of lungs. Try to relax. This is the toughest part. It shouldn't be too long before you're down to four feedings."

I devoured the muffin, acting as if I'd never seen food before. Looking up, I saw Pat smiling at me.

"What are your plans for the day?" Pat asked as I swallowed the last of the coffee.

"If I can figure out how to bath Tyler, I'm not going to do another thing except wait for his next feeding."

"Hey bathing him is no big deal, certainly nothing to be concerned about. It's easy and a lot of fun. Babies love the feel of warm water. I think it has something to do with time in the womb."

"Not concerned? Are you crazy? This is the first baby I've ever touched, let alone bathed. I'm terrified."

THE BUTTERFLY

Pat stood, pushed his chair aside, rolled up his sleeves, and proceeded to fill the small basin on the kitchen counter with warm water. He asked where Tyler's soap and towels were as he headed for his crib.

"What are you doing?"

"I'm going to give you a demonstration on how to bath a baby."

I watched as he undressed Tyler, talking to him in a soothing tone as he placed him in the warm water, and with a gentle touch, soaped his body, and then rinsed him off placing him on a bath towel on the counter. Pat wrapped Tyler in the towel patting him dry and keeping him warm.

"See. Wasn't that easy? Now, all you need to do is dress him and put him down for his nap."

Pat poured the last of the coffee and drank it in one long gulp. "Gotta go. I'm due at the hospital. Call me day or night if you have any concerns or need any more demonstrations." He walked toward the door. "Take care of yourself, Michael."

I stood beside the door, Tyler in my arms still wrapped in his towel. "Thanks, Pat. Thanks for everything, including the muffins." I was sad to see him go.

Monday was hectic. I'd been up before six trying to get Tyler and myself ready to leave. The drive to the office took longer than usual since I drove slower, with a lot more caution than usual. Everyone was excited to see the new baby, and nobody mentioned that I was quite late. By the time the day ended, I began to realize just how difficult this was going to be. When I heard cries from the broom closet we'd turned into a nursery, I'd cut short a telephone conversation with "Sorry I'll have to call you back." Hardly a way to resolve a dispute. I refused to make appointments that took me out of the office.

At the week's end, I'd been less than productive. I wondered how long they'd put up with this arrangement. By week two, things took a dramatic change. Tyler acquired three new mothers. Clara, Elaine, and even on rare occasions, Maria, all agreed that if I was in the middle of something, they'd care for Tyler. They were heaven sent. Things didn't get easier as the day's passed, but I was learning not to panic.

I had no need to call Pat, so I was surprised to hear his voice on the phone as I prepared to leave the office on a Friday evening, several weeks later. He asked about Tyler and how I was doing, just a friendly exchange. I thought the conversation was over when Pat asked if I'd have dinner with him on Saturday.

"That would be nice, but I'm sorry I can't. I have no one to leave Tyler with."

"Well, if the mountain won't come to Mohammad, then Mohammad will come to the mountain. I'll bring dinner."

"You're kidding," I said, laughing.
"Nope. I'm dead serious. I'll be there at seven with take-out in hand. I'm a lousy cook."

At well past seven, I heard the doorbell ring. I opened the door to find Pat's smiling face. He was holding a plastic bag in one hand and a six-pack of beer in the other.

"Sorry I'm late. I had an emergency. A three year old with a rash over ninety percent of his body."

I took the package to the kitchen. "Is he okay?"

"Yeah. They have a new puppy. My guess is the kid's allergic to dog hair. Anyway, I apologize. This isn't the dinner I'd planned, but running late, it's the best I could do. How are you doing?"

"I'm managing. Sort of."

Pat took two bottles from the carton and removed the caps. "Here," he said as he handed me a beer. "This should help."

We settled down on the sofa. It was good to see him. I had no social life these days. Having someone to talk to that wasn't work related was really nice.

"How's the little tiger doing? It's about time for his first office visit."

We'd finished the burgers and fries. I'd turned down a second beer when the conversation turned serious. Pat asked if I'd spoken with my parents yet?

"Not yet."

"So I guess you're going to wait until he's old enough to knock on their door and announce 'I'm your grandson.'"

"That's not fair, Pat. Besides why should you care?"

"Because I do. It's going to be harder the longer you wait." He paused before he said, "How about I drive you and Tyler to your folks house next Sunday."

That took me totally by surprise. I knew I had to face them sooner or later, and I wasn't looking forward to the long drive by myself, but suddenly Pat had forced me to make a decision. "Let me think about it. I'll let you know in a day or two. I appreciate the offer, but it's really not your responsibility."

"I don't see it that way, but think about it. It's not going to be any easier if you continue to put it off."

I think Pat sensed at that point there was nothing left to say. He stood and headed toward the door. I started to hand him the remaining bottles of beer as I thanked him for dinner and the company.

"You keep them. I might just drop by again sometime in need of a brew." He gave me a thumbs up, then turned and walked out the door.

THE BUTTERFLY

I tried to figure Pat out as I closed the door. He was fun to have around. He seemed such a blithe spirit. I knew he was talented and serious about his commitments to his patients, but this seemed way beyond patient commitment. Why was he going out of his way to be helpful? Could it be because I was Jean's sister, but even that didn't make sense. I only knew I felt better after his visits. He always seemed to show me the sunny side of life.

Chapter 20

Sunday found me sitting beside Pat, Tyler secured in his carrier in the back seat of Pat's Ford Explorer, dreading the task ahead. I grew ever more concerned as we got closer to my parents' house.

Pat seemed to sense my unease. "Just remember, they love you. It's going to be a shock so don't be too concerned by their immediate reaction. Put yourself in their shoes and try to understand how you'd react."

"They're going to ask a lot of questions I'm not prepared to answer."

"Then say so. Tell them maybe someday, but not now."

"God, Pat, you make it seem so easy."

"Not easy, just necessary, Michael. How could anyone look at your handsome son and be anything but overjoyed, even though they might not admit it at the moment. They're the jury. Let the lawyer in you convince them."

We turned onto the block where my parents lived and I thought nothing about the neighborhood had changed. Everything looked the same as it did when I was a kid. So many thoughts were going through my head. My dad prodding me on, always expecting excellence from the high-achieving daughter he was so proud of. I had a feeling this wasn't going to be one of my proudest moments.

Pat stopped the car in front of the house, reached over and took my hand. "You're tough. You can do this. I can go visit my parents until you want me to come and get you, or I can wait here."

"Don't go. Please wait. I'll feel better if I know you're here."

Pat came around and helped me with Tyler. "I'll be right here waiting. Take as long as you like. I'm in no hurry."

"Thanks," I said as I walked up the driveway alone with my son secured in his carrier sound asleep.

My mother opened the door, surprised to see me, and confused to say the least by the baby in the carrier. She never took her eyes off Tyler, waiting for an explanation. "Come in Michael. What a pleasant surprise. Why didn't you let us know you were coming?"

I walked into the living room and sat on the sofa placing the carrier beside me. My mother looked uncomfortable as she called to my father. "Philip, Michael is here. We're in the living room."

My heart was beating faster than normal. My hands shook as I watched my dad enter the room.

"Good to see you, my dear." He stopped dead in his tracks as he saw Tyler. "You have an explanation for that?" he said as he pointed toward the baby.

"I've brought your grandson for you to meet." My answer sounded lame, but it was the best I could do.

He paused as if trying to make sense of what I just said. "What do you mean, you've brought our grandson? Explain yourself."

I took a deep breath and tried to think about what Pat had said. "There's nothing to explain. His name is Tyler. He's seven weeks old."

"That's it." The anger in his voice shook me to my core. "His name is Tyler and he's seven weeks old. That's all?"

My mother stood on the opposite side of the room holding onto the back of a chair, tears running down her cheeks.

"Dad, it's a long story. One I'm not ready to share at the moment. He's here, he's mine, and that will have to do for now."

I knew the look on my dad's face, the same look I'd received if a test paper was graded A instead of A plus. The disappointed look if I hadn't proved to be the best at everything.

"If you expect your mother and me to accept that as an answer, you're mistaken. The child has a father. Who and where is he? Are you married? If not is he planning on marrying you? Is he even contributing to the child's support? You're a lawyer, Michael. You know your rights."

"Please, Dad. Please understand. I'm not ready to go into the details. You'll just have to trust my judgment."

"That's a laugh, Michael. If this child is an example of your judgment, I guess your mother and I have failed." His words were like a slap across the face.

"Please, Philip," Mother said wiping away her tears. "Let it be. She'll tell us when she's ready. He's our grandson."

"Stay out of this, Mother. Until Michael is ready to give me some answers I can understand, he's just a bastard, the unfortunate result of my daughter sleeping with a man she wasn't married to. Throwing away a promising career. Making a joke of the education we paid dearly to give her, and the moral lessons I thought we'd instilled."

He shook his head, wringing his hands as he spoke. "What were you thinking, Michael? If you were going to sleep around, at least you could have used birth control pills. You've heard of them, I'm sure. I can't believe you were foolish enough to carry this child to term when abortion is legal."

Red faced, my father started to walk out of the room ordering my mother to follow him. She hesitated, but then followed him. His word was law. He turned toward me saying, "Goodbye Michael. What happens next is up to you."

I knew they wouldn't be pleased, but I didn't expect what I'd just heard from my father. I picked up the carrier and headed for the door, leaving me without a free hand to wipe away my tears.

I understood my father was hurt. He'd pinned his dreams on me. But how could he be so cruel? The word bastard rang in my ears

Pat opened the car door and met me halfway, taking the carrier out of my hands, and tickled Tyler under his chin as the baby smiled back at him. All the shouting must have awaken him.

There was no need for Pat to ask what had happened. The length of the visit and my tears said it all. I was grateful he didn't ask.

Pat started the car and drove off as I paid little attention to the direction we were traveling, still feeling the sting of my father's words.

Chapter 21

I looked up surprised to see we'd come to a stop in front of Pat's parents' house.

"Why are you stopping here?"

"Because you need a little cheering up. The first Sunday of every month is family night at the O'Malley's. The rule is if you can, you just show up for dinner."

Pat opened the front door. "Hey, Mother Molly. I have a visitor you'd like to meet."

Mrs. O'Malley came from the kitchen, wiping her hands on her apron. She kissed Pat, said hello to me, and grinned at Tyler as the lilting sound of her Irish brogue filled the room.

"What have we here? A bonnie wee one?"

"He's Michael's son. Do you think we can find a quiet place for him?"

"Of course we can. Come along, Michael. We'll put him in Patrick's old bedroom."

I followed her up the flight of stairs and down a hallway as she opened the door to a sunlit room with twin beds, a nightstand in between, a double dresser, and a rocking chair in the corner.

"He'll be safe here and it will be quiet away from the rowdy bunch I call family." She was so different from my own mother – so kind and welcoming.

As I placed the carrier on the bed, Tyler began to stir. I checked my watch. "It's time for his bottle."

"Go, my dear, and fetch whatever you need. I'll keep an eye on the wee one."

I thanked her and ran down the stairs and out to the car to retrieve my bag. Pat was waiting for me as I returned to the house. "Everything okay, Michael?"

"Yes. Its just time for Tyler's bottle. Are you sure it's all right my being here?"

"Of course. The O'Malleys are known worldwide for their hospitality and for feeding hungry strangers. Once the family arrives, you'll blend right in." He put an arm around me. "You're more than welcome here."

Having warmed the bottle, I hurried upstairs to find Pat's mother sitting in the rocking chair, Tyler in her arms looking up at her as she sang ever so softly, "When Irish Eyes Are Smiling."

"It's been a while since I've held a baby in my arms. Such a handsome little one and strong, too. See how he's holding on to my fingers. You go on and visit with Patrick. I'll feed him and put him back to sleep."

"I couldn't impose."

"Hush. You'd be doing me a great favor. I'm always happiest when I have a baby in my arms. Go along with you. "She'd already taken the bottle in my hand.

I'd just reached the bottom step when the door opened and a man and women and two young boys entered, the boys making a mad dash to the living room calling, "Papa, we're here."

Pat introduced his sister, Emma, and her husband, Mike. After they moved toward the living room, Pat whispered, "You finished feeding the tiger so soon?"

"Your mother insisted she wanted to feed him. You should have seen her with Tyler in her arms. She seemed so happy and he seemed so content."

"Was she singing, 'When Irish Eyes Are Smiling?'

I laughed. "Yes. How did you know?"

"Ask any of her grandchildren if they know the words to that song, and I bet they can sing it without missing a beat. If you're an O'Malley, it's your family anthem."

More family members began to arrive. Soon the house was filled with laughing, happy people. The older grandchildren were outside playing a game of touch football with their grandfather supervising.

At five o'clock, the family began to gather around two tables, one for the grownups and one for the children. Steaming bowls of lamb stew with dumplings, mixed green salad, wine and beer were passed around. I'd never witnessed anything like it. The siblings teased one another, all in good fun. They engaged in heated political discussions and seemed to be having a wonderful time.

Pat turned toward me asking if I was all right as I hadn't said a word.

"I'm fine, maybe just a little overwhelmed, but this is just what I needed. I'd forgotten that fun loving, happy people are what life was all about. It's been a while since I've been surrounded with laughter. Thank you."

We reached home near midnight. I still had a baby to take care of and tomorrow was a workday, but it had all be worth it. I thanked Pat for a wonderful time and for not asking what had happened between my parents and me.

"I'm glad you enjoyed yourself. A change of pace is good therapy. As for your parents, I'm sure you'll tell me what you want me to know. I'll call you soon. Take care of yourself, Michael."

Chapter 22

Days turned into weeks, weeks into months. Tyler was finally sleeping through the night, but he would soon outgrow the closet as he spent more time awake requiring attention. I didn't know what I was going to do.

Pat was my sanity check. He'd drop by every so often for a beer and a short visit. We took Tyler along with us to a family style restaurant on a couple of occasions, and Pat arranged for a nurse friend to babysit while he took me out to dinner on my birthday.

After an exhausting day, I'd opened the door to the townhouse and put Tyler down in his bed, thinking TGIF. My problems were mounting and the solutions were escaping me.

With Tyler fed, bathed, and down for the night, I poured a glass of wine and walked into the living room. The small room had been made even smaller with the addition of a new playpen, leaving no space in the middle of the floor.

I considered not answering the ringing of my cell phone, but I couldn't do that to Pat. I knew it was him, nobody else ever called. I heard his familiar voice asking if I'd like some company?

"Not tonight. I'm really tired and in a funky mood. I'm not sure I'd be good company."

"Let me be the judge of that. People in funky moods need cheering up, besides my undergraduate degree is in cheering up funky, moody people. See you in a bit."

A smile crossed my face as I hung up. I combed my hair, put on lipstick, and realized I'd be glad to see him.

THE BUTTERFLY

The doorbell rang as I heard a voice call out, "Pizza delivery." I opened the door as Pat with the usual broad grin on his face, handed me a box from Giovanni's Real Italian Pizza Parlor. "I guessed you haven't eaten yet."

"You guessed right. Come in. The pizza smells wonderful."

"Then let's eat while it's hot." Pat opened the refrigerator searching for the supply of beer he kept in reserve. Grabbing a bottle, he sat at the small dining table while I placed the pizza between us still in the cardboard box.

As always, Pat seemed to bring a sense of calm to my life. The nagging worries I'd been dealing with all week seemed to disappear for the moment. I was surprised when he said, "I'm concerned about you, Michael. You look tired, and it's obvious you've lost weight. You're thin enough as it is. You have to start taking care of yourself if for no other reason than for Tyler."

"Really, you needn't be concerned. I'm fine."

Pat pushed the empty pizza box aside. "I've noticed a change in you the past few weeks. What's up?"

"Nothing. I'm fine. Besides, I'm not your responsibility." I gathered up the plates taking them to the kitchen. Pat followed after me.

"Come on, let's talk. Things seem better when they're out in the open." He motioned toward the living room and I followed. "Come on, tell the doctor what's going on."

I took a deep breath. I really did need to talk to someone. "I can't juggle work and having Tyler at the office any longer. He's requiring more and more attention, and I can't keep asking the girls at the office to stop working to care for him while I'm busy or away. My boss has indicated it has to stop. I knew the arrangement was only meant to be temporary. Sooner or later I'd have to find another solution. I need to figure out a way to solve the problem.

"But as you said, you knew the arrangement was only temporary."

"I just didn't think it would happen so soon. I'm in a bind. I can't afford a nanny and decent daycare is expensive. Plus, I'm going through my savings a lot faster than I thought."

I started to cry. The pent up emotions were getting to me. "I don't know what I'm going to do."

Pat put his arm around me and I clung to him. The tears wouldn't stop.

He ran his fingers through my hair and whispered, "You could use a day off. How about I arrange for a sitter and pick you up tomorrow morning about ten. We'll go someplace quiet and talk this all out."

I started to say, "But Pat," as he stood. "No buts. I'll be here by ten. Now get some sleep. We'll figure something out."

The next morning, my cell phone pinged just as I was finishing feeding Tyler. A text message read, "Jeans, walking shoes, and a warm jacket. Carol Jones is on her way. You'll have plenty of time for instructions. See ya at ten."

Carol was at least fifty, a pleasant enough woman who seemed component and comfortable with the responsibility of taking care of infants.

When Pat rang the bell, Carol told me not to worry. "Go and have a nice day out. Don't worry about the time you return. Your baby will be fine with me."

As Pat opened the door of his Ford Explorer, I noticed how different he looked in jeans, a half-zipped grey sweatshirt, and a pair of old, tired looking hiking boots.

"You haven't said where we're going."

"Do you care?"

"Not really. You were right. I do need a day off."

I recognized the entrance to Highway 1. We were headed south. The radio was playing soft jazz as we drove along neither of us having much to say. We'd been traveling about forty-five minutes along the coast, the scenery breathtaking, when Pat broke the silence. "Have you ever been to Big Sur?"

"No. Is that where we're headed?"

"We should be at Big Sur Lodge in a few minutes. If you're up for a hike, you're in for a treat."

Pat parked at the lodge and reached into the backseat to retrieve a wicker basket and a blanket. "Lunch," he said in answer to the questioning look on my face.

We started to hike the trail Pat called Buzzard's Roost, part of Pfeiffer State Park. Hiking was new to me, as we walked along the trial I had to admit I'd never seen anything more beautiful. Everywhere I looked a forest of ancient redwood trees surrounded us, with ferns growing in their shade. Moss covered rocks were scattered along a trail that wound through the redwoods alongside the Big Sur River. The area had an aroma all its own filling my nostrils with a mysterious scent of the unknown.

"Years ago, when I was an Eagle Scout, I led a bunch of kids through the park. I couldn't get over the feeling this place evoked in me and promised I'd come back someday. Today seemed like the perfect time to return and the perfect place for a quiet day off." Pat bent down and pointed to a green leafy plant with a touch of red, "That's poison oak. Don't go anywhere near it. You don't want it to touch you or your clothes as it can produce an itchy, red rash that can bring days of misery.

"I can't believe it's so quiet here," I said as we climbed side-by-side up an incline. "I'd have thought the place would be overrun with tourists and hikers."

THE BUTTERFLY

"It's late in the season. We may luck out and have this whole wonderland to ourselves."

I walked alongside Pat as he pointed to a falcon, saying if I stayed alert I might see a bald eagle. There were deer at the edge of the woods almost hidden from sight. The sound of a woodpecker somewhere in the distance made the place seem truly magical. As a city girl, I'd never experienced anything like this before.

We hiked for close to two miles before finally reaching the top of Pfeiffer Ridge. I was glad I didn't have to go any further. I was desperately in need of a rest. I hadn't realized how out of shape I was. At least the return trip would be all downhill.

"This is incredible, Pat. I can see the Pacific Ocean from here as well as the mountains. It's a whole different world."

"That's the Santa Lucia Mountain Range," Pat said as he spread the blanket on the ground. "How about we rest here and have lunch?"

The words were music to my ears. I was starved and thirsty. With our backs to a stand of dwarf redwoods sheltering us from the wind, I watched Pat open the basket and take out sandwiches, cookies, and a bottle of red wine.

"The problems of the world seem to fade away up here, Michael." When he finished uncorking the wine, he turned toward me, "Maybe it's time to tell me what's troubling you."

I took the plastic cup filled with red wine Pat offered and thought about how much I should tell him. It might feel good to share my concerns with somebody. Taking a deep breath I began, "I guess when you boil it all down it's about money. I don't earn enough to cover my living expenses, and I know it's only going to get worse. The Alliance exists on a shoestring. They can't pay me anymore than they do already. I've been paying the hospital in installments for the part my insurance didn't cover and making up the difference between my paycheck and my living expenses with money from savings. That's not going to last too much longer if I have to pay for daycare."

I sipped my wine and took a bite of the brie and ham sandwich, breathing in the fresh air and wondering if I'd made a mistake telling Pat my problems. After all we were nothing but good friends.

"There are a couple of ways to solve the problem, Michael. The simple fact is, with your background, you could easily be making enough to support yourself if you simply looked for another job. A good paralegal earns three times what you do."

"But Pat, I love what I'm doing. I'm making a real difference in peoples' lives...hard working people who fall through the cracks, which is a whole lot more rewarding than reviewing contracts."

Pat looked at me for a long time before he spoke. "This isn't all about you any longer, Michael. You chose to bring a child into the world, and you have a duty to give him not only your love, but also the kind of stability that's within your power to provide. I don't know if you're punishing yourself or what your reasons might be, but Tyler comes first."

I took a bite of the sandwich. I wasn't happy hearing what Pat had to say. Our relationship had always been light. He'd never spoken to me like this before. In a way, even though I invited it, I resented his intrusion into my life. Down deep I knew he was right.

"You don't understand, Pat. Maria has been so good to me as have Elena and Clara. I can't just walk away."

"Please, Michael. Get real. Don't tell me Maria didn't understand when she hired you that you wouldn't be there forever. She was happy for whatever time you gave her. Think about where you live for just a moment. How are you going to manage in that tiny apartment with a growing child? He deserves his own bedroom. You don't even have a bathtub to bath him in. Sure the sink is more than adequate for now, but he's going to grow."

Everything he said was true. I needed time to think. I put the sandwich I'd barely touched back in the basket and walked away. I thought this was going to be a peaceful day, away from stress, not a look at the bitter truth.

A few minutes later, I heard Pat move before I felt his touch on my shoulder. He stood beside me. "I do have a solution."

"Tell me. I'm lost. Everything you said was true even if I didn't want to hear it. I just don't know which way to turn."

"Let's not wait for the boat from China to arrive."

The puzzled look on my face said it all. "Pat." I had no idea what he was talking about. "What does China have to do with anything?"

"Do you remember the tall tale I told Dr. Hoffman about your parents being missionaries, and how we were waiting for them to return from China so we could get married?" He paused, "It's my inept way of saying marry me."

I didn't know what to say. A proposal was the last thing I'd expected. I stood and turned my back to him. The conversation was getting difficult. I couldn't face him.

"Pat, you can't be serious. You don't know anything about me. Good God, you've never even kissed me."

"Please look at me, Michael. I'm dead serious. I know all I need to know about you, the rest isn't important. I've lusted after you since almost that first day. But damn it, I knew if I tried to kiss you it would be the end of our relationship, not the beginning. But lust has turned to love. I love you, Michael. I love Tyler as if he were my own. Don't say anything. I know it came as a surprise. I didn't plan it this way. Just think about it before you answer."

I started to gather the remains of lunch putting, everything back in the basket. I couldn't cope with his talk of marriage on top of everything else. "I think I'd like to go home now." As I turned to leave I noticed a magnificent blue butterfly, resting on Pat's shoulder making no move to fly away. I couldn't take my eyes off it. Was this some kind of sign, a message, I was supposed to understand?

I finished packing the basket, keeping one eye on the butterfly. It still hadn't moved. Unnerved, I left everything for Pat to carry and started down the trail as fast as my feet would carry me. My head was spinning. I didn't want to think about any of this, not my problems, not the future, and definitely not Pat's proposal.

One unguarded moment and I'd turned my whole life into chaos. Was the butterfly meant as a warning I should run again or just my imagination getting the better of me?

The beauty of the surroundings was now lost to me. All I wanted was to go home and pull the covers over my head. Pat was astute enough to leave me alone as he followed close enough behind to make sure I made it back to the car without incident. He stowed the blanket and basket, then started the engine, but instead of taking the road leading us home, he drove off in the opposite direction.

"Where are you going? Please, I'd really like to go home." The panic in my voice was obvious.

"One more stop and then I promise to take you home."

Ten minutes later, he turned off onto a dirt road stopping close to the water's edge in a totally isolated part of the park. I fidgeted as minutes passed before Pat spoke. He began in a slow, quiet manner, seeming to choose his words with care.

"I've a story to tell you if you have the patience to listen." When I didn't respond he went on.

"Many years ago, Michael, a young doctor received an invitation to attend a seminar in Ireland. His ancestry being Irish, he was badgered by family members to look up a few remaining relatives. And as the tales been told, he extended his visit to spend a few days in Dublin. He was treated royally and just by chance, at one of the family gatherings, he spied a beautiful redheaded young lady. He couldn't take his eyes off her and finally found the courage to introduce himself and ask her name.

"She smiled, her blue eyes sparkling, and he was lost. He invited her to lunch the following day as he was leaving on a night flight for home."

I couldn't help but be intrigued by the story. Pat's mother was right. He was a great storyteller, but I couldn't figure out where his story was going.

"The long and the short of it was they had lunch the following afternoon, the four of them, the beautiful Colleen, her mother, and her older sister.

"Our young doctor flew home, but couldn't get the beautiful young woman off his mind. They exchanged a few letters before he wrote and asked her to come to the States and marry him. And that's how Daniel Patrick O'Malley and Molly Ann Flannigan became man and wife. They couldn't really have been in love, as they knew very little about each other. He too had never kissed her, never even held her hand or spent a minute alone with her before he asked her to marry him. But as the days and months and years went by, the bond between them became stronger and stronger, the depth of their love for each other grew to a point that knew no bounds. End of story."

"It's a lovely story, Pat, but I don't see how it applies to you and me."

"I'm only trying to say that if two people want it to happen, it will. I think I'm kind of a likeable fellow, not too complicated. Maybe not the handsomest guy in the world, but I've been called kinda cute by a few girls. And more than anything at this stage of my life, I'm ready for a home, a wife, and a family. I love you, Michael. I want you to be that wife."

This wasn't what I wanted to hear. I considered Pat a friend. The last thing I wanted was a romantic entanglement. Not now or maybe never. I wasn't ready to cope with Pat's proposal.

"Pat continued before I could say a word. "Look, I can give you and the little tiger a home. You could even volunteer at the alliance a couple of times a week if you choose. I know we're a good match." He started the car. "Give it some thought. You can't keep running away from your problems. It's about time you planted your two feet on the ground and made up your mind to solve them."

He turned toward me and smiled. "I'll take you home now if you want."

"Please. I need some time to think. This wasn't something I'd expected."

"It's not what I planned either, but there in that spectacular setting, just you and me alone, I knew I had to put my feelings into words. Enough said. Besides I've run out of stories." The boyish grim crossed his face and I felt myself smiling back.

Chapter 23

I shut the door after the babysitter left, relieved to be alone. Tyler had been fed and was asleep. The room was quiet. The only noise came from the children playing across the street. I sat on the sofa and looked around, the playpen a visual indication of how small the space was. Pat was right. I'd already outgrown the tiny townhouse, but there was no way I could afford more. Looking for a position with a law firm might not be that easy. My resume wouldn't look very good, with three years at one firm, and a year at the Alliance.

But the time had come when I had to accept it was no longer just me. It was us. There was a little boy who had no say in my decisions, but whose well-being depended on my choices. But marrying Pat seemed like a cop out. Could I ever feel the rush of emotions I'd felt for Berto, or was Berto just a fantasy and Pat was what real love was all about?

In no way could I compare the two men. Pat made me laugh, made me feel comfortable, even secure in his company. We had so much in common. We'd grown up in the same town, went to the same school, and had the same values. None of that could be said for my relationship with Berto, but could Pat ever send shivers down my spine?

I stood and walked into the tiny kitchen to look for comfort food, something I seemed to do whenever I was really upset, at a crossroad. Finding nothing in the refrigerator I opened the freezer. Half a chocolate birthday cake sat on the top shelf in a clear plastic container. I grabbed a fork and stood at the kitchen sink eating, unable to ignore Pat's proposal. I owed him an answer, but I didn't want to go there tonight. With my musings running in a million different directions, I put what was left of the cake back in the freezer, remembering it was Pat who arranged for the cake on my birthday. I turned on the television hoping to lose myself in some senseless program.

I spent most of the next working day calling daycare facilities. Those that came highly recommended were either too damn expensive or full with a long waiting list. Clara told me she had a niece who'd just arrived in the country and spoke no English, but she loved kids and might make a good sitter, I wasn't ready to go in that direction.

The whole week went by without a call from Pat or his dropping by. I tried to put off any thoughts of his proposal. No matter his feelings toward me, marrying me didn't seem fair to him. The weekend passed as well without a call or a text. I wouldn't admit it, but I missed hearing from him. In the sober light of day, he probably realized how ridiculous marriage between us would be and was sorry he'd made the offer.

I spent the weekend cleaning house and doing chores. Thank God the complex had coin-operated washers and dryers, but I still needed to shop for groceries, all of which was dictated by Tyler's schedule. Monday morning I received a call from one of the daycare centers I'd contacted. They'd had an opening for an infant if I could make an immediate decision and pay the deposit that day. I jumped at the chance and promised to stop by and fill out the paperwork. The decision was made. I had no choice though this would put an even bigger dent in my savings. If Maria was right and God would provide, I needed his intervention now.

The center was located in a large older house about two miles from the office. I rang the bell and waited for the door to open. A woman answered, neatly dressed in navy blue cotton pants and a short-sleeved white cotton shirt. She appeared to be in her late forties or early fifties, I introduced myself, and she said her name was Carrie Rogers. We exchanged a few words as she offered a tour of the facility. The place seemed clean, if maybe a little sterile. A small group of children were drawing pictures in what was called the playroom. Other children were playing outside. I saw a sandbox, swings, and a large grassy area, the entire play yard enclosed by a tall anchor fence.

The bedrooms were upstairs. Mats had been placed on the floor for naptime. The largest of the bedrooms held six cribs, all but one occupied. A couple of the infants were asleep, another propped on its side sucking on a bottle. The others were awake, but I saw no one in attendance. I was assured the young ones were carefully tended, fed and changed on time, but there wasn't enough staff to spend the day playing with them. I found this a red flag.

I left after signing some paperwork and receiving a list of rules. The place seemed well run, though I wasn't happy with the lack of attention to the infants or any sort of stimulation, but I was in a bind. I'd promised Maria I'd find a place for Tyler, and I only had one week left to honor that promise.

The cost of daycare was equal to my rent. I had no idea how I was going to manage. I'd put the deposit on my credit card. I'd figure something out later.

The mornings were now a mad dash trying to get Tyler to daycare and myself to the office on time. Evenings were impossible. If I didn't pick Tyler up by six, I had to pay an extra charge. I quickly discovered it was almost impossible to make the six o'clock deadline as a lot of our clients came at the end of their workday.

I still hadn't heard from Pat. I assumed our relationship was on hold or had ended. I missed him, and was more than pleased to hear his voice when he called one afternoon.

"Thought I'd check in and see how things were going. Hope my little buddy's doing well." I could hear a certain hesitation in his voice. I felt nervous as well.

"We're fine. How are you?" I felt stupid. Couldn't I think of something better to say, maybe even that I was glad to hear from him?

"I've been busy. For some reason December is always a big delivery month and I'm dealing with two preemies that are touch and go. Pat paused and then continued. "What I really called about is Christmas. Have you and your family patched things up yet?"

"Not really. My mother sent a birthday card with a hundred dollars in cash enclosed instead of a check. I guess she didn't want my dad to know. Mom and I have talked on the phone a few times, but that's it. She's made no mention of my father.

"Does that mean you have no plans for Christmas?"

"To be honest, I haven't given a thought to Christmas. Tyler is too young to understand the holiday

"Then you've probably overlooked the fact that it's five days away."

"Five days. I had no idea. I guess I'm taking a pass on the holidays this year."

"Come on, Michael. Nobody can be allowed to overlook Christmas any more than they can overlook the sun rising or the moon setting. I'm officially inviting you to Christmas at the O'Malley's. More food than you can consume and more fun than you can imagine with the entire bunch of us together."

"Really, Pat, it's a family affair. I'd feel out of place."

"Well, I have an ulterior motive. I'm still hoping you'll be family one day."

I took a deep breath not knowing what to say as Pat continued. "I've cleared it with Mother Molly, and she's looking forward to you and the tiger coming."

"Really, Pat, I couldn't."

"Really nothing. I'll pick you up early. I need time to have a few words with my dad before the tribe arrives. See ya then." Before I could say anything else, he hung up.

By eleven on Christmas morning, we were on our way. I had no concerns about the long drive knowing Tyler would sleep the whole way. The motion of the car seemed to hypnotize him. Our conversation was light, more of an exchange of what we'd been doing since our day at Big Sur. I had to admit I was glad for his company. Things always seemed brighter when he was around and I realized how much I'd missed him.

Pat stopped in front of his parents' house, the exterior amass with Christmas lights, a huge holly wreath full of red berries at the front door. Once we stepped inside I looked around in awe, every inch of the interior seemed decorated as well. An enormous Christmas tree filled a whole corner of the living room, at least a dozen bright red Christmas stockings with names embroidered on them hung from the fireplace mantel, and greenery wound round the banister.

I was admiring the dining room table set with Christmas decorations when Pat's mother rushed out of the kitchen to greet us.

"I'm so glad you could come, my dear." Turning her attention to Tyler, she smiled. "My how the wee one has grown. Come. Let's go upstairs and get him settled in before everyone arrives."

I followed Molly up the staircase. When we reached Pat's old room she excused herself, saying she still had things to do in the kitchen and left.

I looked around, examining the trophy on the bookcase, first prize for the one hundred-meter dash from Burlingame High School. Pictures of him with the Stanford track team, in his cap and gown, photos with friends and family. His Phi Beta Kappa undergraduate degree from Stanford was framed and hanging on the wall. Impressive to say the least, but I wasn't surprised.

I made sure Tyler was fed and asleep before I headed downstairs. I'd almost reached the bottom step when I heard voices coming from the den. Pat and his father were having a heated discussion. Hearing my name, I stood frozen, curious and positive I wasn't meant to overhear their conversation.

Pat was telling his father he'd asked me to marry him.

"Are you sure you know what you're doing, Son? What about the child's father? Is he out of the picture?" I could hear the concern in his voice.

"Michael says he is, and I believe her."

"Really, Patrick, what do you know about the woman? Do you have any idea what the circumstances of the affair were?"

I caught my breath. The word affair cut to the quick. Knowing I shouldn't be hearing any of this I still couldn't move away. I heard Pat say, "I've no idea, Dad, and I don't want to know. I'm only interested in what happens from here on out."

"Patrick, you've waited a long time to get married. There are plenty of attractive women who'd be happy to marry you. You're talking about taking on another man's child. It could end badly you could get your heart broken."

"Norms have changed since you and mom were married."

"That well may be, but you could get your heart broken. Maybe you should just walk away, or at least give it more time. I admit she's very attractive, but you've said yourself you don't know all there is to know about her."

"I can't walk away, Dad. I love her. I've got to take the chance. Besides, she hasn't said yes, so maybe I'll get my heart broken anyway."

I turned and quickly walked in the opposite direction not wanting to get caught eavesdropping.

Chapter 24

One by one, six O'Malley children, their spouses, and numerous grandchildren, all boys, arrived. When everyone was accounted for, the grandchildren ran to the living room eager to open the presents Santa had left. The whole experience was so different from the quiet reserved Christmas celebrations of my youth. Squeals of joy filled the room as wrapping paper flew in all directions, boxes ripped apart as children were eager to see what was hidden inside. Grandparents were hugged and thanked. The joy was contagious. When all the gifts had been opened, the parents moved to the family room for cocktails leaving the kids to play with their new gifts, and the debris to be cleaned up later.

Pat introduced me to his brother Terrance. "You might remember her she's Jean Madison's little sister." He had everyone howling with laughter as he related the story about Terrance being the best kisser ever. His wife, Jenny, agreed and the title of the family's best kisser was bestowed. Terrance took Jenny's hand and led her to a spring of mistletoe above the dining room doorway and the family all clapped and cheered as he kissed her passionately. She blushed, it was all in fun and she didn't seem to mind being part of the family's amusement.

I checked on Tyler just before dinner was served. Finding him fast asleep, I came back downstairs just as everyone was finding their places at the table. The children's table was decorated with chocolate Santa Claus candy and an array of coloring books and crayons. The older children were in charge.

A buffet had been set up and Pat was right, there was enough food to feed several armies. Platters of roast beef, roasted potatoes, ham, sweet potatoes, brussels sprouts, glazed carrots, breads and muffins. Everything homemade.

THE BUTTERFLY

The O'Malley's were a happy lot. It was wonderful just being with them even though I didn't take part in the rowdy back-and-forth. Pat's father raised his glass after we had all been seated, and as if on cue, everyone stopped talking.

"Thank you, God," he prayed, "for the bounty we are about to receive. Mother and I are grateful that all of our family is here to share this wonderful holiday, and we're happy to have Michael join us as well. And as Tiny Tim would say, 'God bless us, every one.'"

I was surprised he included me after what I'd heard him say, but I guessed it was meant to please Pat. This had to be one of the nicest Christmases I'd ever had.

The children were excused after they'd been served ice cream and cookies in the shape of Christmas trees. Everyone else remained at the table to take part in more good-natured fun as Christmas cake and a Sherry Trifle were served. I was told these were traditional Irish Christmas desserts. Even though I was stuffed I still managed to finish a large helping of both.

After dessert, Pat's father poured snifters of port wine for the men as the women cleared the table. Everybody seemed to have assigned tasks, and I felt like a fifth wheel. One of Pat's sisters suggested I look after the baby saying, "Go check on the him. We can handle the clean-up. We've all been there and children come first in the O'Malley households. If he's awake, why don't you bring him downstairs. You can put him on a blanket on the living room floor. We'd all like to meet the little fellow."

It was almost nine o'clock by the time we started on the long drive to Monterey. Tyler was exhausted. I'm sure from sensory overload. Between the twinkling Christmas lights and the children playing with him, he'd been awake far longer than usual. He seemed happy with all the attention and never stopped smiling.

"I hope you enjoyed yourself, Michael. The O'Malley's can be a little overpowering."

"It was delightful. I've never had a better Christmas and your family is wonderful. They couldn't have been more welcoming. Thanks so much for insisting I come." I settled back in my seat after checking on Tyler. As I suspected he was fast asleep.

"You know you could become an O'Malley with just one simple word."

"I know, Pat, and it's tempting, but it's complicated."

"How complicated can it be? We're great together."

"All that's true, but I can't be sure what I feel for you could ever be anything more than friendship," hopping I hadn't hurt his feelings.

"I'll take my chances. I love you enough for the both of us. Just say yes, and we could be married next month. A January wedding would mean we'd be starting the New Year together."

"Pat, you must be kidding. Why so soon? Shouldn't we think about this?" I was echoing his father's advice. "Maybe we should take time to know each other better."

"The longer you have to think about it, the more reasons you'll find to wait even longer. I know everything I need to know about you. The rest we can work out over the years."

We were almost home and questions were swirling around in my head. I turned toward Pat and said, "You must know this whole conversation is ridiculous. We're talking about marriage, and we've never even held hands, let alone kissed."

"I can guarantee my parents never kissed before they married and there are still cultures where the bride and groom don't even see each other until the wedding."

Was there no end to his comebacks? "Another problem Pat, I'm not Catholic?"

"And why would that be a problem?"

"Well, aren't you Catholic?"

"No. What makes you think so?" He turned toward me a broad smile on his face.

"You're Irish. Aren't all Irish Catholic?

"Not necessarily if they come from Dublin. Trust me, Mother Molly, given enough time, will relate the whole of Irish history until you become an expert on the subject."

I was relieved when we finally stopped in front of my townhouse, and the whole marriage conversation was about to end. Pat carried the sleeping Tyler inside and gently placed him in his crib.

"I'll be by after my morning hospital rounds. I'm not going to quit until I get a yes or no answer." He reached over and kissed me gently on the cheek. "I promise we'll hold hands tomorrow," with a twinkle in his eye he said goodnight, and then he was gone. As the door closed behind him I had to laugh. His Irish charm was hard to resist.

By the end of the following day I'd given in and agreed to become Mrs. Patrick O'Malley. Pat would have made a great lawyer as he presented his opening and closing arguments all the while holding my hand as promised. This wasn't how I imagined I'd become engaged, but so far nothing in my life was how I'd imagined.

THE BUTTERFLY

Under the circumstances, with the strained relationship I had with my family, I told Pat I didn't feel comfortable with a formal church wedding. He was sure his family would be disappointed, but assured me they'd understand. Even offering to speak to the pastor of the family church about a small private wedding or forgetting the whole formal affair and having a justice of the peace marry us. The decision up to me.

Pat was bound and determined our marriage would take place in January and he wasn't going to leave until we'd settled on a plan. "I'm not letting you off the hook even if I have to camp out here." He was smiling, but I knew he was dead serious.

I fed Tyler and put him down for his afternoon nap and started to make lunch. Pat was explaining between bits of his sandwich that his bachelor digs weren't big enough for all of us, and it was a given my place wouldn't do. I had no idea what we should do trying to consider all the options when Pat excused himself, saying he had to get something from his car.

He returned and placed a large manila envelope on the table in front of me. Much to my surprise it contained a bunch of advertisements for houses for sale. Leaving the dishes we sat on the sofa looking them over together. Pat had his arm around me as I thumbed through the advertisements.

"We should put down roots. Tyler needs the security of a home and a neighborhood to grow up in, and I'm tired of rentals and of moving."

Pat really was serious about home and family, I thought, as I looked at the pages he clipped from various realtor's offerings thinking he must have been pretty sure I'd say yes. In the weeks that followed, every spare moment was spent looking at property. I began to admit the prospect of a home of my own was more than appealing. I tried to visualize myself living in each house we visited and began to think maybe I didn't need to prove I could go it alone. Maybe I was ready for the white picket fence and a man to share my life with.

After walking through dozens of properties, Pat and I agreed on a wonderful older home in a settled neighborhood. I knew the minute I opened the front door this was the one. Pat made an offer on the house and it was accepted. For better or for worse, I was about to be a married homeowner.

Chapter 23

We held hands after exchanging gold wedding bands before a justice of the peace, hardly an auspicious occasion as the justice mumbled the lines he'd memorized with as little emotion as possible. He couldn't have been more disinterested. All I remembered was, "With the power invested in me by the State of California, I now pronounce you husband and wife."

If Pat's family was concerned or upset by his choice of a wife, they hid it well. Believing family came first, they'd wished us happiness, I'm sure they were hoping for the best. I knew how disappointed Mother Molly was at our decision to forego a church wedding, but she seemed forgiving after we'd promised she could hold a reception for family and friends. I'd written to my parents without a response.

We left the courthouse following the afternoon ceremony for a long weekend in San Francisco. Tyler was staying with Pat's parents. Somehow the fact that we were married seemed unreal. Maybe it was the lack of ritual that left me with an incomplete feeling. Something was missing. I wondered if Pat felt the same way. Wondered if I'd made the right decision to forego a church wedding.

We'd driven for some time before Pat noticed I had a quizzical look on my face as I was slowly turning the gold band around my finger.

"If something seems unusual about your wedding ring, Michael, you're right the ring isn't new. I planned on explaining everything this evening at dinner.

"Explain what? What are you taking about?"

"Mother Molly gave me the ring when she heard we were to be married. She wanted you to have it. The ring was her mothers."

"This is your grandmother's wedding ring?"

"Yes. I hope you're not disappointed."

"How could I be disappointed, I'm overwhelmed. But why would Mother Molly give the ring to me instead of one of her daughters?

"You'll have to ask her. I do know she's had the ring for decades. All she said when she handed it to me was She waited for God to tell her who should have her Sainted Mother Mary's ring. You were the one she wanted to have it. I should have told you. I'll buy you a new ring if you prefer."

I was too stunned to speak. Mother Molly had given me a treasure. The gift a sign of acceptance. I told Pat I'd treasure the ring for the rest of my life and vowed to never take it off for any reason.

There was nothing more to say a myriad of thoughts were running through my head. It had all happened so fast, but for better or for worse I was on my honeymoon with a man I respected and liked, but didn't know if I loved.

"Your very quiet Mrs. O'Malley. No regrets I hope."

"No regrets just a bit nervous, I guess." I managed a smile as he reached over to hold my hand.

The weather was dank and cold as we arrived at the Fairmont Hotel. I wore a winter coat over the grey wool dress I'd chosen for the ceremony. I'd been much too concerned about money to treat myself to a new dress. I wanted to come to the marriage debt free. I looked on as Pat signed the register, Dr. and Mrs. Patrick C. O'Malley. Pat began to laugh as we started across the lobby.

"What's so funny?"

"I just realized as I signed the register, almost every Irish joke begins 'Pat and Mike walked into a bar.' That's us kiddo, Pat and Mike forever."

I wheeled my suitcase to the bank of elevators and began to feel a sense of anxiety as we walked down the long hall toward our room on the tenth floor. The unease grew more pronounced as I viewed the hotel room, decorated in black and white with touches of gold. The large windows looked out on California Street and a view of the cable cars. Everything should have been perfect, but I couldn't hide the discomfort I felt when I saw the king sized bed sitting in the middle of the room.

I started to unpack hoping my concern wasn't too obvious. Thankfully, Pat suggested we have a drink in the bar in the hotel lobby. I jumped at the idea grateful for whatever it took to change the uncomfortable feeling I had of the two of us alone in a bedroom.

The Laurel Court bar was subdued. A few people were scattered about the large sitting area, a few more seated at the bar. A pianist played a selection of classics as we took a seat on a small sofa. Pat had made a dinner reservations for seven o'clock. We had a bit of time to kill.

When the flutes of champagne Pat ordered were placed in front of us, he raised his glass and smiled at me. "Mother Molly has a saying we kids heard over and over again whenever we were concerned about something. She'd say, 'If you put your mind to it, each day will be better than the last.' A toast to you, my love. That's kinda how I see our life together.

I was surprised how well he knew me and by now how well he read my reactions.

"I know you're concerned, but I promise you won't be sorry. Each day we spend together will be better than the last."

Any girl would be happy to have a man like this, I thought as I sipped my champagne.

Dinner was excellent, as was the wine. The tensions were almost all wiped away as I laughed while Pat related story after story of the many comical mishaps of his siblings' weddings. He seemed to make every adversity a reason for hope.

Returning to the hotel, I passed on a nightcap. The day had
been busy getting myself and Tyler ready. I was tired.

Pat had turned back the spread and was already propped up in bed when I finally finished in the bathroom, having taken more time than usual, putting off as long as I could the inevitable.

Knowing my old T-shirts and sweats were hardly appropriate for our wedding night, I'd splurged and bought a short peach colored silk nightshirt. I thought I owed Pat that much. On edge, I approached the bed and slipped under the covers. Pat reached over and turned off the bedside light, then kissing me gently on the forehead he rolled over on his side with his back to me. "When you're ready, I'll know. Until then it's all up to you. Goodnight, my love. Sleep well."

That caught me completely off guard. Tired as I was, sleep wouldn't come. I could hear Pat's rhythmic breathing, feel the warmth of his body close to mine. I couldn't believe he'd put his feelings aside sensing my unease. I closed my eyes thinking I could really learn to love this man. I lay still thinking about Pat and how much he'd meant in my life since that first day in the hospital. Maybe I did love him and just hadn't realized it. What did the word love mean anyway?

I snuggled up against him, tired of going it alone, all of a sudden needing to be loved and having someone to love in return. I kissed the back of his neck. "Are you awake?" I asked.

"I am now." He rolled over on his back as I put my arms around him. I didn't have to say a word.

His kiss remained long on my lips, delivered with passion, as he whispered, "How was that? I've been taking lessons from Terrance."

I couldn't stop laughing. The nervousness was gone. Everything would be fine. I knew I wanted him.

As the rays of the morning sun streamed in through the windows I was still wrapped in Pat's arms, happy and content knowing I didn't have to face life alone. Maybe this was how love felt.

After showering together we dressed and took the cable car down California Street to Union Square and spent Saturday sightseeing and shopping. We held hands walking through Chinatown, taking in the sights and smells. Then we took a cab to Fisherman's Wharf for lunch. I felt complete, safe in Pat's company. I'd never felt this way before.

Returning to the hotel in the late afternoon, I kicked off my shoes and stretched out on the bed dead tired at the end of an enjoyable day. Pat lay down beside me. It didn't take long for him to reach over and start unbuttoning my blouse, while I wiggled out of my jeans. We couldn't shed our clothes fast enough. We couldn't keep our hands off each other. Our passions ran higher than last night. Afterwards, I rested my head on Pat's chest while he held me tight. I heard him whisper, "I love you," as I fell asleep.

By the time we awoke, the sun had long gone down. After showering and changing, Pat suggested we walk across the street to the Mark Hopkins Hotel and take the elevator to the Top of the Mark for a drink. The bar on the nineteenth floor had one of the best views in the city. We had a couple of drinks, shared food from the bar menu while looking out over San Francisco's specular skyline, complete with a fabulous view of the Bay and the Golden Gate Bridge. Anyone who saw the way we looked at each other had to know we were in love.

Morning came all too soon, and along with it came the time to return home. Our conversation on the long drive home was so different. This time it was all about our plans. The future looked so much brighter.

Chapter 24

A week later, with all the papers signed, the house had become ours. Now with keys in hand, we stood at the front door of our new home, a two-story white stucco with a red tiled roof. As the advertisement read, a Monterey Colonial style popular in the thirties. Pat opened the ornate wooden front door and picked me up his arms to carry me over the threshold, smiling as he stepped inside the home where our life together would begin.

With all the prior owner's furniture gone, the challenge was evident. Between us we had a limited amount of furniture and not nearly enough to fill all the spacious rooms. The Saltillo tile floors, the open beamed ceiling, and the large stone fireplace in the living room spoke to a more traditional style, not even close to either of our current lifestyles. I was sure the large dining room would remain empty for some time. Thankfully, the kitchen had recently been updated, a washer and dryer left behind in the adjoining laundry room. Thank God, I wouldn't be spending any more of my time at Laundromats.

All I could see, as I walked from room to room, was dollar signs. The den off the main hall was lined with empty bookshelves, the windows overlooked mature fruit trees, now leafless, but sure to be spectacular in the spring. The house was all one could ask for, but furnishing all the rooms would be expensive

I followed Pat up the stairs to the second floor with its four bedrooms. Our room was a large master bedroom. There were two bedrooms nearly the same size and one smaller room I thought would be a perfect nursery for Tyler. The two bathrooms were both a little dated.

Pat put his arm around me as I stared out at the large backyard. "What are you thinking? You look so serious."

"It all seems a little overwhelming." I rested my head on his shoulder only realizing what it would take to make this home.

"Yeah, I know, but each time I see the house I'm more and more convinced it's the perfect place for us to put down our roots. Raise our family."

"You're right of course. My life has been so topsy-turvy these last couple of years, I guess I'm just afraid I'll wake up and find this is all a dream."

We walked outside and stood on the stone patio looking at the fenced backyard with its large, well-tended lawn. "Great place for a swing set for our little tiger don't you think, Babe?" So many things were going right about our marriage calling Tyler ours had to be at the top of the list.

The next morning a U-Haul van pulled into my driveway. Today was moving day. While waiting for the closing on the house and trying to get organized for the move, Pat and I had been living separately for the longest two weeks of my life. Hearing loud talking, I opened the door to Pat and his three brothers.

"O'Malley movers at you service," they all said in unison.

"Come in. This is wonderful, I had no idea the whole family would be here."

"The clan takes family matters seriously," Pat said. "Okay, guys, where should we start?"

I couldn't believe how fast everything was piled into the van. I slipped the keys through the mail slot and said goodbye to a very trying time in my life.

As fast as the brothers were in loading, they were equally organized in unloading. They'd obviously done this before. When everything was in place, it was even more than apparent just how little furniture we owned and how a big house we'd acquired.

We ordered pizza and Pat grabbed beer for all of us. I sat on a blanket on the cold tile floor in the empty dining room surrounded by laughing, joking, O'Malley men clowning around like a bunch of kids, thinking about how lucky I was. No matter what they might think of me, everything was all about family, and now Tyler and I were family.

There were hugs and kisses and wishes for nothing but happiness in our new home as the brothers prepared to leave. Pat and I stood, arms linked, as we waved goodbye. I couldn't stop the tears running down my cheeks.

The next few weeks were hectic, as we tried to adjust to living together. We'd missed out on the getting to know you dates and long engagement. We met, became friends, and seven months later we were husband and wife. There was still at lot we needed to learn about one another.

I liked the way Pat would sleep alongside me one arm across my waist. I felt a sense of security being with him, surprised at how eagerly I awaited his return home every evening. His sense of humor made everything less stressful, though I must admit I found it hard learning to share a bathroom.

Pat was up early every morning leaving before breakfast for hospital rounds. I worked two days a week at the Alliance. By the time I paid the sitter, I wasn't making much money, but I felt an obligation to at least finish the cases I'd started. I'd rush home in time to fix dinner. Thank God, Pat wasn't a fussy eater as I was anything but a good cook. We had dinner with Tyler sitting in his new highchair. He was growing so fast.

We fell into a routine where I'd clean up in the kitchen while Pat put Tyler to bed. His attachment to Tyler was wonderful, and Tyler loved Pat's attention. The nursery was the only room in the house completely furnished. We'd even hung pictures on the walls. Now that Tyler had his own bedroom I no longer had to undress in the dark for fear of waking him or having my sleep disturbed by his every move.

One evening having finished in the kitchen earlier than usual I headed upstairs to say goodnight to Tyler. As I approached the doorway of the semi-darkened room, I spied Pat sitting in the old rocking chair I'd purchased at the thrift shop with Tyler cradled in his arms as he sang "When Irish Eyes Are Smiling." I tiptoed down the stairs, hoping he wouldn't know I'd been at the door. More tears flowed, as I realized how much I really did love Pat, though I hadn't' spoken the words out loud as yet.

Standing at the bottom of the stairs I thought how completely happy I was. I'd never felt this kind of happiness before. For the first time in my life I wasn't trying to achieve something. I wasn't trying to ace a test, or looking for happiness in excelling in everything I did. I was happy being Pat's wife and Tyler's mother. I didn't miss any part of my old life.

Chapter 25

The days became weeks, the weeks began months, and the months became years. By our second anniversary we'd managed, little by little, to furnish the house, until now it reflected the beauty of the place we called home. We'd made friends among our neighbors and the local medical professionals, but I still hadn't made peace with my parents. My mother sent cards, and called on rare occasions, but she never answered my letters. I'm sure my father pressured her to be done with me.

Tyler, who Pat more often still called Tiger, was two and we were about to announce that Pat and I were expecting a baby of our own at our next O'Malley family dinner.

Tyler was excited about going to the family dinner. Being the youngest, he was the center of attention and loved every minute of it. I was surprised when we turned off the highway at a different overpass. Pat had decided the time had come to end the nonsense where my family was concerned.

"This isn't the way to your parent's house."

"You're right. Were stopping by to see your folks first."

"Really, Pat, we can't just drop in. My father will slam the door in our faces."

"Not likely. I spoke with him a few weeks ago, and he agreed that it was time to put things to rest."

I could feel tension begin to build. "Why didn't you tell me?"

"For one thing, I didn't want you to be concerned about the meeting. Knowing you, you'd have twisted yourself into knots. Now we're here. It will work or it won't, but at the very least we have to try." Deep down I knew he was right.

I took Tyler by the hand as we walked up the brick path to the front door of my parents' house. "Tyler," I explained, "we're going to visit your grandparents. You have to be a very good boy. Then we'll go visit Mother Molly and Papa, okay?"

"No. Tyler go now." No and why were fast becoming his favorite words.

Pat took Tyler's other hand and swung him up the two steps to the front door. "Listen to your mother and be a good boy for just a little while."

My hand was shaking as I rang the bell. My mother opened the door and threw her arms around me. I saw tears in her eyes and she was barely able to say the words, "Come in."

"Mom, this is my husband, Patrick, and you've met my son Tyler."

She put out her hand to shake Pat's as he put his arms around her. "Handshakes are for strangers. Hugs are for family."

My mother beamed as I smiled at Pat. He was so good at disarming people with his genuine warmth and good nature. Every day I spent with him I knew how lucky I was.

"Let me have a look at my grandson. How old is he now?"

"Two."

"What a handsome boy." She never took her eyes off Tyler, "I'm your grandma, Tyler."

"No. Mother Molly is my Grandma."

"That's what all of us call my mother," Pat explained quickly. "He'll understand soon enough that he has two grandmothers."

I looked up and saw my father standing in the doorway.

Without so much as a second glance, Pat walked toward him and put out his hand and introduced himself. I'm Patrick O'Malley, sir, your son-in-law. Thanks for the opportunity to have this meeting."

I noticed my father eyeing Pat with his red hair and blue eyes, and then quickly glancing at Tyler. His expression was as good as a thousand words. No way was this olive skinned, dark haired, brown-eyed child Patrick's.

"Hello, Dad. How are you?"

"Fine." The chill in his voice couldn't be missed any more than his ignoring Tyler. "Well, Patrick, seeing as we've never met, tell me about yourself," Dad said as he moved toward the living room. In typical fashion, he didn't invite Pat to follow. He just expected him to.

Mother took Tyler by the hand and headed for the kitchen with the promise of a cookie. I followed, knowing Pat could hold his own with my father.

"I'm so glad Patrick called your father, Michael. I've missed seeing you. I hope you'll come often. Patrick seems like such a wonderful man."

"He is Mom. I hope we can come again. It's all up to Dad."

"You know how stubborn he can be, Michael. It may take some time, but he'll relent. He adores you in his own way."

I brushed the cookie crumbs off Tyler's shirt. "I know I disappointed him. I just hope he doesn't hold it over my head forever."

We chatted for a bit, as I got caught up on all the news of my sister and her family, until Tyler began to get antsy, having had his fill of cookies.

I walked back into the living room to find Pat and my father deep in a political discussion, father's favorite subject although it seemed more like a one sided lecture.

"I think it's time to go, Pat. Tyler is getting fussy."

"Are you going to tell your folks the good news before we leave?"

Before I could speak, my dad asked. "What good news?"

"Your daughter and I are expecting a child in about five months, a little girl. You're about to become a grandfather again."

My mother hugged me. "What delightful news. I can hardly wait."

Dad grunted and said, "Congratulations."

I couldn't wait to leave and started for the front door. Mother called out, "Come again soon, children."

My dad patted Pat on the back. "Nice to meet you, Patrick. Come again. I look forward to debating the current political situation with you."

After fastening Tyler into his car seat, we were on our way.

"God, that was painful. My dad didn't say one word to me or to Tyler."

"He'll come around. He just doesn't know how to say he's sorry. His pride keeps getting in the way." I hoped Pat was right.

My mood changed as soon as Pat parked the car. The monthly O'Malley dinner was its usual loud and joyful family gets together. Needless to say, they were overjoyed at our announcement. Mother Molly was beside herself. "So little Kathleen, our first granddaughter, is on her way. Take care of yourself, Michael. The world needs more O'Malley's."

Everyone laughed, but what I knew to be true was Mother Molly had spoken, and unless I was ready to walk through the gates of hell, our child would be named Kathleen.

Kathleen Anne O'Malley, with a cap of auburn hair and blue eyes, came into the world with her father at my side. Pat held her in his arms moments after she was born, with tears in his eyes and pronounced her the most beautiful child he'd ever seen. The look on his face told me if he had his way this wouldn't be the last O'Malley.

Pat opened the door to my hospital room several hours later carrying a large bouquet of pink roses tied together with an enormous pink bow. He reached over the side of the bed and kissed me on the forehead. "She's perfect. I checked her from head to toe. No signs of anything to worry about, and she does have a powerful set of lungs. We'll have no trouble hearing her call in the middle of the night. We can take Miss Kathleen home tomorrow morning."

Miss Kathleen took over the nursery and Tyler graduated to a bedroom of his own. Pat was more than eager to share the night feedings, and he was the one who explained the new baby to Tyler. He was the one who told him all about the do's and don'ts and his responsibility as her big brother.

Even though Kathleen was a good baby, I had my hands full, and with regret, resigned from the Alliance, but left the door open to answering any questions or giving any advice over the phone.

Everything in our life was perfect. I couldn't have asked for more. Never dreaming life could be this good. On occasion, Pat would be called to the hospital at night for either a newborn in distress or one of his regular patients needing his care. The few times when he couldn't save an infant broke his heart. He'd grieve along with the parents, wishing he could have done more

He came home very late one evening, having missed dinner, with tears in his eyes. Even though he seldom drank hard liquor he poured himself a large glass of straight scotch, and walked upstairs to check on the children asleep in their beds.

I questioned Pat when he came back downstairs and listened, as he told of the preemie he'd been looking after for days. "The baby's parents are older than most, Michael, and they've been trying for years to have a child. After several attempts at in-vitro fertilization, the woman finally conceived, but the child was born three months premature with a multitude of problems. I did everything I could, but I couldn't save her. Her little heart just gave out."

The look on Pat's face was one of despair as he drained the last of his second drink. "They wanted that baby so much and there wasn't anything I could do. Maybe I missed something. I just don't know."

"You can't blame yourself. I'm sure you did everything humanly possible."

Pat put his arms around me and I clung to him hoping to ease his pain as he whispered, "Babe, we just don't realize how lucky we are. I thank God every day for giving me you and the kids."

"Sweetheart, we're the ones who should thank God we have you."

Chapter 26

We received a call from Pat's older brother, Sean, saying Mother Molly was in the hospital and it seemed serious. He had no real news to relate only that Pat's father was awaiting the results of a battery of tests and wasn't willing to speak with anyone until he had an answer. I left the dinner dishes on the table and called the sitter, rushing to change clothes awaiting her arrival. We had little to say as we drove to Burlingame's regional hospital.

We were the last of the family to arrive. Even though it was late, we found the whole family still gathered in the waiting room on the fifth floor. I'd lost track of time, the family on edge their concerns noticeable when Pat's father finally appeared, his shoulders sagging, his face ashen. Before anyone could say a word he spoke, his voice uneven as he tried to deliver the news without breaking down.

"Children, I'm sorry to say it's serious. Your mother has advanced stage four pancreatic cancer."

No one said a word, shocked looks on their faces. "How could this happen Dad," Terrance said. "Ye gads, she's married to a doctor. Didn't you suspect something was wrong?"

"I'm sorry to say I didn't. Its onset is masked. It's a silent killer. There were no symptoms until very recently. She never complained. It wasn't until I noticed her losing weight I grew concerned. I had to drag her kicking and screaming to a doctor. You know your mother. She'd never admit she was anything but well and happy.

"What's the prognosis? What are they going to do?" We all had questions.

He sighed, almost unable to speak. In a tone just above a whisper he said, "Terminal. Unfortunately, there's nothing anyone can do at this stage except keep her comfortable. She'll be coming home in the morning. I've arranged for a full time nurse."

The silence was heartbreaking. Each seemed lost in their own thoughts reluctant to speak. Mother Molly was the glue that held the family together. I took Pat's hand, not knowing what to say.

"Can we see her now?" Emma, one of Pat's sisters asked."

"Yes, I've just come from her room. She knows, but knowing your mother, she wouldn't appreciate long faces or the shedding of tears. Hold it together while you're with her, please. I suggest just a few at a time and don't stay long. She's had a tiring day."

While the others decided who would visit Mother Molly first, Pat walked over and put his arm around his dad. "How are you doing, Dad?"

"Not well, son. She's the light of my life. I don't know how I'll make it without her. We've been together well over fifty years, never spent a night apart." He broke down and started to sob as Pat held him in his arms. My heart broke for both of them.

With the end in weeks, rather than months, the O'Malley women decided they take charge of the monthly family dinner that weekend. They declared it mandatory that everyone be there. That meant every grandchild and great grandchild.

We all pitched in, bringing prepared dishes from home as well as cooking in Mother Molly's kitchen. The tables were set and all was ready as the clan began to find their way to the dining room.

We were all seated as Pat's dad helped Mother Molly to her place at the head of the table. She looked tired -- dark circles under her eyes. She'd lost a great deal of weight and the gray hair she'd hidden for years was now visible at her temples and hairline. The smile on her face and the twinkle in her eye told us her spirit was strong.

"If you'll be kind enough to fill my glass with wine, please, Sean," she said to her eldest son seated on her left. "I'll be needen' a sip." She stood, supporting herself with one hand held firm to the arm of her chair. "Before we begin our meal, there are a few things that need be said. I want no long faces or tearful greetings. If the good Lord says it's my time, then who am I to argue?"

My admiration for this woman knew no bounds. Our relationship had been special ever since she gave me her mother's wedding ring. I loved her as if she were my own mother, and was doing all I could to hold back the tears as she continued.

THE BUTTERFLY

"I've had a good and long life. I've never missed a meal. I've never felt the cold for lack of a warm coat or a roof over my head. I've been loved by a good and wonderful man who put up with my arrogance and stubbornness, and figuratively strewed rose petals along my path every day of our life together. With his help, I've brought six O'Malley's into the world, who have made us so proud."

Her grip tightened on the arm of her chair. Her voice seemed a bit weaker as she continued.

"My sons brought wives to our table who were fair of face and good of heart. My daughters married handsome men worthy of their love. We have been blessed with sixteen grandchildren and three great grandchildren. Who could ask for anything more from life? It's all about family."

She raised her glass, her hand shaking a bit as she smiled. "God bless our family."

We all raised our glasses, repeating her words. "God Bless our family," when one of the grandchildren's voice could be heard, "And God Bless Mother Molly."

I wasn't sure the wine could get past the lump in my throat, but I was determined to hold back the tears.

We began passing platters of food around the table. I noticed Mother Molly picking at her food, barely eating a mouthful. When it seemed we'd all finished, leaving only dessert and coffee to be served, Mother Molly rose and thanked everyone for making this evening so special and nodded toward her husband. "Dear man, if you'd be so kind as to help me upstairs. I'm feeling a wee bit tired."

That was the last meal she shared with us. Within less than three weeks, she was gone. The funeral was set for Saturday afternoon at the local Presbyterian Church. The family gathered beforehand for a last goodbye before the coffin was closed. The tears in Pat's eyes broke my heart.

By the time we entered the church, every seat not reserved for family was taken and people were standing along the walls. Sean, the eldest son, and Emma the eldest daughter, gave the eulogies. Thankfully they were done with warmth and humor, Sean and Emma spoke of her Irish humor and love of Irish history, and how from a very early age, they could all sing the words to every classic Irish song from "Danny Boy" to "Sweet Molly Malone."

Sean told the story of how it came about that the family called her Mother Molly. In her Irish way, Sean related, at least once a day she would refer to her mother as my dear departed sainted mother Mary. When Terrace, was still learning to talk, he couldn't say, "My dear departed sainted mother Molly," it was far too many words. "Mother Molly" was all he could manage, and it stuck. Since that day she'd never been called anything else.

Sean ended, a catch in his throat, by saying, "She taught us the difference between right and wrong. To her, it was black or white, never any room for gray. The love she and dad had for each other was the example for us to follow in our marriages. She will be missed." I held tight to Pat's hand.

When the service ended, we followed the hearse to the cemetery for a family-only burial. Pat's father clutched a box containing soil from Mother Molly's home in Dublin, which had arrived by air express the day before. When the service was concluded, and the coffin lowered, he sprinkled the earth from her beloved Ireland over her coffin, just as she'd requested.

Pat and I lingered with the rest of the family over the plot. No one spoke. We all knew nothing would be the same now that she was gone. We weren't ready to move on, but it was time to return to the family home and greet those wishing to pay their respects.

Pat's father was having a hard time keeping it together in front of friends and family. For a strong man, this had knocked the pins out from under him. When he couldn't take any more, he grabbed a half empty bottle of whiskey off the bar and went upstairs. Sean checked on him periodically. The report was the same each time. He was sitting on the bed in the unlit bedroom still holding the unopened bottle with tears in his eyes.

Hours passed until there was no one left but family. We filled our plates with the remains of the buffet and the wine and beer flowed freely. I listened as the siblings sat around telling funny and touching stories of growing up. They spoke of tales about leprechauns and other magical creatures they believed would punish them if they did wrong. The stories of Mother Molly's views on Irish history were told and retold. They spoke of a house where joy and laughter abounded.

We stayed the night in Pat's old bedroom not ready to face the long drive home. I awakened in the middle of the night to the sound of Pat crying and pretended not to hear. I'd leave him to his grief. There was nothing I could say that would take away the loss he felt.

Chapter 27

Almost a year to the day of Mother Molly's death, our second daughter was born with a few wisps of red hair and eyes that were sure to remain blue. We named her Molly. No other name would have been appropriate.

Kathleen was now in nursery school three days a week, Tyler was turning six and attended public school, and a wonderful Hispanic women did the heavy cleaning once a week leaving me with free time. I called the Alliance volunteering to give them two days a week of legal service without pay. Of course the offer was accepted with glee.

Pat's reputation had spread over a wide area of the central valley towns and his services were in high demand, his practice growing by leaps and bounds. We managed to have Friday night dates, nothing but an emergency could stand in the way.

The O'Malley family dinners had come to an end. We held one after Mother Molly's death, but it didn't go well. The fun was gone and a touch of sadness surrounded the whole evening. We were concerned that the family's close ties would begin to fray so a pledge was made, each sibling promising the family would come together once a year for Thanksgiving. Needless to say, packing up three children for the long drive to Burlingame was a chore, but we held to our promise.

My relationship with my parents had improved. My father hadn't completely given in, but Tyler was hard to resist and Kathleen was the apple of his eye. With my sister now living on the east coast, my children were the only grandchildren they had close by. My mother couldn't do enough. She showered the children with affection and gifts.

I had a beautiful home, three wonderful children, and a husband who adored me. Life was good, and I felt so lucky. How could anything go wrong?

I was surprised to see Pat's car drive into the garage just before noon. He never came home for lunch. I watched for him as he entered through the back door, as I was busy putting Kathleen's peanut butter and jam sandwich on a plate.

"You're home early. What's up?" The look on his face told me something serious had happened.

"Sit down. You're not going to believe what just happened. Put on your lawyer hat. I need advice."

"If someone's suing you for malpractice your insurance company will provide all the legal help you need."

"It's worse than that." I'd never seen him look so worried before, the sound of disbelief in his voice. "I'm being accused of sexual misconduct."

"What? No way. That's impossible."

"That's what I thought, but the Human Resources department of the hospital sees it differently."

I sat down at the kitchen table, not believing what I had just heard. If there was anyone who was incapable of sexual misconduct, it was Pat. "Maybe you'd better start from the beginning."

He pulled up a chair and sat down beside me. "The beginning. It's complicated. It all started when the head of HR left a message for me to come to his office before I left the hospital this morning."

"Go on."

"He didn't keep me waiting. After the formalities, he asked me to have a seat and proceeded to tell me one of the nurses had filed a complaint against me."

"What was she claiming you did?" I was slipping into my lawyer mode.

"He was vague, saying he'd asked her to put her complaint in writing, which she agreed to do."

I felt relieved. "If she puts it in writing we'll have something to go on. I know you could never be guilty of such an act. Did he give you the nurse's name?"

"No. He said he'd show me the written complaint as soon he received it, but he was suggesting because of the grave nature of what she had told him, my hospital privileges would be suspended until the matter was resolved. The written complaint would be turned over to the ethics committee."

"He can't do that." Without realizing it, I'd raised my voice. The Lawyer in me had taken over. "He can't rescind your privileges."

"That's what I said. I've got four preemies in neo natal intensive care and a five year old patient who may have a brain tumor. I can't just abandon them."

"My God, this is beyond belief. I suggest we find a lawyer right now. This is way beyond what I can help you with. Besides, I'm your wife, the last thing I need to be is your lawyer."

"Jesus, Babe, I don't even know what kind of a lawyer would handle something like this."

I took a deep breath, trying to think straight. Who did we know, that we could call? Pat's older brother was an attorney, but he lived too far away. Our friend, Josh Kimball was a nice guy and I was sure a good lawyer, but he didn't seem aggressive enough.

"Wait a minute. We might know just the right guy. Remember Howard Cummings, the guy we met at the United Way Charity event last year?"

I could see Pat trying to visualize the guy. "Tall, dark, swarthy kind of guy. Yeah, I remember him. You thought he was an arrogant asshole if I remember correctly, Babe."

"That's him. Just the kind of barracuda you need at the moment. Call him now." Pat reached for his cell phone as I asked if he wanted to share a peanut and butter sandwich with his daughter?

By four that afternoon, Pat and I were seated in Howard Cummings law office. We'd exchanged pleasantries and were on a first name basis. Pat explained the circumstances of our visit.

"The complaint is ridiculous. I'm not worried. I've done nothing wrong and I'm sure you can deal with her idiotic complaint, but at the moment, it's my hospital privileges that are my prime concern. You've got to make sure they stay intact. I've patients under my care in the hospital right now, and I'm the only pediatric cardiologist on staff."

"Hold on." Cummings sounded irate. "They threated your privileges before they even had a written complaint in hand? That's bullshit. What's the name of the Human Resources dude? Let's get him on the phone right now."

I breathed a sigh of relief. Howard Cummings was just the barracuda we needed.

By the time Howard had hung up, having threatened a multi-million-dollar lawsuit, one aspect of the problem was resolved. Pat's hospital privileges were intact. Howard continued to question Pat about the so-called misconduct at length.

"Have you any idea who might be making the claim?"

Pat shook his head. "None. I've thought of nothing else since I left the hospital. I'm a friendly guy. I joke with the nurses, but never with any sexual content. That's not who I am. We've all gotten along famously the nine years I've been at the hospital."

"Sometimes friendliness can be misinterpreted. Ever lay hands on one of the nurses?" Howard didn't mince words.

"Good God, no. Never."

"Well then, I guess we'll just have to wait for the written complaint. My guess is whoever made the charge may not want to put it in writing." After a pause Howard looked up from the notes he'd written on a yellow legal pad in front of him. "Until you hear further, we'll just let it ride. Let me know if anything else transpires."

Pat promised to keep in touch. We shook hands and left. Driving home, we both felt much better.

"What do you think, Babe? Is he still an asshole?"

"Yes," I said with a smile, "but now he's our asshole."

At least two weeks passed before the written complaint was finally shared with Pat. He handed me a copy when he came home. Standing at the kitchen sink, I give it a quick read. It seemed obvious that none of this could be true, but the more I read, the harder it became to control my anger. "Do you know this woman?"

"Yes. She's a rather new addition to the unit. She's been there only a few months." He paused briefly, "She's been more or less stalking me."

"Stalking? I can't believe the nonsense she's accusing you of. Grab a beer and lets talk about this. The kids can wait a bit for dinner. Tell me about her and what you mean by stalking."

Pat followed me into the living room, beer in hand, and sat down next to me on the sofa. "I don't know what to tell you, Babe. The whole thing is a pack of lies."

"Let's start with is she pretty, young, outgoing? You know, how would you describe her."

"Actually, I never gave her much thought. Yeah, I guess you could call her attractive. She's young, a bit of a nuisance. Always following me around asking questions."

"How did you react?"

"What do you mean?" Pat took a swig of his beer, a puzzled look on his face.

"Did you answer her questions, ignore her, what was your response." I was behaving as if I was interrogating a client. I needed to change my tone this was my husband after all.

"In the beginning, I answered her questions. They seemed legitimate enough. She seemed eager to do well. This was her first job after graduating from nursing school."

"Okay. So how did she go from asking questions to stalking you?"

Pat took a long drink of beer before he spoke, seeming to weigh his words. "As I think about it now, she seemed to know my routine. She'd show up in the cafeteria every morning at about the same time I finished my rounds. Most mornings I stop by the cafeteria for a cup of coffee and a donut before I'd leave for the office. It's the same thing I've been doing for as long as I can remember. Almost as soon as I'd sit down at an empty table, she'd stop, smile, and sit next to me."

My legal instincts were in play as I tried to draw a picture in my mind of what was occurring. "Not across from you, next to you, right?"

"Yeah. At first it didn't seem strange. Sitting alone can be unpleasant for some people, and I was a familiar face. But when she began to turn up everyday, I stopped eating in the cafeteria and stopped at Starbucks instead."

"Did she make you feel uncomfortable?"

The question seemed to startle him. "Why would she make me feel uncomfortable? She was just beginning to be a real pain in the ass, intruding on the only quiet time I had for a cup of coffee and quick glance at a newspaper before I had to dash off to a waiting room full of kids." I could relate to that.

"Anything else you can think of?"

"Not really, except she did ask if I was married. You read her complaint. She's sick. None of what she claims ever happened. You have to believe me."

"Of course I believe you. I never doubted you for a minute. The whole damn thing is bizarre." I stood up, and started to walk back toward the kitchen. I still had a family to feed. "You'd better call Howard while I put dinner on the table. We'll go over her complaint again after the kids are in bed. Don't worry it will all work out."

Chapter 28

The next afternoon, I sat next to Pat in Howard's office, the complaint in front of him on his desk. The crux of the matter was she wanted fifty thousand dollars to go away. Otherwise, she'd sue the hospital claiming it was an unsafe environment in which to work, but she wasn't suing Pat for sexual harassment. To me that made no sense. What was her lawyer thinking? She should be suing Pat as well as the hospital. The complaint itself wasn't very well written, there were a few misspelled words, and it lacked punctuation. As I continued to read the complaint it was obvious no lawyer had written this.. My guess was she hadn't even consulted a lawyer.

We sat without speaking while Howard finished reading her claims. As he turned to the last page, he looked at Pat and asked if any of it is true.

"Well, it depends on how you read it. Yes, she sat next to me in the cafeteria on several occasions, but I didn't invite her to have coffee with me. She just showed up. But, good God, I never ran my hand up her leg or caressed her crotch. I never followed her around the unit. It was the other way around. I may have said something about her looking nice, but I would say something like that to all the nurses at times." Anger was beginning to replace frustration.

Howard was taking it all in, making notes on his yellow legal pad as Pat continued.

"She asked me if I was married. I never brought up the subject. There was no reason to. Did I ever tell her my wife had let herself go after our children were born? That I was no longer sexually attracted to my wife and longed for a relationship with someone as attractive as her? Christ, no."

THE BUTTERFLY

Howard folded his hands across his chest, as he looked straight at Pat. "It would seem the young lady has a vivid imagination, if what you tell me is true."

Pat looked distressed. "True? Believe me, Howard, every word I'm telling you is true. Ask anyone. Michael and I have a great relationship. I'd never do anything to hurt her. Anything as stupid as an extramarital relationship would never cross my mind. There's nothing lacking in our sex life. I love my wife."

"What about the incident in the car. What's that all about?" Howard questioned.

"Jesus, she really set me up, didn't she? To tell the truth, all I remember is coming out of the hospital late one afternoon after checking on one of my patients. The kid had a serious fall down a flight of stairs. After being admitted by emergency, I was called to take over his care as his physician. I left for home just after the change of shifts. I remember the weather was awful, pouring rain. Jenny, that's her name, was standing under the overhang in front of the building talking on her cell phone. I'd started to walk toward my car in the parking lot when she called out to me by name and asked if I could give her a lift home, saying she didn't live very far from the hospital. Her boyfriend had just called to say he couldn't pick her up." What Pat described seemed innocent enough to me.

"Okay," Howard looked straight at Pat. "So she gets in your car and what happens next?"

"Nothing. Just as she said, she lived close to the hospital. I dropped her off, she said thank you, and I drove home." His anger was returning.

"You never kissed her, grouped her breasts and tried to rape her?"

"You must be kidding. I already told you, I'm a happily married man. I adore my wife. I love my kids. But even if that wasn't the case, I'm not stupid enough to try to rape some nurse from the hospital in my car in broad daylight. You do believe me, don't you?" Pat looked directly at me.

"It's not my job to believe you, it's to defend you. We've got a she-said he-said situation here. Part of what she's says you admit is true, part you say is fiction," Howard summed up.

Pat looked ashen as he reached for my hand. "This could ruin me, Howard. Not only the money, but the loss of my reputation."

"I'm pretty sure the hospital isn't going to pay her off, Pat. Why should they? She can always sue them. You could offer her some money to try and make this go away, but there's no assurance she wouldn't keep coming back for more. If everything you say is true, Jenny may be attempting to blackmail you.

"No way. Nothing about her complaint is true. Nothing ever happened between us. She's not getting one dime in hush money from me." Pat looked at me. "You do agree don't you, Babe?"

I nodded yes.

"Well," Howard said, checking his notes. "I think the first thing we do is to have my private investigator check her out. We need to look into her past, so just sit tight until we hear from him. Go home and try not to worry. So far it seems she hasn't hired an attorney, which is a good sign."

On the drive home I asked if Pat had spoken to his partner as yet. He said he had, and Ron was behind him one hundred percent. Anyone who knew Pat knew the charges had to be false.

It was good to be home. Once we'd closed the door behind us, it felt as if nothing could touch our world. Pat paid the sitter and picked up Molly, swinging her around in circles, her red haired curls swirling around her face. He kissed her on the forehead and reached for Kathleen, kissing her as well. "Your daddy loves his girls more than anything else in the world except maybe Mommy and Tiger."

As the days dragged on, I could see the situation was taking its toll on Pat. The happy warrior was gone and a sad depressed man was taking his place. He'd never complained about our chaotic home before, but now he was short with the kids, and not sleeping well at night. Word had spread at a rapid pace. The gossip mongers were out in full force, not only on the neo natal unit, but throughout the whole hospital. Pat thought it wouldn't be long before it spread to the entire medical community.

He said the atmosphere in the unit was cool toward him. Almost toxic. The nurses tended to believe Jenny. What would she have to gain by lying? Of course no one had heard about the money she was demanding, only that she had been attacked by an important, all-powerful doctor. Howard had advised Pat not to discuss the case with anyone, so the only story people heard was Jenny's.

Days dragged on until they'd turned to weeks and still with no word from our attorney. Pat was getting nervous. His income was beginning to suffer as fewer new parents were being referred to him. What if Jenny had a clean reputation? Where would that leave him in a he-said she-said situation? Pat worried that, even if she was proven a liar, people would still believe he'd done something wrong.

THE BUTTERFLY

One evening, noticing the door to the den was closed. I knocked once and entered. Pat was sitting in his easy chair, a beer bottle in his hand, an unopened book on his lap. "It's time to go, the sitter's here already."

"Go on without me, Babe. Send Kasey home, I'll stay with the kids." I was worried. His depression had gotten to the point where I could no longer reach him.

"But Pat, Tyler has been working on this school project for weeks. He's so excited to show you what he's done. All the other parents will be there."

"He can explain it to me later."

"Pat, it's important," I tried again.

"I'm not visiting his classroom with the other parents and his teacher looking at me with suspicion."

"What are you taking about? Nobody is suspicious of you."

"God damn it, Michael. How many times do I have to tell you before you get it through your head. I'm not going. Go without me." He was actually yelling at me.

I turned and left the room, stunned. Pat had never raised his voice to me before tonight. I wiped the tears from my eyes, said goodnight to Kathleen, and handed the sitter a few dollars and told her to go home. Pat would watch the girls.

I'd tried as hard as I could to be confident and to keep Pat's spirits up. Apparently I was failing if he was refusing to go to Tyler's school. He was even beginning to dread going to the hospital.

Returning home, I sent Tyler into the house ahead of me and called Howard on my cell phone.

"Glad you called, Michael. I was about to get in touch with the both of you. My P.I. reported in yesterday. As far as he can tell, the young lady is squeaky clean. She hasn't been here long. She's a farm girl from Iowa. This is her first job. She does have a boyfriend he's looking into, but to date no reason why she would make up such a story." Howard stopped so his words could sink in.

"You're not saying you don't believe Pat, are you?"

"No. I'm just at a loss to understand what she hopes to gain without the help of a lawyer who could if nothing else, file a lawsuit in her behalf. Howard assured me he planned to talk to the hospital's legal counsel tomorrow and see what he thinks, and what he plans on doing. "So far she hasn't gone public, but the hospital has to be worried about their reputation. I'll call you both as soon as I have something tangible to report."

"Thanks, Howard. You need to understand how much this is impacting Pat and taking a toll on our marriage. I don't know how much more we can endure before there is serious damage to our relationship. The sooner it's resolved, the sooner we can get our lives back. I'll wait for your call."

I'd never taken a case to trial, but my instincts said something was missing. Jenny never reported the so-called assault to the police. That would be the first thing I would do if someone attempted to rape me. Then she asked the hospital for money when it made more sense to ask Pat. Something was off, I just knew it. But what?

I went upstairs to make sure Tyler and Kathleen were getting ready for bed. The door to the den was still closed.

I turned over as I felt Pat slip into bed hours after I'd turned off the light. I could smell the alcohol on his breath.

"Are you awake, Michael?"

I thought about pretending to be asleep, but that wouldn't be fair. "Yes," I answered.

"There's no excuse for the way I treated you this evening. I'm so sorry. Hurting you and Tyler was the last thing I wanted to do. I just don't know how to handle the situation anymore. I'm getting strange looks from the other physicians at the hospital, or maybe it's just my imagination. I've never been in a position where my morals or integrity have been questioned. The whole thing is like a dark cloud hanging over me. Coloring everything I do."

"I know you didn't mean it. I can't wait for this mess to be over. I want my happy warrior back. I turned slightly so I was nestled next to him and told Pat about my conversation with Howard and my gut instincts about the whole situation. Something just didn't add up.

"God, Babe, I feel the same way. I just don't know what we're missing."

A few minutes later, I heard his steady breathing. The exhaustion and alcohol finally taking over.

Howard called the next evening and Pat placed the call on speaker so I could hear the results of his conversation with the hospital's chief council. Howard said the young lady was still looking for a monetary settlement and was upset that the hospital was allowing an unhealthy work environment to continue. She claimed it was unfair that she was forced to work every day alongside the man who assaulted her and was threating to take her complaint to the nurses' union.

Howard finished by saying, she's talking about holding the hospital responsible for keeping a man on their staff that is a threat to women. She wants Pat removed from the hospital staff."

I could tell Pat was having a hard time holding it together, trying to keep any hint of his Irish temper in check.

"Pat, one more question," Howard said. "Have you ever had any physical contact with the nurses, any touching?"

"If you mean in a sexual way, good God no, but as I said before, and Michael knows, I'm a friendly guy. My emotions are all on the surface. I've hugged a nurse on occasion. In fact, I hugged the whole team months ago when we sent a baby home who had been with us for six months. It had been touch and go. When the day came for the infant to finally go home, there was so much joy on the unit I thanked everyone and gave them all hugs."

"Did anyone report your behavior?"

"Hell no. What are you talking about? They hugged me back. Up until now, we've all worked together as a happy team."

Pat was fuming, his face red with anger. I could tell by the sound of his voice he was losing control. The strain was taking its toll.

"This is so much crap, Howard. The woman is ruining both my career and my life, and you don't seem to be doing anything about it. Christ, I've worked hard to get where I am. Can someone just destroy everything I worked for with a pack of lies? God Damn it, Howard, what the hell are you doing to put a stop to this crap?"

Howard ignored his outburst and said, "Hold on, Pat. I know how you feel, but two things are in our favor. First, my P.I. says the boyfriend is dirty. The two of them grew up in the same town, and she moved here to be with him. He was recently dishonorably discharged from the Army and is deeply in debt. It seems he likes to gamble."

"That's interesting," I said. "Maybe he's behind the whole thing."

"My thought exactly, Michael. Second, I've arranged for a face-to-face meeting between all of us in the hospital attorney's office. She's accepted the invitation to attend the meeting and has been informed she can bring anyone she wishes, including an attorney, but she's not been advised you will be there as well."

"Does that mean we're finally getting somewhere?" The look on Pat's face as he spoke was one of relief. "When's the meeting set for?"

"Day after tomorrow at four in the afternoon. Oh yes, I want Michael to be there as well."

Chapter 29

For the first time in weeks, things were beginning to look up and at least something was happening. Pat stopped the car in front of a refurbished cottage on Munras Avenue, the law offices of the hospital's attorney. The street was full of old cottages, which had been converted into office space. We climbed the three steps to the front door, both of us hoping this would bring an end to the whole mess. Howard had requested we come a few minutes early, as he wanted me hidden from sight until he decided if he needed me or not. I had no idea what his plan was.

Howard was waiting for us in the reception area. He and Dan Cameron, the hospital's attorney, had met earlier. Howard said Cameron had not had any indication that Jenny had hired a lawyer or that she was bringing anyone with her.

Pat and Howard were ushered into Mr. Cameron's office while I waited in an adjoining room, the door slightly ajar so I could hear everything that went on. The meeting couldn't start soon enough for me. The anticipation was killing me.

A few minutes after four, the receptionist announced Miss Wallach's arrival. I wished I could see what she looked like, wanting more than anything to observe her demeanor. I'd been taught you could tell a lot by watching how people react. I expected her to be nervous, but law school taught me to watch for other signs, they could be a giveaway to how honest the person was being. Why was I worried? Howard and Mr. Cameron had far more experience than I'd ever had.

I heard Dan Cameron introduce himself as Jenny was escorted into his office, introducing Pat's attorney as well. He pointed to Pat who was sitting in a chair on the far side of the room, "You know Dr. O'Malley, of course."

Dan offered her a seat and asked if she'd like coffee or water.

"No, I'm fine," her voice a little shaky.

Then, with the same nonchalance, the same tone of voice, Dan asked if she had any objections to recording the proceeding. Before she could reply, he explained, "That way you will have a record of what was said." he made it sound as if it was no big deal and really for her benefit.

I kept my fingers crossed. California law requires both parties to approve recording their conversations before the recording could be used as evidence.

Jenny agreed easily enough.

Dan clicked on the recording device and began the conversation.

"Thank you for coming, Miss Wallach. Would you please state your full name?"

There seemed to be a pause before she answered. "Jennifer Ann Wallach, but everyone calls me Jenny."

Dan continued, "Thank you. We hope to resolve your complaint today, Jenny. It's dragged on far to long. I'm sure you will agree. So lets begin."

He paused again, before speaking. "So, Miss Wallach, when and where did you first come into contact with Dr. O'Malley?"

Through the long back and forth, questions and answers about their frequent interactions on the unit, Jenny could not relate any specific instance where Pat's actions were improper, just that they were. She agreed with Dan's assertion that Pat was friendly and went out of his way to answer her questions. Then Howard asked an extensive list of questions about Pat's interactions with the other nurses. Had she witnessed anything that seemed improper?

Dan Cameron took over the questioning and began to ask about the events that took place in the cafeteria. Jenny admitted that Dr. O'Malley hadn't exactly invited her to join him. She was vague about their conversations, saying she couldn't remember word for word what they talked about, but it didn't have anything to do with his patients. That was followed by several questions about Pat's behavior. Had he held her hand? Had he put his arm around her? She was asked about her assertion that Pat had run his hand up her leg to her crotch and touched her. She was vague, again, about anything precipitating what she claimed, but still she accused Pat of touching her and acting in an inappropriate manner. I was beginning to get angrier by the minute. She was lying, accusing Pat of something he would never do.

Dan asked Howard if he had any questions. Howard turned toward Jenny and began to ask about the uniform she wore. What color was it? Did she wear the same type garment every day? He got her to admit that, as part of her regular attire, she wore slim fitting long pants, a matching short sleeved blouse, and comfortable shoes. Saying the uniform was a type approved by the hospital

"Tell me, Miss Wallach," Howard spoke in a quizzical manner, much the same as you would use to confront a child you knew was lying, "how was it possible for Dr. O'Malley to run his hand under your long slim fitting pants while sitting at a table in a crowded cafeteria without anyone noticing? It sounds like a gymnastic feat at best."

All she would say was, "It happened."

He went on to ask who left the table first. She admitted it was always Pat.

"So he runs his hand up your pant leg to your crotch and then just gets up and leaves the table. Is that what you're saying?" Howard's tone spoke volumes.

I could hear her answers becoming more disconnected and a more nervous tone to her voice than before. Either she hadn't done a very good job of preparing for the meeting, or she didn't think she'd be questioned like this.

Under Howard's further questioning, she admitted Pat stopped going to the cafeteria after a while, that he hadn't invited her to meet him in the cafeteria, nor had he ever invited her to meet him anywhere else.

The questions were then directed toward their conversations. Miss Wallach recited a story about Pat telling her he no longer had any sexual interest in his wife. She said he'd told her his wife had let herself go after the birth of their last child gaining so much weight he found her unattractive. He told her he was lonesome, found her very attractive, and was interested in a romantic affair.

"When did he tell you this story, Miss Wallach?" Howard stared at her in a dismissive manner.

Jenny hesitated, her answer rambling. "I think the second time we had breakfast together in the cafeteria. No, maybe it was some time later. I don't remember. I just know what he said."

Howard had her in his sights. "And yet you kept coming back even though he professed to being interested in an affair. You never said it was inappropriate or you weren't interested. Oh, and by the way, did he pay for your breakfast?"

When she said no, Howard continued. "Didn't it seem strange to you that the guy who was asking to take you to bed wouldn't even pop for a cup of coffee?"

In a way, I almost felt sorry for Jenny. Those two seasoned attorneys were setting her up and tearing her apart.

The questions then turned to the supposed assault. She had no explanation as to why she hadn't gone to the police. Howard started to ask a few questions about her boyfriend, but she refused to answer, saying he had nothing to do with the situation.

THE BUTTERFLY

Dan Cameron took over and ended his remarks by asking if Jenny knew how many years Dr. O'Malley had been part of the hospital's staff? When she answered no, he explained that it was going on ten years. How could she explain that in all those years there had never been one complaint or even one suggestion of inappropriate interaction with any of the female staff?

A minute or two went by before Jenny answered, "Maybe it's because he finds me more attractive than the other nurses. They're much older than me, or maybe because he finds me much more attractive than his wife."

That was the cue Howard was waiting for and he went in for the kill. He called for me to come into the room. I opened the door and walked in taking a long look at Jenny Wallach. I saw a look of concern, as if she knew she was in trouble. I suspect she knew she should have been better prepared for today. Her expression, the way she kept wrapping and unwrapping a lock of her hair around her finger, told me the meeting was taking its toll.

"Michael," Howard said, "is also an attorney. She may have a few questions. Michael, may I introduce Jenny Wallach."

"How do you do, Jenny, I've heard a lot about you." I tried to sound as pleasant as possible as I looked at the woman whose lies were tearing my family apart. Howard interrupted me before I could ask her anything.

"Jenny, just for the record, take a good look and tell me how you would describe Michael."

Jenny seemed confused by the question. I continued standing while she looked me up and down.

"Well, Jenny what do you say?" Howard pressed.

"She's very pretty, nice clothes. She must be smart if she's a lawyer." Jenny clearly puzzled by the question.

"Would you say she's damned attractive by any man's standards?"

Jenny hesitated. The questions she was being asked seemed to be causing her great alarm. Her tone was hushed. She seemed exhausted. "Yes," Jenny replied. "She's very attractive."

"For your information, Jenny, Michael is Dr. O'Malley's wife." With that Howard leaned back in his chair. He'd won.

Jenny's response was visible. She seemed deflated, looking like a balloon that was suffering a sudden almost fatal, loss of air. I almost felt sorry for her.

With their backs turned away from Jenny, the two lawyers had a short exchange of words. Howard said he had no more questions and Dan Cameron indicated the same. The girl looked exhausted. She was asked to step outside for a few moments while the lawyers held a short meeting to discuss the details of her request.

After Jenny left the room, Howard spoke first. "What do you think, Dan? How should we handle this?"

"Well, looking at the inept way she's handled this, plus the way she responded to easy questions, I'm sure she'd wilt if questioned by the District Attorney."

"Especially if we bring the boyfriend into the picture," Howard said.

Dan nodded in agreement. "I suggest we tell her we're joining hands and contacting the District Attorney asking that he charge her and her boyfriend with extortion.

Dan looked at us. "Are we all in agreement? Pat, what do you think?"

"I say go for it." The relief on his face was obvious

"What about you, Michael," Howard asked.

"I say go for it as well."

"Okay. Then we're all in agreement." Dan said. "As the hospital is the one she hit up for money, let me speak first, then you can speak for Dr. O'Malley, Howard."

Howard stepped outside and asked Jenny to return.

Dan went over, with great care, the charges he would expect the District Attorney to bring against her and then he laid out the proposition he and Howard had agreed upon.

"Jenny, you have a choice to make. You can drop the charges, write a letter of apology, and leave the hospital's employment at once, or we will contact the District Attorney's office asking them to charge you with extortion, a form of blackmail, which is a felony. Dr. O'Malley will be filing charges against you and your boyfriend for defamation of character and monetary damages. He paused for effect, then reminded her, "Don't forget, Miss Wallach, we have recorded all your answers."

I knew that was meant to scare her.

"The offer to let you off the hook is good for the next five minutes," Howard added. "You leave the room without agreeing to the terms and the offer's rescinded."

Jenny looked shell-shocked. I'm sure she arrived at the meeting expecting to walk away with a sizeable amount of money. Maybe not the fifty thousand she'd asked for, but a large amount, and here she was facing the possibility of being charged with a felony as well as a lawsuit.

I could only imagine what was going on in her head. I was positive it was her boyfriend that convinced her the complaint was a slam-dunk, and she was naïve enough to believe him. She wasn't conniving enough to have come up with the idea on her own. She didn't make a lot of money, and her boyfriend was broke, where would they get the funds to even hire a lawyer?

Tears ran down her cheeks as she said she'd write whatever we wanted if we'd just let her go home, admitting this was all her boyfriend's idea.

Wiping away her tears, Jenny couldn't look at Pat. "I'm sorry, Doctor O'Malley. I didn't mean to hurt anybody. We just needed the money so we could get married. My boyfriend told me the hospital had insurance so nobody but the insurance company would be out the cash."

Dan called for his secretary and dictated a letter, the terms of which we'd all agreed to. We waited until Jenny's recanting of her accusations was signed before we left. Thank God, the whole nasty ordeal was over.

Chapter 30

Neither of us was ready to go home and face dealing with our three young children. Instead, I called the sitter, and said we'd be home later than we planned. She was happy to feed the kids and put them down for the night if we weren't back by their bedtime.

Needing time to let what just happened sink in and to celebrate the lifting of the dark cloud that had engulfed us we decided to drive to Rocky Point, a restaurant we used to favor. Because it was some distance from town, it had been years since we'd been there. As the name implied, the restaurant was located where the land ended at a rocky point, a sheer drop to the Pacific Ocean below, making the view from the bar and dining room spectacular. At night, the lighting was such that we could see the waves crashing against the rocks. Rocky Point was not a place you brought children. We were sure it would be just the sort of idyllic setting we needed to let all that happened wash over us like the waves below.

The stress we'd been through had taken its toll on both of us and would take time to overcome. We'd been like a sailing ship falling deep into the troughs of one wave only to be thrust onto the crest of the next. The lows had been painful.

After deciding to wait at the bar for a table with a view, Pat ordered scotch on the rocks as I hesitated, wondering what to order. The bartender, a pleasant enough man in his fifties, suggested a Paloma. "It's new. It's a very popular cocktail with the ladies."

I was taken aback. It was almost as if I could hear Berto's voice suggesting a Paloma as the perfect ladies drink that first night we had dinner together. It had been years since I'd thought of either Mexico or Berto. A cold chill ran down my spine as if fate had a surprise in store for me. I dismissed it as nonsense and ordered a Martini instead.

The evening was just what we needed. The food was incidental. We shared wine and enjoyed being together without a sense of despair hanging over us, something we hadn't experienced ever since Jenny appeared on the radar.

Lingering over our coffee, Pat was staring at me as if he had a question he was hesitant to ask.

"Something bothering you, Pat."

"In a way, yes," he admitted.

"Well, out with it. How many times have you reminded me we don't keep secrets from each other?"

"It's just that I saw how talented you were as I watched you engage with the attorneys, and I couldn't help but wonder if you were satisfied being home with the kids? If maybe you feel all the years and hard work it took to earn your degree are being wasted? I don't know, is being home with the kids really enough for you?"

"You're serious?" I had to laugh.

"Yeah, Babe, I am. Because if you'd like to go back to practicing law it's fine by me. All I want out of life is for you to be happy."

"But Pat, I am happy. I've never been happier in my whole life, and raising our kids is the best job I could ever hope to have. Maybe when they're all off to school full time I might be tempted. But for now, I wouldn't give up being a full time Mom for anything."

"You're sure?" He didn't seem convinced.

"Positive. I'm glad it's my choice. So many women don't have that luxury. Remember, I was a working mom for a short time, and it was rough. Besides, I think my dad was more interested in my becoming a lawyer than I ever was."

We drove home relieved that our life would go back to normal now. What more could possibly happen?

The next evening Pat came home happier than I'd seen him in weeks. The hospital was abuzz with the news of Jenny's absolving him of any wrong doing and asking for forgiveness for making false charges. As the reason for Jenny's departure was made known, Pat said the rest of the nurses went out of their way to be pleasant and engage him in conversation. The animosity they'd displayed earlier was gone.

Dinners with the kids were fun again because their dad was in his usual jovial mood. Laughter was once again part of every meal. Pat represented fun and games, whereas I was the schedule keeper, and the disciplinarian.

With March fast approaching, Pat proclaimed with a flourish one night at the dinner table that the time had come to learn "The Wearing of the Green." When he was growing up, he said, Mother Molly required everyone to sing the song to celebrate Saint Patrick's Day, which he informed the kids, would be celebrated in a few weeks.

"Wow," Tyler asked, "you have a day named after you, Dad? That's really cool."

Pat winked at me with a broad smile on his face, as he explained Saint Patrick's Day was named after a different Saint Patrick.

"Good work kids." Pat gave a round of applause after even Molly learned to sing the first chorus. "We O'Malley's have to remember our Irish roots or my dear sainted mother in heaven will send the leprechauns."

I watched with delight as Pat in his best Irish brogue had the children spellbound at his description of the Leprechauns, dressed in their little green suits, who were capable of all sorts of evil tricks when they came after you.

"What about me, Dad?" Tyler asked. "I'm not an O'Malley. Will the leprechauns come after me, too?" Tyler seemed dead serious.

I could see by the look on Pat's face, he was upset. He hadn't meant to exclude Tyler. He considered him every bit his child as he did the other two.

"You're safe, Tiger. You are officially a honorary O'Malley and don't you ever forget it." I was certain I was the only one who heard the sadness in Pat's voice.

Tyler seemed satisfied. I learned long ago kids don't stay focused on any one thing for very long, but could tell Pat was still upset by his faux pas.

As dinner ended and the kids were about to scamper off, I looked at my family, a happy lot. They always found delight in the wild tales Pat recited in his own inimitable way. This was a moment to cherish, one to hold precious and recall as the years went by to remind myself of how lucky I was that Pat came into my life.

I did the dishes while Pat got the kids ready for bed. After they were all tucked in for the night, we settled down for some quiet time together.

Pat turned on the evening news as I stretched out on the sofa. "I'm sorry, Michael. I didn't mean to upset Tiger."

"Nothing to be sorry about. I don't think he's upset, and I know it wasn't something you meant to do."

"You know, I'd adopt him in a minute, if I could."

"I know. It's unfortunate it can never happen. But he'll understand when he's old enough to be told the whole story." At least that's what I told myself.

Chapter 31

There was nothing unusual about the morning. Pat left at his regular time. I got Tyler ready for school, and Kathleen ready for nursery school. I planned on taking Molly with me to shop for groceries as soon as the beds were made and the kitchen cleaned. I found it easier looking after one child in the supermarket rather than three.

I heard the phone ring, wondering who would be calling at this time of the morning. Picking up the receiver, I noticed it was an international call. The voice on the other end, with a strong Hispanic accent, asked to speak to Michael Madison. "That's my maiden name. Who am I speaking with?" I answered with a sense of suspicion.

"Hola, Senorita Madison. This is Anna, you remember, the secretary to Senor Ortega?"

I felt a sense of unease as I answered. "Yes, of course, Anna. I remember you very well, but why are you calling? And how in the world did you get my telephone number? I'm married and my names not Madison any longer."

"I was desperate. I hired a private investigator in the United States. He traced you from your old company to your parents, and your mother gave him your telephone number. Senor Ortega is very ill."

"I'm so sorry to hear that, Anna, but you still haven't told me why you're calling."

"Senora Michael, Senor Ortega speaks of you so often it breaks my heart. A few weeks ago he told me if he could have one wish before he died, it would be to see you once again."

I didn't know what to say. The same eerie feeling I had the other night when the bartender offered a Paloma had returned.

"Are you telling me he's dying? Anna, that can't be. He's still a reasonably young man." The whole phone call felt uncomfortable. The last thing I wanted was a conversation with Anna about Berto.

"He has cancer and there are no more treatments. His doctors have done everything they could, even a bone marrow transplant with no success."

"I'm so sorry." I was at a loss for words. I'd pushed all thoughts of Berto out of my mind years ago.

"I can tell you, Senora Michael, he has never been the same since you left. He hoped that after he wrote of his wife's death you would come back. I know how many letters he sent to you because I mailed each one myself." I couldn't tell Anna I tossed them all away unopened.

"Well, I understand you've gone to a great deal of trouble to let me know he's ill. I'm truly sorry at the news, but what can I do?" I was confused. What could Anna possible want from me?

"You can come back to Mexico. Spend a few days visiting with him. Give him his dying wish. I would do anything for him, Senora Michael, but it isn't me he wants, it's you. If it means shaming you into coming to see him I will do that as well." Then she did just that. "He's all alone."

All sorts of things were running through my mind. Berto had meant so much to me once, but that was years ago. My life had changed since then. I couldn't think straight. His dying wish to see me would have to go unanswered.

"Anna, this is too much for me to deal with at the moment. Give me your telephone number, and I promise to call you back later. I need time to think about what you're asking of me."

"I understand. I'm sure my call comes as a shock, but if I don't hear from you I will call until you give me an answer. I owe him that."

"I understand how you feel, Anna, but this has taken me by surprise. I promise to call tomorrow."

I stood with the receiver still in my hand, bewildered by my emotions. I felt a sense of doom rather than sorrow. Fate was bringing back everything I wanted to forget.

I hung up the phone in an utter state of confusion. I'm a happily married woman with a family. Mexico was another time, another world, another me. I didn't owe Berto anything. Or did I?

My leaving without a word of goodbye might have been the coward's way out, but it happened out of desperation. If I'd gotten over him, I was sure he had gotten over me. I'd never opened any of his letters, never answered one of his

THE BUTTERFLY

calls, knowing I had to move on. He has a family and many friends. Anna had to be exaggerating. How could he possibly be alone?

I sat down at the kitchen table, not knowing where to turn. Why was all this coming back to haunt me now, after all this time? I'd never told Berto about his son. Maybe that was wrong, but I made my choice and it's too late now to change anything.

As I finally pushed back my chair, I glanced at the kitchen clock. I still had shopping to do, and Kathleen would be home from nursery school in a couple of hours. I had to pick up Tyler after school -- my afternoon to carpool. I had to pull myself together. I'll think about Berto tomorrow. My family had to come first.

Somehow I made it through dinner, and between us the kids were bathed and put to bed. I started to walk down the hall after closing the door to Kathleen's room when Pat came up behind me pulling me close. With his arms wrapped around me he said, "What's bothering you, Babe. You're not yourself tonight."

"Just a bit of troubling news. I'm really tired. What say we talk about it tomorrow?" I wasn't ready to have this conversation.

"If you say so, but you know we don't keep things from each other." He kissed my cheek and hugged me tight. "If there's a problem, I'm here to help."

"Tomorrow, I promise. You have my word. I would never keep anything from you."

"Fine, it can wait until tomorrow. Run along to bed. I have a journal article I haven't finished reading. I'll be upstairs in a little while."

I got ready for bed and slipped beneath the covers turning off the light, hoping I could wrap my head around the situation better in the dark. The more I thought about Anna's comments, the more confused I became. Visions began to race across my mind like a river in a storm, overflowing its banks and drowning everything else in its path.

Would I even have the courage to follow through if I thought going to Mexico was the right thing to do? It would mean opening up events and feelings I'd put aside long ago. Traveling to Mexico alone would be asking Pat for a leap of faith. How would he react to my rushing off to spend time with my former lover, Tyler's father? I rolled over on my side willing sleep to come. I'd sort it all out tomorrow.

I didn't sleep well. I dreamt of running barefoot through the sand at the beach house. The dream was so real I could feel the warmth of the sand between my toes. So many visions played out in slow motion like an old movie -- the good times I spent with Berto, as well as the loss of self-respect I felt at the time. The movie kept running over and over again like an endless reel.

I fed the kids. Molly was still in her pj's when I sent Tyler off to school. Kathleen was watching Sesame Street on TV. I'd wait for a quiet time to call Anna.

As usual, Pat had left early for his hospital rounds so the result of my telephone call and any decision would have to wait until tonight.

By early afternoon, Molly was down for her nap, and Kathleen was playing with a friend next door. I hesitated about calling Anna, but I'd promised. I doubted anything she could add would change my mind. By the time I awoke this morning, I knew what I had to do. Deciding to see Berto again was not an easy decision. There were so many unknowns. Foremost was the nagging concern that if I went to Mexico would I be hurting the ones I loved the most? Maybe this was my punishment for causing my family such pain and for causing pain and embarrassment to Berto's family as well. I knew my going would hurt Pat. But how could I avoid going? When all was said and done, didn't Berto have right to know he had another son?

I picked up the phone, held my breath, and dialed Anna's number. She answered the phone on the first ring.

"Anna, it's Michael. I've decided to come to Mexico. I'll call you as soon as I've made plane reservations for Guadalajara." I must have taken her by surprise because it took a moment before she to spoke.

"I'm so glad you're coming. I'm relieved to tell you the truth, but Senor Ortega isn't at his house in Guadalajara. He is staying at the beach house."

That threw me for a loop. The last place I wanted to visit was the beach house. I didn't want to relive any of those moments. I could have handled Guadalajara, but I wasn't sure about the beach house.

"Fine, I'll let you know when to expect me. One more thing. I need a favor. If I bring my son with me, Anna, is there someone who could watch him while I visit with Senor Ortega?"

"Si. I will be happy to look after him myself." There was another long pause before Anna spoke. "Thank you for coming. It will mean so much to him, but I won't say a word until you're here, in case you change your mind. He couldn't stand the disappointment. I'll arrange for the houseman to pick you up at the airport. Come soon. There isn't a lot of time left."

"As soon as I can make reservations."

I fed the kids early and had them bathed and in their pajamas by the time Pat came home. I put Molly to bed before we had dinner and told the other two they could watch a movie. I made it clear we were not to be disturbed.

THE BUTTERFLY

I'd set the table with our best dishes, lit candles and poured the wine I'd opened earlier. As Pat sat down he had a look of surprise on his face.

"Well, this is special, dinner for just the two of us. What's the occasion?"

"It's not a celebration, just a small gesture to let you know how much I love you."

"Is this about whatever was bothering you yesterday?"

"In a way. Let's enjoy dinner together, and we'll talk about the rest after the kids are in bed."

The whole meal seemed to be an exercise in procrastination, with me stalling for time before facing Pat with my decision. He seemed to know whatever was coming was serious, but put off asking any questions. Pat knew me better than anyone and he knew not to push me before I was ready to talk.

We put the kids to bed and returned to the living room. The one room in the house was off limits to the kids. I poured the last of the wine and handed Pat a glass as he settled into his easy chair while I sat across from him on the sofa, placing my wine glass on the coffee table. I hoped and prayed one last time that he'd understand. The last thing I wanted to do was hurt Pat.

"Okay, let's get this over with. I can't stand the suspense. Have you robbed a bank or something, Babe?"

I took a deep breath and started to speak hoping for the best. "I received a telephone call yesterday from Mexico. Tyler's father is dying, and he wants to see me."

There was a long pause, a look of concern on Pat's face as he said, "And?"

"And I have to go. I know you've never asked about Tyler's father or anything about what happened between the two of us. I never thought speaking of our relationship was important, especially because you never seemed interested, but now I think it's time you know the whole story." I spoke quietly my nerves on fire. Pat didn't move or make a sound. For once, I couldn't read his body language.

I downed half a glass of wine before I had the courage to go on, embarrassed by what I had to reveal and scared of Pat's reaction.

"I was sent to Mexico by my law firm to oversee the final details of a merger between the American company we represented and a Mexican company called Grupo Ortega. Berto was the president of the Mexican company."

"Berto?"

"Yes, that's his name, Umberto Carlos Luis Ortega, Tyler's father."

Pat looked uncomfortable. He crossed his arms across his chest as I continued, but didn't speak.

"He was lonesome, and I was vulnerable, and oh so naïve. It started off innocently enough. We'd go out to dinner after work once or twice a week. He took me sightseeing. It was nothing more than co-workers spending time together in the beginning. Berto was a very wealthy, attractive man some twenty years older and unlike anyone I'd ever met before. He was charming, worldly, urbane. It seemed innocent enough. We'd never so much as held hands in all the time we'd spent together, though I must admit I found him attractive.

"He invited me to spend the Independence holiday at the family's beach house. I was led to believe his wife and children would be there. Of course there was no one there but the two of us. That's when the affair began."

Pat never took his eyes off of me. I couldn't read his mind, but as I'd expected he didn't look happy.

"Are you sure you want me to hear the rest, Michael?"

"Yes, I'm sure. It's important you know the whole story." I swallowed and began again, as I tried once more to gauge Pat's reaction.

"Our being together became more difficult after the week at the beach. Dinners weren't enough any longer. I went with him on a business trip to Italy before it became evident that his family knew about me. That's when I realized it had to end. The whole situation was making me feel uncomfortable, even cheap. He was Catholic and divorce was impossible."

I went on to tell Pat that no matter what Berto promised or what the norms were in Mexico among his social set, I couldn't see myself as someone's mistress. Though it was difficult at the time, I told Berto it was over between us and how he insisted he'd find a way for us to be together.

"When I heard his wife had fallen down a flight of stairs in their home and might not recover, I became desperate. I wondered if it was possible he could have been responsible."

Picking up my wine glass I drained every last drop, trying to guess what Pat was thinking, but his expression still hadn't changed.

"I called my law firm to tell them my work was finished and I would be returning to the States. I'd completed the project weeks before, even though Berto had convinced my firm that I needed to remain longer. Anyway, I came home without giving him so much as a goodbye. I didn't know I was pregnant until I'd returned. I never told him, never opened the letters he sent, and made up my mind to close the door on the affair. I haven't thought of him in years." I realized I was shaking.

"So what you're telling me is you're planning on going to Mexico to spend time with him." Pat seemed shocked.

THE BUTTERFLY

"Don't you see, I have to go and I'm taking Tyler with me. I owe him that." Somehow my words rang hollow.

Pat uncrossed his arms, got up from his chair and walked toward the fireplace. With his hand resting on the mantel he stared at me. As I fully expected, he disagreed with my decision. "I don't think you should go, Babe. You said yourself you haven't thought about him in years. You were very young and as you said, naïve. I really think he took advantage of you. But what worries me most is you don't see how this could drive a wedge between us. What if you going, changes the feelings you and I have for each other? Why take the chance. Stay. Better to let the past be the past."

Pat who was always so low keyed seemed taken aback, deadly serious. "You're married, you have a family. You can't just run off and visit your ex-lover."

That hurt. While I'd held out hope, was I asking too much of him?

I pleaded with him to understand. "Pat, don't you get it? His secretary say's all he does is speak of me. His dying wish is to see me. I bore the son he doesn't even know exists. I owe him this."

"I don't give a shit about his dying wish. I care about you and me and our family. Obviously, I can't stop you, but I beg you, please, Babe, don't do this. Don't go. There's too much at stake."

Pat grabbed a jacket from the hall closet saying he was going for a drive and slammed the front door behind him. Storming out like that was so unlike him. I knew he was hurt. Was I putting all I held dear in jeopardy?

While I should have expected this kind of a reaction, Pat had always been so easy going, so willing to let me do whatever I wanted, always so understanding. Deep down, I knew you couldn't trample on someone's feelings and expect everything to be okay. There was a limit, and I'd exceeded it.

Chapter 32

Our goodbye in the morning was anything but pleasant. Pat was not only disappointed, he was furious. He'd begged me not to go, and I was ignoring his plea. Without his usual hug and kiss, Pat let us leave without a word. He didn't offer to drive Tyler and me to the airport. Instead, he left me to handle the bags and Tyler by myself.

We arrived at the airport in good time. I parked in long-term parking, and Tyler and I wheeled our cases to the airport check-in. Tyler was one excited little boy, he'd never flown before. Although he was having a hard time understanding why we were on our way to the beach to what he considered a vacation in Mexico without his dad and his sisters. When I gave him some nonsensical answer saying it was complicated, he stopped asking questions.

It took six hours before we landed in Puerto Vallarta. The familiar airport and the sounds of Spanish spoken by everyone around me only added to my apprehension. Part of me was saying get on the next flight headed back to the States. Go home to your family.

I had reservations at the Sheraton in town on our first night. Berto's houseman would pick us up early in the morning. Tyler was taking it all in chattering away like a magpie. He asked a million questions faster than I could answer.

We had an early dinner at the hotel's beachfront cafe and went for a walk afterwards. Every other word from Tyler was wow or cool as he watched the street entertainers and the strolling musicians. He seemed surprised that I could speak the language. We'd gone quite a distance when Tyler begged me to let him walk on the beach. We took off our shoes and walked back to our hotel along the water's edge while I tried to explain what would happen tomorrow.

It was hard pulling him away from all the sights, but I knew he was tired, and so was I. He fell asleep the minute his head hit the pillow. I'd sent a text to Pat earlier to say we'd arrived safely. When I hadn't received an answer, I dialed the home phone, but the call went directly to the answering machine. This wasn't at all like Pat.

I'd organized everything, hoping to make Pat's job easier, and had the sitter on standby in case he had an emergency. I only expected to be gone over the weekend, planning on being home by Monday at the latest.

After a fitful night, I awoke early dreading the events to come. Tyler and I grabbed a quick breakfast, and we were ready and waiting in the lobby by eight for our drive to the beach house. The houseman looked familiar. I was sure he was the same man who worked for Berto when I was there.

Tyler was all eyes as he stared out the window at the sights. I stared along with him. Everything was all too familiar. I remembered the drive from Guadalajara with the top down, the warm sun shining on my face, the slight breeze blowing through my hair. As we got closer, I could feel my heart pounding, a knot in my stomach, my nerves on edge. This was crazy. What was I doing here? Had I made a huge mistake ignoring Pat's pleas? But it was to late to turn back now.

The houseman honked the horn as the car stopped in the driveway. Anna came rushing out to greet us. She threw her arms around me. And I found myself hugging her back. She had tears in her eyes. "Thank you for coming. Senor Ortega is waiting for you. I haven't seen him this happy in months. You have lifted his spirits. Come, I'll take you to him."

"Anna, this is Tyler. Can you watch him while I visit? He brought his swim trunks, and I'm sure he'd enjoy a walk on the beach."

"Of course." The surprised look on her face as she greeted Tyler said it all. One glance was all it took for Anna to know this was Berto's son.

"He's such a handsome boy, Senora Michael. Don't worry, I will guard him with my life. We'll have a good time together on the beach."

I followed Anna down the hall as she led the way, stopping at the door to the master bedroom. I spoke to Tyler. "Please go with the Anna and promise you'll be a good boy and listen to her. I'll only be a little while. Okay?" The earlier conversation about of the beach had won him over as he took Anna's out stretched hand.

I'd explained once again, as we were driving toward the beach house that I was going to be visiting an old friend who was very ill, maybe too ill to spend time with a little boy. I bent down and gave Tyler a hug as Anna led him away promising a walk on the beach.

I stood for a long time outside the bedroom door trying to get my emotions under control. Memories began creeping back, reminding me of what had taken place in that room. I tapped on the door. Was I about to open Pandora's box?

My heart skipped a beat at the sound of the familiar, mellow baritone voice, saying, "Entrada." After all these years the sound of his voice still sent a chill down my spine. I opened the door to find a darkened room, the drapes drawn across the glass doors blotting out the sunshine.

"My little butterfly. How wonderful to see you. Please forgive me if I don't get up. I'm not too steady on my feet these days."

"I'm glad to see you as well, though I'd prefer it be under different circumstances. Why is the room so dark, Berto, and why are the doors closed to the outside on such a beautiful day?"

I tried to get my nerves under control as I walked to the wall of glass doors and pulled back the drapes. "I know how much you love the sound and smells of the bay."

I opened the doors pushing them back like the folds of an accordion and stacked them against the side walls, letting the sunshine brighten the atmosphere. "There that's better." As I turned to face Berto, I realized why the room was dark. He didn't want me to see him in the full light of the day.

What I saw broke my heart. I hardly recognized the figure sitting in the chair beside the bed. Dressed in a maroon silk robe that appeared miles too big for his frame, his body now a mere shadow of his former self, the huge loss of weight was evident. His black hair had turned silver gray, and there were dark circles under his eyes. The Adonis I once knew looked pale and drawn, like a dying man.

Though I tried to hide it, he could see the shock on my face.

"One can't control fate, my dear, but let me look at you." He smiled at me as his eyes took in my being. He seemed pleased by what he saw. "The young girl has grown into a far more beautiful woman. Come let me give you a kiss."

I walked to his chair as he took my hand pulling me close to him as he touched his lips to my cheek. It was a tender kiss that nearly broke my heart. I bit my lip trying not to cry.

"Just to have you close to me is something I've dreamed about for years. Come sit beside me and tell me all about yourself. I want to hear everything there is to tell about what your life since you left."

I had no idea how I would feel when I saw him, but at the moment I felt only sorrow. I walked to the other side of the room, walking past the bed I'd shared with him, and picked up a small upholstered chair, placing it alongside him. Reaching out, he put his hand on top of mine. I felt a rush of emotions at his touch.

I didn't know where to begin. The way Berto stared at me was upsetting. He had such a sense of longing in his eyes.

I took a deep breath and began to speak. "You know, of course, I'm married, and I've been blessed with three beautiful children. My husband is a wonderful man. I have a good life."

"I want to hear more. Tell me about your husband, your home, your children."

Berto seemed interested in everything I had to say. He'd smile and nod seeming to enjoy each small detail as I sketched my life. We must have talked for hours, until the conversation was interrupted by a knock on the door and the entrance of a uniformed nurse.

I knew enough Spanish to understand she was asking if he was tiring, or in pain, suggesting he rest for a bit. He ordered her out, telling her he'd let her know when he needed her.

"Really, Berto. You should rest for a while. I'm here for the whole day. We can talk later."

"I have so much to say to you, Little One, and so much I want to know. Your being here brings new energy to my life. I can rest tomorrow and soon for all of eternity, but I can't waste a moment of your time here with me." There was no point in arguing with him.

We talked for another hour or so until Anna came to say the cook had prepared lunch, and Senor Ortega was due for his medication. She said the nurse insisted he take a short rest and then he could have more time to visit.

"Please do as the nurse says. I'll still be here, I promised."

"Only if you promise you won't sneak away again without saying goodbye."

"I promise." I left the room as Anna closed the door behind me and asked, "Where's Tyler?"

"He's changing out of his wet bathing suit. He wanted to swim in the pool first. We'll walk the beach this afternoon."

"Thank you Anna. I hope he's not being a problem."

"No, he's a very sweet boy, so smart and so well mannered. Can I ask why you brought him?"

"I'm sure you've already guessed."

"Yes, one look at him, and I knew he was Senor Ortega's son. Are you going to tell him?"

"I want to. We'll see how things go, but please don't mention anything to Tyler. He doesn't know."

Lunch was set at the beautiful forged iron table I remembered so well on the patio under the Palapa.

Anna went to fetch Tyler. I saw him running ahead of her. His excitement was obvious.

"Mom, this place is really cool. We should have a pool in our backyard. Wouldn't that be amazing?"

"Yes, it would be." His enthusiasm was contagious. "Sit down please. Lunch is ready."

The cook placed dishes of rice, beans, shredded beef, tortillas, lettuce, and homemade salsa in the middle of the table. Tyler gave me a funny look. "Could I have a peanut butter and jam sandwich? This doesn't look like lunch."

"This is my favorite Mexican lunch, Tyler. It's called tacos. Here, I'll show you. First put some beans and rice on your plate and then take one of the warm tortillas and put some beef in the center, you can put a bit of salsa and lettuce on it if you like, then fold it over like this and take a bite."

I watched him assemble his taco and take a bite, the salsa dribbling down his chin. "Mom, this is really good." He ate every bit of the taco and had second helpings of the rice and beans, then pushed his plate aside and reached for the ice cream and cookies the cook brought out.

Having finished the last cookie, Tyler said. "I like your friends, Mom. They're really nice."

"I'm glad. Anna said the two of you were going for a walk on the beach this afternoon. Be sure to wade in the surf and look for seashells to take home."

"When do we have to go home?"

"Tomorrow. Kathleen and Molly will be missing us, and you have school on Monday."

"Yeah. Wait till I tell my friends all about Mexico, but I wish we could stay longer."

I suggested Tyler stretch out on the chaise until Anna came to get him. An hour passed before Anna returned to say Senor Ortega was waiting for me. I tapped Tyler on the shoulder to awaken him. "Anna's here. Are you ready for a walk on the beach?"

Tyler sat up, rubbed his eyes and said he was ready. He grabbed Anna's hand as he told her he wanted to look for sea shells.

I left the two of them and walked back into the bedroom. Berto looked refreshed, his hair neatly combed, sitting in his chair. "Did you have lunch? I hope you are planning on staying for dinner. Cook is busy preparing something special."

"I don't think I can. I want to return to the hotel before it gets too late. I have a flight home tomorrow morning."

"Indulge me. I insist you have dinner and stay the night. We have more than enough bedrooms, and every minute I have with you is precious."

"I can't Berto. All our luggage is at the hotel and I have to check out."

"Give me your hotel key. I'll send Anna and my houseman to pick up your things and check you out of the hotel. Besides, my son Carlos is arriving later this evening. I want you to meet him. He is my pride and joy. Every man wants a son, an heir to carry on his name."

Was this the moment I'd been waiting for? I knew when I brought Tyler along that if the time were right, I'd have Berto meet our son. I figured it was now or never. He had a right to know. I owed him that much

"You're twice blessed as you have two sons." I spoke clearly as I looked into his eyes.

His expression was quizzical. He sat up straight in his chair and said, "What are you taking about, Little One?"

"I brought a little boy with me. He's your son." There I finally said it. I had no idea what would happen next.

Dead silence filled the room. I could see by his shocked look Berto was having a hard time understanding what I'd just said.

"Michael, are you saying we have a son? How can that be?" There was another long pause before he said, "Is that why you left without even a goodbye? Little One, you know I would have taken care of you. How could you have gone off and not said a word." His face was flushed, I could see the veins pulsing in his temple. "I had a right to know."

"Please, Berto, try not to get excited, stay calm, and I promise I'll tell you the whole story." My heart was pounding, and my hands felt clammy. This wasn't going to be easy. I stood and walked toward the wide-open glass doors leading to the patio. I couldn't face him.

"I didn't know I was pregnant when I left. I didn't find out until several weeks later. By then, I'd made up my mind to put our affair behind me. I knew our relationship had to end before everyone involved was hurt or hurt more deeply. If I'd let you know things would have been even more complicated, so I kept my secret. It wasn't until I planned on coming to Mexico that my husband knew any of the facts of our relationship."

I turned toward him. "I'm truly sorry, Berto. To deprive you of any word of my pregnancy or the birth of your son might not have been the right thing to do, but at the time it was the only way out I could see." I hoped he understood.

"Oh, my little butterfly, you flew off and got caught in a giant spider's web. Does your husband treat the boy well?"

"He adores him. He was the physician who discovered a defect in Tyler's heart just hours after he was born. Pat has been in the boy's life from his very first day on earth."

"A problem with his heart. My God, Michael, is the boy well, healthy?" I heard the alarm in his voice.

"They found a small hole in his heart and operated on him just days after he was born and were successful in closing the opening. He's a perfectly normal, healthy boy."

"Am I going to be allowed to meet my son?"

I nodded, "If you want to. That's why I brought him with me. My way of trying to make it up to you for withholding information you had every right to know. It's important to me that Tyler meets you as well."

"Will you call the nurse and give me a few minutes before you bring him to me?" The matter was settled. Berto would finally meet his son.

Chapter 33

I went in search of Anna and Tyler, but didn't have to go far. I could hear Tyler laughing as Anna was washing sand off his feet and spraying him with the warm water at the outdoor shower. "Hurry, Tyler, you need to get changed. There's someone I want you to meet."

I wrapped Tyler in a beach towel and took him by the hand leading him back to his bedroom to change out of his wet trunks. I wanted to make sure he looked presentable. I combed his damp hair, much to his displeasure, and tried to answer his questions about the man he was about to meet.

"You're about to meet the gentleman who owns this beautiful house. His name is Umberto Ortega." I smoothed his hair one more time.

"Wow, that's sure a funny name. What am I supposed to call him?"

"Senor Ortega might be a good place to start. It's very important that you be polite and on your very best behavior." Tyler just rolled his eyes at me. I was always insisting he be on his best behavior.

I started toward Berto's bedroom, surprised to see him sitting in one of the oversized chairs in the living room. He was no longer wearing a robe, but dressed in starched white shorts several sizes to big, held together at the waist by an oversized belt clinched tight around his waist, a navy blue polo shirt, and huaraches on his feet. There were purple needle marks visible on the veins in his arms.

Berto smiled. "Well, young man, welcome to my home. I hope you are enjoying yourself."

"This place is really cool. I wish I could live on a beach," Tyler replied.

"We haven't been introduced as yet. Tell me you name."

"Bertram Tyler Madison, sir. My mom and my teachers call me Tyler, but my dad and my friends call me Tiger."

"Then may I call you Tiger? I'd very much like to be your friend, and you can call me Berto just as my friends do."

Tyler shrugged his shoulders and said, "Sure, that's okay with me."

"Would you like to sit down, Tiger? Now that we're friends, I'd like to know all about you." Berto never took his eyes of him. Holding on to every word with sheer joy.

Tyler plopped down beside me on the sofa and sank into the deep cushions, his feet dangling, his legs too short to reach the floor.

"So, Tiger, your mother's name is O'Malley, but yours is Madison."

"Yeah. My Mom told me it's complicated. You see dad is my dad, but he's not my father because he didn't make me." I was intrigued by the way he explained the difference.

"I see. Yes, that is very complicated. Tell me about your dad."

Berto listened carefully taking in Tyler's every word. "Well, he's a kids doctor, and he was in charge of my heart when I was a baby. He's funny, and he teases me a lot, but then he tells me I'm the greatest kid in the whole wide world."

"You like him a lot?" Berto asked.

"Yeah, I like him a whole lot, but I love him, too."

I felt a lump in my throat. I was so proud of Tyler and touched by his feelings for Pat.

"What would you say if I told you I was your father? The man that made you."

I turned toward Tyler. How would he react?

"I'll have to think about that."

I could see Tyler trying to figure out what Berto had just said. I watched, as he seemed to process the comment. After a moment, he laughed. "I'd think that was funny. A really funny joke."

Berto changed the subject and the two of them talked about

School, his sisters, and what he liked to do. Berto took in every word with delight. Fatherly pride radiated from his face as he beamed at his son. The conversation came to an end when Anna called us for dinner.

"Please forgive me, Tiger, if I don't have dinner with you and your mother. I hope you'll say goodbye before you leave tomorrow. It's been very special for me to meet you and to have you as my most special friend. Thank you for coming all this way."

THE BUTTERFLY

"My father told me a long time ago, Tiger, when I was just about your age, that a son's job is to respect his mother and always to take care of her, and so I pass my father's words on to you. It's important that you always take care of your mother."

Berto motioned Tyler to come to his chair. I could see he was tiring as he reached out his hand and took Tyler's small hand in his. "Is there anything you'd like to know before you leave?"

Tyler replied without a moment's hesitation, "You bet. Would it be all right with you if I came back for visit? This place is really cool."

"Well, you'll have to ask my son Carlos tomorrow. The beach house will be his very soon."

I knew Berto wanted to hug his son, but he held back, settling instead for a handshake.

"Enjoy your dinner. He remained seated as I wondered if he could walk without help. "Cook has been busy all day preparing a special meal for you and your mother. Michael, will you come and say goodnight before you go to bed?"

I promised I would. By the time we finished dinner the hour was late. I got Tyler bathed and in bed. I'd expected questions about Berto saying he was his father, but you never know what kids are thinking. I guess he really thought Berto's comment was a joke.

As I tucked him in, all he wanted to know was could he swim in the pool before we had to leave in the morning?

As promised, I knocked on Berto's bedroom door to say goodnight. A handsome, dark-haired young man was sitting beside him as he lay in bed. The resemblance to his father was evident. I could envision what Tyler would look like as a young man.

"Ah, come in Michael. I want you to meet my son, Carlos. He arrived a few hours ago from New Haven where he's a student at Yale. Carlos this is Michael O'Malley, an old friend from the States."

He rose and took my hand, "Mucho Gusto."

"I'm glad to meet you too, Carlos. Your father is very proud of you." I smiled not knowing what to say next. Though I was a bit unnerved by the way he was staring at me.

He pointed to a framed picture on the opposite wall I hadn't noticed before. "You're the butterfly. I recognize you from my father's sketch."

I glanced over at the picture. My God, it was the drawing Berto had done of me years ago during my stay at the beach house. I could feel my checks redden. How much did Carlos know?

"How long are you staying, Mrs. O'Malley?"

"I leave tomorrow morning. My son and I are booked on a flight back to the States. I just came to say goodnight and probably goodbye, as we will most likely be leaving before your father is awake."

"Then I'll leave now. Goodnight, father. I'll see you in the morning."

As the door closed behind him, I remarked on how handsome he was. "He resembles you so much."

"Turn off the lights, please, Little One. It's much to bright in here." I did as he asked, leaving only the soft glow of the bedside lamp.

"Come here and lie down beside me."

I hesitated. It seemed more than awkward and I wasn't sure it was a good idea.

"I'm harmless. Please, I would love to feel you close. To close my eyes and remember the beautiful moments we had together in this room, on this very bed. Come. I promise I won't lay a hand on you."

I lay down beside him, only a satin sheet between us and held my breath.

"I wanted to tell you after the ugly night of the charity ball, just how sorry I was for any pain I caused. You must know it was never my intention to hurt you. I loved you, but you left, my Little One, and never gave me a chance. Had you read any of my letters you would have known I've never stopped loving you. I could have put an end to your fears as my wife admitted she'd caught her heel in the hem of her gown causing the fall. "You would also have known I wanted you to return and marry me after my wife died. We could have been so happy together. You gave me back my youth and made my life so joyful for the short time we spent together."

His voice just above a whisper as he continued. He was having trouble keeping his eyes open. "I would have given you anything my money could buy."

"It never would have worked, Berto. As far as your family and friends were concerned, they'd have hated me for having your child. They would never have forgiven you for being so unfeeling that you couldn't wait until your wife was cold in her grave before you married your mistress. The one who had your bastard son." I knew I was right.

"My son," he whispered. "How can I ever thank you. Now I know we are forever bound together. I wish I had time to know him better. He's a fine young man. A gift I thank you for. Some piece of our love will live long after me."

A long silence followed. I had nothing more to say as Berto reached for my hand.

"Stay beside me until I fall asleep. The medication is beginning to take hold. Then once again you may fly away, my little butterfly."

THE BUTTERFLY

I felt nothing but sadness as I waited until I heard the steady rhythm of his breathing. I stood up with care, not wanting to awaken him, and left the room. Somehow, I managed to close the door behind me before the tears began to flow.

Chapter 34

Knowing I couldn't sleep I tip-toed through the silent rooms and opened a door to the patio. I walked past the pool, down the steps to the gate that led to the beach. The moon, low in the sky, seemed to illuminate the bay water, which glowed iridescent in various shades of blue. I kicked off my shoes and walked barefoot through the warm sand. The beach, the moonlight, the sound of the water ebbing and flowing made the whole scene seemed surreal, much as my relationship with Berto had been. Never real. Always a fairy tale.

A sense of sorrow came over me knowing I'd never see him again, but the longer I walked the more I knew it was time to close the door forever on what had happened between us. I finally understood whatever had occurred between us wasn't love.

I turned and walked back to the beach house knowing the only man I'd ever loved was my husband.

I was up and dressed before I awoke Tyler, helping him to get ready, as he was still half asleep. Trying to explain we didn't have time for him to swim.

I wheeled our suitcases out to the parking area, where much to my surprise, it was Carlos I saw waiting by the car.

"My father wanted me to drive you to the airport. He thought I should meet Tyler."

Carlos started to put the luggage in the trunk of the grey sedan we'd arrived in, while Tyler had his eye on the convertible.

"Could we take the red car? It would be really cool if you could put the top down."

THE BUTTERFLY

Carlos looked at me as if to ask was it okay.

"It's up to you, Carlos."

Having received my approval, Carlos started to move the luggage to the convertible. "Okay kid, let's take the red car." Tyler was beyond excited.

I climbed into the back seat, telling Tyler he could sit in front.

With the luggage secured, Carlos turned toward Tyler. "Put your seatbelt on, kid, and I'll put the top down."

Tyler settled into his seat and began to talk to Carlos as if they were old friends. It was Carols who said. "By the way, kid I'm Carlos, Berto's son. What's your name?"

"Tyler. I'm Berto's friend, but my friends call me Tiger. Your dad said I had to ask you if I could come back to the beach house for a visit sometime. He said the house was going to be yours."

"Would you like to come back?"

"Yeah. This place is really cool."

"Then my answer is yes. You can come back whenever you want."

Tyler turned his head toward me a big smile on his face. "Mom did you hear what my friend Carlos just said? He told me I can come back whenever I want. That's cool.

Tyler was excited about driving with the top down, something he'd never experienced before, telling Carlos his car was really cool. Of late everything seemed to be cool with him.

Tyler was taking in the sights asking questions of Carlos. The two seemed to be getting along famously. I was glad to be excluded from the conversation, which was impossible from the back seat with the top down. I recalled with mixed emotions the time I'd spent in this very same red convertible.

I'm sure Carlos was aware that Tyler was also his father's son. If he hadn't been told, all he had to do is look at him and he'd know. The two of them looked like brothers. The same dark hair, the large, dark-brown eyes, the long, thick, black lashes, and the same body structure.

As we were about to enter the airport, Carlos reached out and put his arms around me. I was pleased with his embrace. It seemed so natural. Something family would do. I guess in some small way we were family.

"Bless you for coming, Michael. I know there was unfinished business between you and my father that under the circumstances needed to be addressed. Things that needed to be sorted out between the two of you. He spoke often of his love for you, how happy you made him. His feelings for you were very special, he never looked at another woman after you left."

Carlos said he was too young to know all that happened and now it really didn't matter, but he planned to keep in touch, saying he was sure that someday Tiger would know the truth about who his father was and he wanted to stay close to him. He knew that would make his father happy.

My eyes were filled with tears as I thanked him. "It would make me happy, as well, if you stayed in touch. Your father will always have a special place in my heart."

I took Tyler's hand, and we entered the doors to the airport on our way home. No matter the consequences, I knew that coming and bringing Tyler had been right thing to do, but I grew more anxious the closer we got to home. I had so many things I needed to tell Pat, hoping beyond hope I hadn't jeopardized our wonderful relationship. Tyler kept me busy with his never-ending questions, but it seemed like it was taking forever to land.

I sent a text message to Pat as the wheels touched down on the runway, telling him we'd be on our way soon, that I missed him, and could hardly wait to be home. The text went unanswered. Now, I really began to worry. My cell phone showed the message had been delivered. That wasn't like him.

I drove a lot faster than usual only slowing down when I turned onto our street. Pulling into the garage, I grabbed our luggage from the trunk, and hurried into the house as Tyler ran ahead. By the time I entered the house, Tyler was babbling on with a great deal of excitement about the plane ride, showing Kathleen the wings the stewardess had pinned to his jacket. I was glad to hear the happy sound of kid's voices, glad to be home. I gave Pat a kiss on the cheek, saying I missed him, but the hug I expected never materialized.

"Have a nice visit?" The remoteness of his voice was unlike him. The smile was missing. He had a strange look about him I couldn't quite figure out. It wasn't the kind of look I got from my father when he was disappointed in something I'd done. This was more a look of sadness. I tried to overlook the chill in the air and sound upbeat even though I had a sinking feeling. This was the first time I'd ever felt uncomfortable in Pat's company the familiar warmth was missing.

"It was one of the most important two days of my life. I'll tell you all about it after the kids are in bed."

"I can hardly wait," Pat answered. His sarcasm was hard to ignore. It sounded more like something he was dreading, like being told about a death in the family.

If I could only hold it together until evening, I was sure he'd understand and everything could go back to normal. I tried my best to act as if nothing was wrong.

THE BUTTERFLY

When dinner was over, the dishes done, and the last of the children down for the night, I settled onto the sofa and waited for Pat. Anxious minutes passed before he appeared holding a bottle of beer in his hand.

"Before you say a word, Pat, please hear me out." I don't want you to misunderstand what I meant when I said the trip was important." I needed him to understand what I was feeling more than anything right now. "What I meant was how important it was for the two of us."

Pat sat across from me in his favorite chair, his feet up on the ottoman, one hand wrapped around the bottle of beer. "What was so important?"

"It may be hard to explain. Even harder for you to understand, but there's always been a part of me, a part of my brain sectioned off, sort of like a small dark room, with the door slightly ajar. It was a scary place I didn't want to visit, a place where Berto and Mexico lived. I never really dealt with Berto and my time with him. Never really examined my feelings. Now, after all the years that have gone by, and all that's happened in my life, I've finally thrown the door wide open, and exposed the whole experience to the light. I put the event in its proper place in my life. I faced all the room's demons, then shut the door, and turned the key in the lock."

Pat looked at me, his arms crossed against his chest, not saying a word. I took a minute before I continued.

"As I spent time with Berto, I realized it had all been a fantasy, a fairy tale. He didn't love me, he loved what I represented, a love he'd lost. I was the girl he left behind when he was called home to run his family business after his father passed away. I reminded him of his youth, torn away before he was ready."

I looked at Pat, his expression still hadn't changed. I took another deep breath and went on. I had to tell Pat everything if he was to understand what I'd come to realize.

"The more time I spent with Berto, the more I felt pity for him, a deep sense of sorrow. Here was a man who to the outside world had everything, alone, dying, without friends or family. Yet the only feeling I had was a profound sense of sadness. I realized I'd never loved him. How could I? I had no idea what love was until I met you."

I noticed Pat shift in his seat, his expression changing a bit as I continued.

"Look, I was as naïve as they come. My relationships with the opposite sex were few and far between. I never had a high school romance, nor did I fall head over heels in love with some boy I met in college. No. I was the nerd, pushed on by her father, the one who spent all her time in the library studying. I was smart, just not smart enough to reach the heights my father expected. But it meant I didn't have much time for parties or dating."

"I had no chance to learn about the interactions between the sexes. Believe me, Berto could be captivating. No man had ever paid me that kind of attention, nor had I ever given sex a serious thought before. That first love affair that carries you away and opens up sexual feelings you'd never had before, that experience had escaped me growing up. My sexual experiences, few and far between, were total disasters.

Pat had uncrossed his arms and seemed more relaxed as he finished the last of his beer.

"When I met Berto I was overwhelmed by both his wealth and the glamour he represented. He was an introduction to a world I'd never known. But it was never love. I never want him to creep into our life in any way ever again.

I stood and walked over to Pat and sat on the edge of the ottoman facing him. "Please, my love, forgive me for hurting you. It was the first time you'd ever asked anything of me, and I went against your wishes. But I couldn't give in. Something in my gut said I had to go."

"Christ, Babe, how did you expect me to react? Was I supposed to be overjoyed you were rushing off to spend time with your former lover? More than anything I was scared, worried sick I'd lose you. So what if the guy was dying, would he be there between us from now on? When I made love to you, would you be pretending it was him." The sadness in Pat's eyes stung. I never meant to hurt him

"You might not realize how fragile men's egos are. Oh, I knew you'd never break up our family, but given the unusual circumstances of our crazy courtship, I was afraid you'd never love me the way I loved you...that the ghost of your former lover would always come between us."

"What are you talking about?" I was lost, confused by what he was saying.

"You know very well how crazy our relationship was before we married. We never fell in love like two people usually do. I was never sure you didn't see our relationship as some sort of a marriage of convenience. Yeah, we get along better than most, but I was afraid any hope of our maintaining what we had between us would end after you spent time with him."

I stood and looked at Pat, my heart going out to him. "It's my fault if you thought for one moment I didn't love you. That anything or anybody could ever come between us. Don't you understand, I never knew what it meant to love someone the way I love you. My happiness is wrapped up in you and it breaks my heart to know how much I hurt you."

Pat walked toward the fireplace, he seemed to be taking in all that I'd told him. I walked toward him.

THE BUTTERFLY

"Please forgive me, Pat." I threw my arms around him and took a deep breath. "I have a favor to ask, and I won't take no for an answer. I want a real honeymoon. Not months from now or even weeks. I want to leave as soon as we can make reservations somewhere. I want a week or ten days alone just the two of us, without children, without your patients, alone in some secluded place where no one can find us. I want to make love every night, sleep until noon, and spend every waking moment with the man I adore."

In the darkness of our bedroom, that night I knew he forgave me as I showed him how much I loved him.

Chapter 35

Pat made reservations at what sounded like the perfect spot, a small inn located on the outer banks of North Carolina, clear across the country. The kids promised to be good for the sitter. That may have had something to do with the tale Pat told them about leprechauns swooping down dressed in their green suits and threatening small children that didn't behave with terrible punishments. I'm sure he'd heard the same story growing up.

We flew to Norfolk and rented a car, driving the eighty miles to the inn. I couldn't conceal my excitement just thinking about the novelty of the two of us alone together for ten whole days.

The inn was isolated. The main building had at some point been a private residence, now surrounded by eight individual cabins. We checked in and were told dinner would be served in the dining room in one hour. Dress was informal.

The cabin lived up to the pictures online -- a king-sized bed, its headboard resting against one wall, and a wood-burning fireplace with logs already in place. There were two comfortable upholstered chairs, with a small coffee table facing the fireplace. The bathroom was modest, but clean, with double sinks and a large shower stall. Two terry bathrobes hung on the back of the bathroom door, with oversized towels resting on a heated rack. The cabin itself was set among a grove of Cypress trees. It looked like heaven to me.

Six other couples were staying at the inn. We met over wine and appetizers in the living room of the main building before dinner was served. While the conversation had been interesting, we opted for a table by ourselves. I wanted time alone.

After dinner, both of us too full of food to call it a night we decided to go for a walk. It had begun to cool off a bit, with patches of fog drifting in. We put on jackets and walked along the beach. We ambled along the water's edge holding hands. There was no need for words. I never felt closer to Pat than I did at that moment.

Returning to the cabin Pat lit the fire and we stretched out on the shag rug in front of the fireplace. I thought back to our first night together at the Fairmont Hotel and how far we'd come.

I realized more than anything, I wanted Pat to make love to me right now. I sat up and began to coyly unbutton the blouse I was wearing. Pat looked at me, a grin on his face, enjoying my performance. He slipped off my blouse as he kissed me with a great deal of passion. The bed could wait for another time. We made love on the rug before the warm fire with joyous abandon like newlyweds. This was the honeymoon we'd never had.

The inn packed a lunch for us each day, and we hiked away from the shore following a path among the trees on the deserted part of the island. It reminded me of the trip to Big Sur, when Pat proposed. I also remembered with some sense of uncertainty the blue butterfly that had remained on Pat's shoulder, then dismissed it as nonsensical superstition.

In the late afternoon we'd sit on comfortable chaises we dragged to the water's edge and talk in ways we never had time to before. I wanted to know everything about Pat. There were so many things one would have expected I would have already known after our years together. Curious to know what Pat was like as a young boy, as a teenager, his college years. Had he been in love with anyone before me? We laughed together that we were finally having a courtship years into our marriage, relishing being together for the very first time without any responsibilities and vowed to do this every year.

The nights were sheer heaven. There were no nighttime feedings, no teething babies, no little visitors in the middle of the night scared about a nightmare or a thunderstorm. It was just the two of us acting like newlyweds, growing closer than we'd ever been.

My trip to Mexico made me realize how much I'd changed. How much I'd matured. Thanks to Pat I understood love is more than the passion we shared. Pat is my best friend, my lover, and my partner. He's the one person whose happiness I put above my own, above all others. What I feel for him grows stronger with each passing day. I couldn't imagine life without him. How could I have been so lucky?

We didn't want to leave, but at the same time, we were both anxious to go home. The time away with all that had happened was just what we had both needed.

Patrick Christopher O'Malley Junior was born almost nine months to the day after our Outer Banks visit. He was another redheaded, blue-eyed O'Malley. We agreed this would be our last child. Pat had his son and four children were enough of a handful.

Chapter 36

We continued to share Thanksgiving with the O'Malley clan. Pat's dad was thinking of giving up his practice and moving into a retirement facility. At almost eighty, the big house was both a physical and financial drain on him. He agreed we'd have one big bash before he sold the house. I was sad at the prospect, the house was the one thing that still kept the family together, although nothing was ever the same without Mother Molly.

We arrived on Thanksgiving to find the house full of laughter and kids running around. It felt good to have all the family together. Everyone acknowledged his or her guilt for not doing a better job of keeping in touch. I had conversations with as many of the family as I could about the idea of their dad moving into a retirement facility. The only reaction I got seemed to have the same rational. If this was what their dad wanted, who were they to disagree. Besides the facilities were capable of providing whatever care might be needed in the future.

I had a hard time enjoying the meal knowing we would never be together like this again if the house were sold and dad moved to retirement home. Helped with the clean up the kitchen I realized how different it was this year, having been a year since we had all been together the sense of camaraderie we'd had seemed strained. We went about the task with more of a sense of sorrow than joy. The laughter and fun we'd shared over previous years was gone. I divided up the leftovers making sure to leave plenty for dad. The ritual we'd happily shared for years was coming to an end.

When the chores were done the family began to leave one by one. No indication meeting again. We were spending the night, as Pat wanted his dad to show us the retirement facility he was considering.

Late the following morning, our family arrived with four children in tow much to the dismay of the manager of Twin Pines. She greeted Pat's father with a warm handshake and indicated how pleased she was to meet his family, although I knew by her reaction that wasn't the case. She eyed the children with suspicion as she reached for a key handing it to Pat's dad. "I'm sorry I don't have the time to show your family the apartment you're considering, Dr. O'Malley, but it's close to lunch time and I'm needed elsewhere."

She walked toward the living area. "Nice to have met you all. You have a wonderful family, Dr. O'Malley." Again, I felt she was less than sincere.

We followed Pat's dad down a long sterile hallway to an elevator. Reaching the third floor, we walked down yet another blank sterile hallway with an uncarpeted floor making wheelchair access easier. Papa unlocked the door to apartment 327. I looked inside with horror. The whole apartment couldn't have been more than six hundred square feet consisting of a living room dominated by a large built-in television set, a tiny kitchen with an eating counter, and a small bedroom and bathroom. The apartment stretched the very definition of efficiency. If I had thought my old townhouse was depressing this had to be the most God-awful place I'd ever seen. The furniture was tasteless. The apartment looked like a hospital room. The whole place lacked any warmth. Pat poked around, but I couldn't wait to leave. I couldn't imagine leaving anyone I cared about in such a dreadful place.

Back downstairs, we looked in at the living room as we kept the children close. The large room was pleasant enough. People were seated at several card tables. There were sofas and lounge chairs scattered around. A baby grand piano took up one corner and flowers and potted plants were placed here and there.

I found the people moving about the room equally depressing. A few women were dressed with a sense of fashion, but most were in pants and practical footwear. There were many more women than men, and too many walkers and wheel chairs.

Papa was too young and healthy for this group. He'd die of boredom here.

We drove Papa home and I fixed lunch for everybody. Once we'd finished eating I started the dishwasher while Pat began to gather our belongings. We piled the kids into the car for the long drive home leaving Papa alone in the empty house.

THE BUTTERFLY

Once we were underway, I whispered to Pat, not wanting the children to hear. "I don't feel right about your dad moving into that awful place. He's too young, too vital for that group. It's not right for him. He'll be miserable. Can you for one minute imagine the grandchildren visiting, see them running around?"

"Yeah, I found the place depressing, too, but what's the alternative?" Pat sounded just like his siblings.

"He can come and live with us."

"Babe, that's crazy. Where would we put him? We haven't a bedroom to spare and no place for him to get away from the kids. It's a nice idea and very generous of you, but it's impossible."

Of course he was right. There was no place we put him? Even if we tripled up the children, there was no place for any privacy. The bathroom situation was complicated enough as it was. Still, the thought of him living in the cold, impersonal situation was really disturbing me. I thought of nothing else on the entire drive home.

Pat parked in front, and we moved four children, two sleeping soundly into the house. By the time he finished unloading everything Pat said, "I'll put the car in the garage and be right back to give you a hand." That's when it hit me. The garage. We could convert the garage into an apartment.

I waited in the kitchen eager to tell Pat my solution as he came in the back door carrying a cooler filled with Saran covered paper platters of food. When I told him all he could say was, "Where will we put the cars?"

"Honestly, Pat, you don't mean that." I couldn't believe what he just said. "We can put the damn cars in front of the house for all I care. What's more important the cars or your dad?"

"Hey, slow down. You're really serious."

"Of course I am. He needs family. The kids will drive him crazy, but at least they'll keep him young and without a chance of being bored."

"You realize you'd be adding one more human being to your already full plate."

"Pat, sweetheart, your family went out of their way to take me in, make me feel welcome, never judging. If nothing else, I owe this to Mother Molly who opened her heart to me. She'd have taken us in if the need were there. Family comes first, remember." I found myself in Pat's arms. "Have I told you how wonderful you are? You're right, of course. If you're game, I'm one hundred percent for it. We'll call Dad in the morning."

As promised Pat spoke with his dad the next day. He was resistant at first, he didn't want to be a burden, but Pat was very persuasive. After a long conversation he agreed, but only after insisting he'd pay for the construction costs.

We spoke with a building contractor whose kids were patients of Pat's. Between the three of us we agreed upon a set of plans that called for a large bedroom and bathroom. A sitting area with room for a desk, and an alcove large enough to hold a small under the counter refrigerator, a sink, and a two-burner stove top, just enough space to make coffee and breakfast.

We sent the plans to Pat's dad for his approval, and he seemed pleased. He'd be able to furnish the place with familiar pieces from his house, something the assisted living facility wouldn't have allowed.

The contractor's estimate was no more than twelve weeks start to finish once we got the plans approved by the city. The contractor helped where he could even going with Pat to the planning commission. A garage conversion in an upscale neighborhood would be a hard sell. It took almost three months to get the permit, practically having to move heaven and earth to get an exception.

At long last the construction was underway. The kids, with the exception of the baby, we'd nicknamed Paddy, were excited at the thought of having their Papa living with us. The O'Malley clan was delighted that their father would have a home with us although I wondered why none of them had offered to have him live with them.

Papa planned to put the house up for sale as soon as his new apartment was ready. Houses, such as the O'Malley's, located in the much sought after Burlingame Hills, seldom lasted more than a week on the market and usually sold above asking price. The area was all part of the booming Silicon Valley.

The construction was a source of entertainment for the kids while I'm sure we all drove the worker's crazy. Every night after dinner, we'd tour the site to see what had been accomplished that day, excited to see the plans come to life.

Of course, our renovation had created an unexpected problem when we realized we had no place to put all the things that had been stored in the garage. Pat bought one of these portable tool sheds from Home Depot and put it in a far corner of the backyard for all the tools and gardening equipment. The rest we crammed into the attic, but were fast running out of space there as well.

As moving day came closer, I started to feel anxious. I hoped I hadn't asked for more trouble and more work than I could manage, and concerned the kids might be an annoyance. Papa had become used to peace, quiet, and order. Something he wasn't going to experience much of with us. What if he was miserable?

THE BUTTERFLY

Finally the apartment was ready, turning out even better than we'd hoped. With its separate entrance on the front and a bank of windows overlooking the garden, the space no longer looked like a converted garage, but a wing of the house that had always been there.

Pat drove to Burlingame the night before moving day to help his brothers with packing and loading the U-Haul. It gave him the opportunity for a final look at the house he grew up in. I'm sure there were bittersweet moments for him as he packed pictures and trophies to bring home.

The U-Haul pulled into our driveway around noon with Pat following close behind, his car packed with the overflow from his parent's home. I wondered where we would put everything. Every bit of closet space was sfull.

The brothers unloaded the furniture and had it all in place in short order. We had lunch together while waiting for Papa to arrive. By three in the afternoon, when we hadn't arrived we all began to worry. Could he have gotten lost? Pat's brothers stayed as long as they could, but finally had to leave. The hours ticked by as Pat and I waited for Papa.

Pat assured me his dad was fine. "He's grown even more stubborn these last few years. He'll show up when he's good and ready. It's probably hard for him to leave the old house, Babe, leaving Fifty-plus years of memories behind. No matter what we say or how we act, he knows he'll be a guest in his son's home, no longer the master of his own house. I'm afraid it isn't going to be an easy adjustment for any of us."

Papa arrived a little past ten in the evening, his car loaded with clothing. Pat rushed out to greet him. "Dad, welcome to your new home. Let me help you get settled."

"No need son. I can manage on my own." I saw the first signs of the stubborn streak Pat had mentioned.

I asked if he'd like something to eat.

"No thank you, my dear. I stopped along the way. It's late. I've had a busy day and I must admit I'm tired, so if you would show me where I'm to stay I'll turn in for the night."

The reserved tone to his voice, gave me a feeling he'd accepted the change with reluctance, and was prepared to make the best of it, but wasn't pleased with his new station in life.

"This way, Dad." Pat led the way to the front door of the new apartment and turned on the lights.

I could see the surprised look on his face. I don't think this was what he'd expected.

"This turned out very well, Patrick. I'd never believe it was once your garage." He seemed pleased to see the area filled with the familiar pieces of furniture from home.

"Is there anything I can get for you, Dad? Michael put towels in the bathroom, and you'll find a coffee pot and the makings on the counter."

"I'll be fine. You two just go on and do whatever you were doing. I don't intend to be in the way."

"Nonsense. This is your home, Dad. We don't expect you to spend your time locked away. We hope you'll join us in the morning for Sunday breakfast. The kids are anxious to see you."

"We'll see. Goodnight to you both."

We closed the door behind us and headed upstairs to our bedroom. It had been a busy day.

"Your dad seemed a little reserved. I don't know what I expected, but what can we do to make him feel at home?"

"Babe, he's always been reserved. The only one he ever let his guard down to was Mother Molly. She had him wound around her little finger. He was always the young man lusting after her. He'll be fine. He just needs time to make the adjustment. The kids will do the rest. Just watch, he'll let his guard down to his grandchildren."

The transition was difficult at first. Papa spent a great deal of his time alone in his apartment. I hadn't a clue whether it was what he wanted or what he thought was expected, but he'd have to work it out himself. I had enough to think about with four children in the house.

Chapter 37

Soon after Papa's arrival, I received a lengthy letter from Carlos apologizing for the long delay in letting me know his father had passed away in his sleep a few weeks after I left. He thanked me again for my visit and assured me that if either Tyler or I ever needed anything, I was to let him know. He'd promised his father he'd make sure we were both taken care of, to be sure we were never in need of anything.

I showed the letter to Pat as soon as he arrived home. "With Berto gone, there's nothing standing in the way of your adopting Tyler if that's still what you want to do." Broaching the idea of adoption felt odd. Pat had been the only dad Tyler had ever known.

"That's great news. I don't mean about the guy's passing away, but adopting Tyler would make our family complete. I'll look into it first thing tomorrow, but I have to get the okay from Tyler first." How like Pat to talk it over with Tyler before moving forward.

I stood in the doorway, silent, staying in the background, as Pat tucked Tyler in bed that evening. This was between the two of them.

"Tiger, there's something serious I want to talk to you about." Pat sat down on the edge of the bed.

"Did I do something wrong, Dad?" Tyler looked worried.

"Of course not. This has to do with our family. Do you remember when you became an honorary O'Malley?"

Tyler thought for a moment before he said, "Yeah, that was cool."

"Well, son, there's now a way to make you a permanent O'Malley, if that's what you would like. You'd no longer be called Tyler Madison, you'd be Tyler O'Malley, and as far as the law was concerned I'd be your father."

"You mean it, Dad? You mean you'd be my dad for real?"

"For real, son. It's called adoption, but it's up to you."

I saw Tyler throw his arms around Pat, tears in his eyes. He was crying, "Okay. Yes. I want you to be my real dad. I want to be an O'Malley."

The tears were running down my cheeks as well,

"Consider it a done deal." I heard the catch in Pat's voice knowing he was close to tears as well.

At dinner the next evening, Tyler told Papa he was going to be an O'Malley soon.

"I have a legal path to adopt him now, Dad."

"Well, congratulations, Tyler, but you've always been an O'Malley to me."

Kathleen piped up, a quizzical look on her face. "I don't understand. Aren't we all O'Malley's?"

"It's complicated," Pat said.

"That's what you and mom always say when you don't want to tell us something. What does complicated mean, anyway?"

"Dear Kathleen, complicated means hard to explain. It's something that will be easier for you to understand when you're older. I promise to uncomplicate it all one day. Okay?"

"Okay, but don't forget, Dad."

We hired an attorney who filed all the necessary paperwork, which included Tyler's birth certificate, our marriage documents and a certified copy of Berto's death certificate to legalize the adoption.

There was a great deal of excitement at breakfast the morning of the final hearing before the judge. Tyler had to appear along with Pat and me, but it was Papa's suggestion that all the children be present in court for the special occasion. He even volunteered to keep watch over them.

Getting everybody ready was nerve wracking. The children were dressed in their best clothes, Tyler in new chinos and a navy-blue blazer. Paddy was my only concern. Keeping him quiet for any length of time would be a problem.

We arrived at the courthouse shortly before ten and met with our attorney in the hall outside the family courtroom. He seemed pleased that the whole family was there.

Entering the courtroom everyone settled in the front row, taking up all the seats.

THE BUTTERFLY

We were first on the docket when court was called to order. The judge, in her black robe, greeted us as Pat and I were asked to approach the bench.

"Good morning. As this is family court, I try to keep the proceedings as informal as the law will allow. I'm glad to see the whole family is in attendance." She smiled and nodded at Papa trying to keep four children quiet.

Putting on the glasses attached to a cord around her neck, the judge turned over the pages of our file taking her time reviewing them. "I see all your documents are in order. Just a few questions. Mrs. O'Malley, are you in favor of Doctor O'Malley adopting your son?"

"I am."

"Do you further favor changing your son's name to O'Malley?"

"I do."

"Doctor O'Malley, are you aware that if you adopt this child, you will be responsible for him until he becomes of age?"

"I am." Pat answered confidently

"You may both be seated. "Young man, Tyler, is it? Please step forward."

Tyler looked toward Papa who assured him it was all right. We passed each other as he walked toward the bench and sat in the witness chair. Although he was growing taller almost overnight his feet were dangling, unable to reach the ground.

The judge leaned over and spoke to Tyler. "How old are you son?"

"Ten." His answer barely audible. I could tell he was nervous.

"Have your mother and Doctor O'Malley spoken to you about the adoption?"

"Tyler nodded yes."

"Speak up, Tyler. The court reporter needs a yes or no."

"Yes." His answer, louder than necessary, make the judge smile.

"Is Doctor O'Malley's request to adopt you something you agreed to, something you want to happen?"

Gone was the nervousness. "You bet. He's been my dad for as long as I can remember, and he took care of me the day I was born. It's complicated being a Madison when my brother and sisters are O'Malley's."

I looked at Pat, and we both smiled at his using the word complicated in his explanation to the judge.

"More than almost anything, I want my dad to be my father."

"Then, son, I see no reason why the adoption shouldn't be granted. Congratulations Bertram Tyler O'Malley." The judge looked pleased.

Tyler walked back toward us a broad smile on his face as our attorney approached the bench and had a short conversation with the judge as we left the courtroom. He met us in the hall to say the judge assured him the papers would be filed by the end of the day. The adoption was official.

Pat hugged Tyler and suggested a celebration was in order. "What should we do, Tiger? It's your day. You get to choose."

After a visit to the aquarium followed by Pizza for lunch, I couldn't help thinking the last hurdle had been crossed. Taking a step back I looked at Pat, the Children, and Papa — they were such a beautiful family. How blessed I was that they were mine.

Chapter 38

With our children growing up, it seemed as if we were all off and running in different directions, always in a rush to be somewhere. Dinners were often the only time we were all together. We began a nightly ritual with each of us sharing what he or she'd had learned or taken part in that day. Pat, as usual, was full of funny stories. The dinner hour was always the best time of the day.

Pat's dad had finally settled in. He started volunteering two days a week at the new VA Clinic, and he liked to putter in the garden. Our landscaping had improved 100% since he arrived. We had newly planted flowerbeds, and the old shrubs were pruned to perfection.

One evening, after the children were all in bed, and we'd settled in the living room, Pat's dad brought three cups of Irish coffee on a silver tray from his apartment.

"I thought we'd have a toast tonight to celebrate the six-month anniversary of my being here and to thank you both for making an old man comfortable with his new status in life."

"We're happy you're here, Dad. Just hope the kids aren't driving you crazy."

"You must be kidding, son. I'd forgotten how joyous the sounds of children's laughter could be. Being surrounded by, as your mother would say, wee ones, it reminds me of my happiest days, now long gone, when all six of you were under foot."

I took a sip of the warm brew. A contented feeling at how well the new arrangement was turning out.

"Patrick, you know you were always your mother's favorite, so I can't begin to tell you what it means to me that you would be the one to open your home to me."

Pat turned toward me. "You're giving your thanks to the wrong person, Dad. This was all Michael's doing. It was never my idea, and I admit to being hesitant, but she was the one who insisted, reminding me it's all about family." Pat raised his cup as a toast to me.

The look on Papa's face was one of dismay. He seemed completely confused. It took him a minute or two to understand what was said. With a smile on his face, he said, "Then, my dear, I owe you an apology on more than one score. If my good fortune to be here was your idea, Michael, I shall be forever grateful." He took a large drink from his cup before he continued.

"I must admit I was dead set against Patrick's marrying you. I was more than a little upset when he ignored my warnings and married you anyway. My concerns were heightened when you didn't have a proper church wedding. It was a great disappointment to your mother, Patrick, that the wedding took place without any of the family present. Even with that disappointment, my dear wife kept telling me I was wrong about you, Michael. She admired you for your strength and courage and thought you'd be the perfect wife for Patrick. Like always, she knew best."

Pat reached over and took my hand.

"As I've watch you with the children, Michael, and I see how happy my son is, I realize just how wrong I was. Please accept my apology for the cold reception I've given you over the years. My dear wife was a far better judge of character than I. Patrick, you couldn't have found a more perfect woman to spend your life with."

Papa paused, the smile remained on his face as he looked at me, "I'm not an outwardly affectionate man, Michael, and maybe a little old fashioned, but I would like to give you a warm embrace."

I rose from the sofa and walked toward him, tears in my eyes as he held out his arms. Though it had taken a lot of years, I'd finally passed the test. He'd accepted me as family.

Later, as we were getting ready for bed, Pat said, "That wasn't an easy thing for Dad to admit. You know how stubborn he can be, and he's even slower to acknowledge he's been wrong, but in the end, he's right about one thing. You are the perfect woman for me to spend my life with. Of course, my dear, you understand a perfect man deserves a perfect woman, and all Irish men are perfect. If you don't believe it just ask one."

THE BUTTERFLY

Almost two years had passed since my trip to Mexico. Paddy was a year old and the delight of his grandfather who spoiled him in every way possible. Kathleen was in elementary school and Miss Molly was four and enrolled in preschool. My life was getting much easier.

I was about to walk toward the car ready to run errands. Paddy was holding on the Papa's hand and waving bye bye, when I noticed the postal truck stop in the driveway. The mailman walked up the path handing me a large bulky certified mail envelope requiring my signature. The postmark and return address indicated it was sent from Guadalajara.

Clutching the envelope I opened the car door, sat behind the steering wheel, and opened the clasp withdrawing the contents. The cover letter was addressed to me from a law firm in Guadalajara describing the enclosed documents as part of the final recording of the last will and testament of Umberto Carlos Luis Ortega Gonzales. The letter informing of the terms of the funds bequeathed to his son.

I unfolded the document, which seemed to be only a portion of Berto's will. The page was divided in half, one side written in Spanish, the other in English.

As I skimmed the legal document, I couldn't believe what I was reading, trying to catch my breath. Berto had bequeathed Tyler a one million dollar trust fund drawing interest until his twenty-first birthday. At which time the trust fund was to be turned over to him to be used as he pleased. I was the trustee until he came of age.

I couldn't believe what I had just read. As I continued to read the document Tyler was also given a ten percent interest in the company, Grupo Ortega.

My hand trembled as I folded the document and replaced it in the envelope. Tyler was now one very wealthy little boy. It was hard to grasp just what this all meant as it came as a big surprise. I hadn't expected or asked for anything from Berto. My God, he had been more than generous. I could hardly wait to tell Pat. I hoped he wouldn't be upset.

A letter from Carlos was also enclosed. I opened the envelope and carefully unfolded the watermarked sheet of paper, which read,

Dear Michael,

I want you to know I whole heartily agreed with my father's decision to change his will in Tyler's favor.

*I was married three months ago
to an American girl I met at Yale. Not
making my father's mistake, I married
for love and not for money.*

*My wife and I would like to establish
a relationship with my little brother
and hope that you will allow him to visit
with us if you think he's old enough to
travel alone and to understand that we are
brothers.*

*We plan to spend several weeks this
September at the beach house and would
like to have Tyler spend the time with us.*

*I will understand if you think this isn't
in his best interest.*

*Regards,
Carlos*

I handed the will to Pat as soon as he walked in the door that evening, suggesting he sit down and read the contents. I watched as he settled into his chair and carefully read the document, a look of amazement on his face as he saw the size of the gift that had been willed to Tyler. He sat up straight in his chair, removed his feet from the ottoman, and placed them on the ground as he smiled at me. He shook his head, a look of awe on his face before he spoke, "Wow. I must say this comes as a surprise. He's been most generous, Michael. Maybe he wasn't such a bad fellow after all."

"Read this next." I handed him Carlos's letter

Pat folded the letter once he'd finished reading the contents and replaced it in the envelope. I couldn't read his expression.

"What do you think? I asked."

"You met Carlos, Babe, how did he strike you?"

I thought for a moment before I answered. "He seemed well mannered, respectful." I tried to remember if there was anything that disturbed me, but we'd spent so little time together I hadn't much to base my opinion on. "I liked him. He seemed genuine, really interested in Tyler. They got along famously. He's certainly well educated. Why?"

Pat's answer came as a surprise. "Because unless you have any objections, I think we should let him go to Mexico in September."

"But Pat, he's so young and it's a long way. What would we tell him?"

"Babe, he's almost twelve, old enough to understand. We tell him the truth, he knows I'm not his real father. Think about it for a moment. The one thing Mother Molly never let us forget was our Irish roots. We were taught to be proud of our ancestors. Tyler needs to be aware of his Hispanic roots as well, and be proud of his Mexican heritage."

"Pat, he's an American."

"But his father wasn't. He has a family he needs to know. I think it says a lot about Carlos that he wants Tyler in his life."

A thousand reasons to say no were on the tip of my tongue. Were my objections based more on holding Tyler close, not wanting to share him, wanting to keep him to ourselves?

"I know you're right, but he's such a little boy, and it's so much for him to deal with."

"I guarantee he's a lot smarter about than you think he is. I'm sure he knows all about the facts of life. Kids today are a lot savvier than we ever were. Trust me, it will be a lot easier for him to handle this now than years from now."

Pat put his arm around me brushing a lock of hair off my face. "What do we tell him at his twenty first birthday when the trust fund is turned over to him? Yes, son, you had a very generous father we never told you about. He made you a very rich young man, and you have a whole family in Mexico you know nothing about." He paused to let his words sink in.

"Oh yes, Tyler, one more thing we forgot to tell you was even though Carlos, your half-brother, wanted you in his life and invited you to spend time with him at the beach house, we withheld the invitation. We didn't want you to get to know him or any part of your family."

That blew a hole in any selfish reasons I might have to shelter Tyler from the truth. Pat was once again the voice of reason.

"I'll write to Carlos and let him know we think it's a wonderful idea for Tyler to visit in September. I know he'll be excited. He loved the beach house and asked Carlos if he could come back for a visit someday."

"The more you think about it, Babe, the more you'll realize the time has come, he needs to know who he is. His adoption is final so there couldn't be any problems whatever with any Mexican laws. Carlos seems genuine to me as well."

As I dropped off to sleep with the trust fund, the interest in Grupo Ortega, and a trip to Mexico all fresh on my mind, a smile crept across my face as I thought of the irony. Berto may be deceased, but it seems he will always be a permanent member of our family.

I felt a sense of relief as I awoke in the morning. The last bit of my past had been resolved, as I'd come to terms with the importance of Tyler knowing the truth and having a relationship with Carlos and the Ortega family.

I slipped out of bed and drew open the curtains to let in the morning sun taken aback with the sight of a magnificent blue butterfly resting on the windowsill. The elegant creature made no move to fly away. Its iridescent color and size reminded me of the blue butterfly that landed on Pat's shoulder that day in the park when he asked me to marry him. I remembered how I'd struggled to decide if the butterfly was a prophecy of good or an omen of evil

I couldn't hold back the smile, I understood at last the true meaning of the butterfly.

Milton Keynes UK
Ingram Content Group UK Ltd.
UKHW020454050324
438776UK00001BB/299